DATE DUE

JAN 1 7 2007	
FEB 1 5 2007	
FEB 2 3 2007	
APR 0 9 2007	
MAY 1 2 2007	
JUN 2 0 2007	
SEP 1 2 2007	
SEP 3 2009	
MAY 2 4 2010	
MAR 1 3 2014	
AUG 1 9 2019	

BRODART, CO.

SUMMER GARDEN MURDER

Books by Ann Ripley

HARVEST OF MURDER

THE CHRISTMAS GARDEN AFFAIR

DEATH AT THE SPRING PLANT SALE

SUMMER GARDEN MURDER

Published by Kensington Publishing Corporation

A GARDENING MYSTERY

ANN RIPLEY

SUMMER GARDEN MURDER

KENSINGTON BOOKS
www.kensingtonbooks.com

KENSINGTON BOOKS are published by

Kensington Publishing Corp.
850 Third Avenue
New York, NY 10022

All Kensington titles, imprints and distributed lines are available at special quantity discounts for bulk purchases for sales promotion, premiums, fund-raising, educational or institutional use.

Special book excerpts or customized printings can also be created to fit specific needs. For details, write or phone the office of the Kensington Special Sales Manager: Kensington Publishing Corp., 850 Third Avenue, New York, NY, 10022. Attn. Special Sales Department. Phone: 1-800-221-2647.

Kensington and the K logo Reg. U.S. Pat. & TM Off.

Library of Congress Card Catalogue Number: 2004110759
ISBN 0-7582-0817-0

First Printing: August 2005
10 9 8 7 6 5 4 3 2 1

Printed in the United States of America

To Marie

ACKNOWLEDGMENTS

Thanks to the professionals and friends who helped with this book: Roylene MacNeil, a forensic accountant, who showed me how she helps uncover business fraud; Professor Kandace Einbeck, of the German Studies Department at University of Colorado; Hal and Selma Altschuler, who inspired my story with a Yiddish curse; Karen Gilleland, Sybil Downing, Margaret Coel, Beverly Carrigan, Jessie Lew Mahoney, Bob Sinclair, Irene Sinclair, Margit Percival, Caty Habsburg-Lothringen and Martha Gray.

1

Returning from the bar with a drink in either hand, Louise Eldridge made the mistake of trying to slide through a narrow space between a wall and a cluster of people.

One of them turned and confronted her, his eyes lighting up like a fisherman who'd snagged a trout. "Hey, Louise, you're lookin' good," said her new neighbor, Mike Cunningham. "And I sure like your bling-bling." He reached out a hand and fondled the gold chain at the neckline of her sleeveless black dress.

Louise brushed his hand away. "Last time I heard, Mike, a flat gold necklace on a black sheath wasn't 'bling-bling.' Now, would you please let me pass?" She took a step away from him, and her rear end bumped into the wall. Trapped.

Cunningham didn't move. They stood eye to eye, she being a tall woman, he, a not-so-tall man. His eyes clamped on her breasts. Steadying the two drinks, Louise considered throwing them into her captor's face. It was a strong face, just short of being jowly, but with good features—languid brown eyes and a nicely formed nose, most likely the product of a nose job somewhere in his past, she thought. The blown-dry hair, however, was a tribute to juvenility, which she knew was a good thing in plants, but not in people. But clients of a high-priced Washington lawyer might like that blown-dry look. On his finger, Louise noticed, he wore his own bling-bling, a gold pinkie ring set with an eye-catching diamond.

"Get three or four more necklaces," Cunningham said enthusiastically, "and wear 'em with this one. Then it'll be bling-bling for sure," once again touching the chain.

She gave him a quick stare, then shoved by, only to bump into a knot of people. The liquid bounced in the glasses and half the contents sloshed onto the flagstone floor.

"Damn," she murmured, and looked down at the puddle she'd created.

Cunningham stood about eight inches away now, both hands up as if to deny responsibility for the spill. "Now, now," he said, "don't get mad, Louise. I was just trying to have some fun with you. You take things much too seriously, do you know that?"

Just in time, Louise spied Bill out of the corner of her eye and headed to her husband's side. She didn't want Bill to see Cunningham cornering her. The man had attended his first neighborhood party a couple of months ago, shortly after he moved into the house two doors away from the Eldridges. He seemed pleasant at first, but as the party wore on, he became tiresome. First he teased her about her job as host of the PBS show *Gardening with Nature,* as if there were something inherently humorous about hosting a nationally syndicated TV garden show. Then, to Bill's annoyance, he began to come on to Louise. By the end of the evening, he'd had the nerve to sweep her into his arms, swing her back and give her a big kiss good-bye. Bill had been about to deck him, but Louise managed to talk him out of it.

She intercepted Bill with a smile and handed him his depleted drink.

"Everything all right?" he asked her, sending a suspicious look at the attorney.

"Oh, sure," she replied. She needed a moment to calm down. They stood in a space in the center of the living room. Ron and Nora Radebaugh's home, like others in woodsy Sylvan Valley, was spare and modern, with lots of floor-to-ceiling windows and a flat roof, a sharp contrast to the prim colonials that populated adjacent northern Virginia neighborhoods. The huge windows were bereft of drapes, serviced instead by nearly invisible blinds that almost disappeared when opened. In this room, Ron and Nora had extended minimalism to a fine art. Two modern white couches, an ottoman or two and half a dozen Charles Eames contour chairs were insufficient to seat the twenty or so guests, so some with tired feet, like Louise, who'd been shoveling dirt in the garden all day, were obliged to stand, or if lucky, lean against a wall.

"I do have to admit," said Louise in a quiet voice, "the man is a piece of work."

Bill looked down at her and frowned. "What'd Cunningham say to you?"

Louise paused. How to explain the offensive touch without inflaming her husband? He clutched her arm and said, "Don't tell me he got fresh again. I'm gonna tell him a thing or two."

"Please don't, Bill," she said, and blocked his path. "He didn't insult me, he just annoyed me. I shouldn't have mentioned it." This party was already a bummer, not flowing and filled with goodwill the way a party should. All it needed now was fisticuffs between Bill, a high-level State Department official, and Cunningham, who was with the prestigious firm of Wilson and Sterritt. "Look at him now," she said lightly. "He's annoying someone else."

Cunningham had brought his house guest, Lee Downing, a business associate of some kind from Texas. A silver-haired fellow, Downing was shorter and stockier, but as glossy looking as his companion. Now the two of them lounged against a couch and smiled down at a long-legged young woman perched on the couch's edge. She looked back at the men with wide eyes, like a doe contemplating flight from imminent danger.

"Oh, brother," murmured Bill. "The two of them have pounced on Hilde." Hilde Brunner was new to the neighborhood. She had come from Europe for an apprenticeship, but Louise wasn't sure from which country. "Mike can't stand the fact that you won't flirt back, so he looks for someone who will." Bill smiled. "Of course, I can't blame him for coming on to you, or to Hilde. . . ." He gave the young woman an appreciative glance.

"She's as lovely as our own daughters," said Louise, noticing how Hilde's long hair, brown with rosy highlights, swung gracefully as she turned her head to and fro. "How old do you suppose she is, twenty? Twenty-two? And yet I don't see anyone besides Mike and his friend acting like horny teenaged boys. Too bad they don't have wives to keep them in line."

While his silver-haired companion focused his attention elsewhere, Cunningham had slid down onto the couch next to Hilde. Louise sympathized, for she knew Cunningham—he wanted to sweep every woman he met off her feet. She could hear Hilde telling Mike how she had come to Sylvan Valley to work as an apprentice to the area's foremost potter, Sarah Swanson. That seemed a safe-enough subject; Louise turned her attention away.

Bill was surveying the crowd. He said, "Parties are supposed to be happy occasions. But I don't see many here who look like they're in a celebrating mood."

"Except them." She nodded at the cheerful group she and Bill had been talking to earlier: Frank and Sandy Stern and their next-door neighbors, Roger and Laurie

Kendrick. The three couples had joked about how their kids' college tuitions were impoverishing them. Louise had shared details of her kitchen renovation, joking that the addition of new granite and tumbled marble might make her a better cook. They challenged her to invite them over for a meal so they could find out for themselves.

"To become a better cook," Sandy Stern had dryly replied, with a shake of her red hair, "would require you to use a cookbook other than that one entitled *Twenty-Minute Dinners*. I intend to give you one." They'd all laughed, even Louise, who knew she was a mediocre cook. She'd confided to the group that the old-world look of the marble tiles had inspired her to buy French accessories for the room: a butter dish inscribed with "*Beurre*," some dishtowels with the Grand Hotel logo and a heavy milk pitcher with the word "Paris" stenciled on it.

"You're like an American tourist gone overboard, aren't you?" teased Roger Kendrick, peering at her over his eyeglasses. An internationally traveled news correspondent for the Washington *Post*, the scholarly Roger would never deign to buy foreign trinkets, she was sure.

"Don't laugh," Louise had warned him, "or I won't come through with that dinner."

As Louise stood companionably with her husband, her gaze passed over the room and settled on a man whose long, oval face was set in a morose pout. "Bill, look at Richard Mougey. What on earth is wrong with him?" Richard, like Bill, worked in the State Department, though until recently this was a cover for his actual job as a CIA operative. Richard languished on a second couch. His petite blond wife, Mary, her wide-skirted dress puffed out attractively beside her, cuddled next to him and held his hand.

"I know what's wrong," said Bill. "Richard's suffering buyer's remorse."

"What did he buy?"

"He decided to take early retirement; don't ask me why."

"Mary doesn't look happy, either," said Louise, "and Mary is always happy."

"She's still working at her job in Washington," said Bill. "I suppose her success is hard on Richard's ego, now that he's retired."

"What a shame. I always thought a retiring husband should be a moment of great celebration." She put an arm around Bill so that no one else could hear what she said. "I know what's wrong with Nora," she said, tilting her head toward their hostess. With her dark hair, flowing mauve-colored caftan and regal manner, Nora Radebaugh was the most striking woman in the room.

Bill chuckled. " 'What's wrong with Nora?' We've had to worry about that from the day we met her and Ron. You can sure tell he's a guy with something heavy on his mind." The handsome host was a very tall, elegant man with a shock of graying hair. He carried out his hostly duties with the air of a dignified servant, not even looking at his wife as he moved about the room. Nor did Nora acknowledge he was there. "Don't tell me it's that same old problem."

" 'Fraid so. Ron's refused to go to another of those awareness seminars in California. I thought the first one helped, but now Nora . . . Oh, well, maybe someday she'll settle down."

Bill laughed. "Don't count on it. Poets like Nora are that way. She'll probably still be writing love poetry when she's ninety, if she doesn't throw herself from a bridge onto a frozen river."

"Bill, that is so unkind, so . . ."

"I know—loathsome. Forgive me. It was a joke. I don't really want or expect her to follow in the shoes of John Berryman."

"Did John Berryman really—"

"Yep, and it must have been a damned hard landing."

She winced.

"Aw, sorry, Louise, no more jokes. Anyway, Nora will recover from whatever's ailing her. She always does."

Their hostess was crossing the living room to respond to the door chimes. The late guests were the Eldridges' next-door neighbor, Sam Rosen, with whom Louise had spent the entire Saturday afternoon, and his friend Greg Archer.

Sam, a short, dark-haired, friendly-faced man, gave Nora a big hug. Greg, who knew her less well, settled for a handshake. Sam was a congressional aide who had been Louise's gardening buddy for years. Today, they'd labored side by side, double-digging a vegetable garden in a crevice of land that lay on the border between their woodsy yards. Her husband jokingly called the two of them "Mutt and Jeff" when the tall Louise and the shorter Sam toiled together in the soil. Over the years, they had bought gardening equipment together and shared its use. An electric golf cart dubbed the "cartita" and a rototiller were the latest purchases.

Sam's life changed three months ago when Greg moved in with him. Archer was a slim, attractive man with high cheekbones and stylish blond hair, quite a contrast to Sam. This newcomer in Sam's life was not interested in gardens, but preferred collecting antique glass. In a quick flash of compatibility with Louise when they first met, he'd given her an erudite lecture on his collection and she'd shown him the small assemblage that she and Bill had in a wall cabinet in their dining room. But once he'd discovered she and Sam were a devoted gardening duo, Greg had kept his distance from Louise.

Instead of immediately joining the party circuit, the newcomers hovered near the front door, as if they couldn't quite decide whether or not they would stay. They were quietly arguing. "Oh boy," said Bill, observing the pair, "another disgruntled couple. This party has so many that I fear the situation's reaching criticality." He turned to Louise. "I hope you didn't make trouble between Sam and Greg."

"Of course not," she said. Then she reflected that she and Sam had spent the past two Saturdays together gardening. "I didn't mean to make trouble."

He took her arm and gave her a tug. "Let's go back to the bar. I need another drink if they're not serving dinner yet." As they approached the bar, however, they ran into two more neighbors with gloomy expressions. "Uh-oh," Bill told Louise, "more couples on the rocks. What the heck's going on around here?"

Mort and Sarah Swanson were another Mutt and Jeff pair. He was probably six-foot-six, wide-shouldered and slim, with horn-rimmed glasses and a completely bald head, features that made him look like a wise investment banker or perhaps a college professor. His wife was short and ample, but obviously muscular from years of throwing pots on a wheel. She had gray hair that fell in wisps of curls about her face and was caught in a fat braid down her back. At the moment, her gray eyes seemed to be holding back tears. Mort, mouth turned down at the corners, was pouring himself a glass of orange juice. This was strange behavior for Mort, thought Louise. He normally did not settle for less than a good belt of straight whiskey.

What was going on around here? Louise wondered. The mood of these close friends seemed to reflect the brooding, restless nature of the country at large. Instinctively, she reached out and gave her potter friend a hug, and a smile broke out on Sarah's face. She pulled Louise away a step or two, seeming to read her mind. "Forgive us if Mort and I are party poopers," Sarah said, "but we're going through a hard time just now. We've just gotten Mort's tests back. The liver, you know. It doesn't look good."

Liver. Pancreas. Louise shuddered to hear of those particular health problems. Torn rotator cuffs, which so many people seemed to suffer, were something one could handle, but liver problems sounded fatal. She felt irrationally obliged to convince Sarah that the worst would not come to be. "I'm so sorry, but I'm sure they will be able to do something. They must be able to do something. He's basically a very strong man. Isn't he accustomed to running three or four miles a day?"

Sarah laughed, desperately. "Yes, and I hope that improves his prospects. They're doing more tests. We're hoping for a magic reprieve, for someone to say, 'It's all a mistake and he's fine.' "

"You're so generous, taking on an apprentice at a time like this," she said, nodding at Hilde. "Maybe it would it be easier if the young woman stayed at our house for a while."

"Thank you, but no. Hilde is turning out to be wonderful. Even though she's quite tall, Mort calls her his 'little one.' Isn't that sweet? She's one of the stalwart Swiss, you know: quite learned, and a young activist, something like your lovely daughter Martha. She took a bachelor's degree in European cultural and political history, one of those young people interested in really understanding the Holocaust. And frankly, Louise, it's better to have another person around. It takes my mind off Mort's health."

"It shows you how well-known your work has become, that you're being sent apprentices from abroad."

"I guess so," said Sarah, glancing over to the couch on which Mike Cunningham and Hilde Brunner now sat side by side. "She's a little naive, I fear. I hope the attentions of the dashing Mr. Cunningham are not too much for her to handle. She's met him before, but he's coming on mighty strong tonight. I suppose no one would take a man like him seriously."

They noted the movement of black-uniformed servers laying food out in the dining room. Sarah said, "Ah, dinner at last. After we eat, I'll whisk Hilde safely home with us. Do come and sit with us."

Together with the Swansons, Louise and Bill edged toward the dining room, murmuring with pleasure when they saw the elegant repast that Nora, who was a real cook, had prepared. Guests were to serve themselves and sit on the patio.

Nora, looking as mysterious as the mythical goddess Circe, intercepted them. "There's a slight delay in serving dinner." She looked around self-consciously, then turned to them and pleaded, "And please, dear friends, this party needs your vital presence. Everyone is so somber. I'll admit that Ron and I are not at our best tonight. But don't leave early, Sarah, I implore you. I heard you saying that you would. I'll be heartbroken if you do." She squeezed Sarah's arm and smiled. "I'm sure we'll all feel more jolly once we've eaten." Then she swirled away as a worried server beckoned to her. With an imperious tilt of her head, Nora relayed a message, which the server hurriedly passed on to her dutiful husband.

The delay apparently was due to a wine shortage. Ron hurried away to get more from their wine closet.

Over the expectant chatter of a crowd about to sit down to a good meal, they barely heard the front door chimes. Nora went to answer it again. Louise could define an intense baritone voice and an insistent high one. The owners of the voices appeared to be jostling themselves right past the amazed hostess.

Louise pulled in a rasping, noisy gasp of air and fell back a step. Standing in the living room archway was a tall, muscular man with graying blond hair, piercing eyes behind gold-rimmed glasses and a mirthless smile on his face. Next to him stood a woman with sharp features and a blond pageboy.

"Hello, folks. Remember me?" said Peter Hoffman. "I'm back."

2

Louise staggered and almost fell against Bill as a wave of faintness overcame her. She gazed at the man in the doorway. He was a brutal murderer, a person she had never expected to meet again. Peter Hoffman might never have been caught had Louise not discovered his grisly crime. And now he was, free as a bird, back into her life like a very bad dream.

She could not stop trembling. Bill took a firm grasp on her elbow and whispered consolingly in her ear, as if soothing a mental patient. "Get a grip, honey. We knew the sonofabitch was leaving that hospital."

"But to think he'd have the nerve to show up here," she said. Hoffman, through the efforts of a pricey legal team headed by Mike Cunningham, had gotten off with an insanity plea four years ago. Instead of the harsh realities of the Lorton maximum-security prison near Washington, D.C., he vacationed at the taxpayers' expense at a mental hospital in the Blue Ridge mountains in southern Virginia.

When the sentence was handed down, Louise had been in her own home, having avoided the agony of sitting out both the long trial and the verdict in the Alexandria courtroom. She'd cried out in disbelief when she heard that he'd been declared insane at the time of the murder. After the trial was done, she had decided that to live a sane life herself she would block thoughts of Peter Hoffman from her mind.

And she'd been fairly successful. Even the news of his imminent release from Western State Hospital had only floated vaguely in the back of her mind, like a dark storm cloud that wouldn't come too near. She never believed she would actually see Peter Hoffman again, especially in her own backyard.

Louise and Bill, like the rest of the guests at the party, stood speechless, not knowing what to do. That is, until the feckless Mike Cunningham stepped forward. He sauntered up to Hoffman and gave him a big hug. "Peter! So good to see you." Cunningham drew his male companion up to Peter and said, "And here's your friend Lee Downing."

Hoffman boomed, "So good to see you, Lee," and gave him a businesslike handshake. Then the handsome Cunningham leaned down to embrace the blonde in the expensive cotton knit suit who stood quietly at Peter Hoffman's side—Peter's wife, Phyllis Hoffman. Louise hadn't seen her since the trial, when Phyllis had sat in a front row and supported her husband. She'd gained either weight or muscle. Mike Cunningham greeted Phyllis with a "Hi, sweetie."

Cunningham turned and stretched out his arms to the crowd, which was frozen in place like a tableau of wax figures. "Folks," he said, "we all have to remember Peter has served his term, paid his debt and been declared ready to resume his place in society."

"Oh, no," grumbled Sarah Swanson, "we don't need a killer in our midst."

"Now, now, Sarah," Cunningham said in a rebuking tone. As if he'd just been elevated to the job of party host, he took Peter's arm and escorted him into the midst of the group. A few people including Sarah's husband, Mort, and Roger Kendrick, gave Hoffman a restrained greeting. He responded with a big hug for Mort and an effusive handshake for the reporter. The others remained silent and still.

Louise's thoughts reeled back to that moment when she'd found parts of the body of Kristina Weeren, the woman Hoffman had murdered, in the bags of leaves she'd gathered from neighbors to mulch her yard. Paid his debt? How could a man who'd massacred someone be free to enter normal society after only four years?

Then she heard Nora's quiet voice. She stood in the living room archway, her face pale with shock. "Peter. Mike. Wait. You must go no further until you talk to Ron. Please honor my wishes."

Hoffman paid Nora no attention, but Mike Cunningham paused, looking ambivalent, probably wondering whether this party-crashing was a good idea. After all, Mike now lived in this neighborhood, in the intimacy of the Dogwood Court cul-de-sac. Would he risk all cachet with his neighbors?

Mike's lawyer's dilemma didn't appear to bother Peter Hoffman an iota, for his attention was elsewhere. His glance darted first to Louise and then to the white sofa.

As Hoffman passed by Louise and Bill, he stopped and stared straight at Louise. Bending his head, he murmured, "You're dismayed to see me, my dear?"

She nodded agreement and looked up at him. "I can't believe you have the nerve."

"It's been a long time, Louise. Maybe we could talk things over and come to a rapprochement. After all, I have done my penance. You might find me a changed person." Then, in a carrying voice, he continued, "Of course we can get together later and talk. I'd enjoy that immensely." He'd implied that Louise had made some overture to him, rather than the reverse. She should have sensed at once the significance of his statement. She gasped and raised her hand to her mouth to hide the fact that she was nearly in tears.

Somewhere nearby, Louise could hear Sarah Swanson protesting Hoffman's presence, while her husband tried to quiet her. Meanwhile, Hoffman swept on through the room as if making a royal procession. His wife trailed well behind, eyes downcast. He approached the white couch where Hilde Brunner sat and stood over her as if she were to be his first dinner course.

Louise thought the young woman, lounging there with her long legs extended before her, looked like a scared deer. And it was no wonder. First, Mike Cunningham had monopolized, no, positively enveloped her. Now a new male was demanding her attention. Her perfect oval face with its big green eyes turned and focused on Hoffman. "Hello," she said quietly.

"Well, who do we have here?" said Hoffman. "Someone new since I left Sylvan Valley." He reached down and took Hilde's hand, as if no one else in the room existed. There was faint air of perplexity on his face. "You, my dear, are like a dream," he said, in his deep, resonant voice. "Botticelli comes to mind, or perhaps Titian."

In this fixed moment, Louise saw Phyllis Hoffman's body stiffen and a blush suffuse her neck and face. Phyllis looked over and met Louise's stare. Even from halfway across the room, Louise could feel the hatred and she trembled despite herself. Perhaps it was natural that Phyllis hated her. She had been the messenger who'd brought the bad news that Peter was the mulch murderer. Louise knew Phyllis no longer lived the life of luxury that she had before Peter's crime was discovered. She had moved from their sleek mansion to a modest house on the edge of the neighborhood a mile away from the Eldridges. She went to work at Saks, selling designer clothing. Louise understood her resentment at the change in her lifestyle.

She exchanged a glance with Bill in which they wordlessly agreed to abandon the party. But then Ron Radebaugh reappeared, and Louise could tell he was sizing up the situation. She told Bill, "Thank God Ron's come back."

Ron strode into the living room and practically bounded over to Peter. "Well, well, what a surprise," he said, in a tone that one might use greeting a long-lost friend. But his actions belied his words. With one arm clamped around Hoffman's shoulders and the other gripping his arm, he propelled the uninvited guest back into the entrance hall. "Peter and I need to talk," he explained to the guests. "You must be hungry. Please help yourselves to the food."

Afterward, Louise realized that this horrible scene had taken only a matter of minutes. Assured by the noises in the hallway that the Hoffmans were being gently kicked out of the party, she and Bill joined the others to serve themselves, then drifted toward the patio to eat.

The outdoor air was thick with moisture and resounded with the songs of cicadas. Louise, who'd found it chilly in the Radebaughs' living room in her sleeveless gown, now found herself sweating in the almost unbearable heat. The cicadas' love songs, usually beguiling to a nature lover like herself, jarred her nerves. Or was it Peter Hoffman's rude appearance that had caused all her bodily senses to shift out of control?

People began talking all at once. "How dare the man . . ." "What nerve . . ." "His poor wife, so humiliating . . ." Louise and Bill sat down with the Swansons at a table for six, and Hilde joined them. Louise looked around for Mike Cunningham. Apparently he was busy at the front door, trying to smooth the exit of the unwelcome guests.

"What colossal arrogance," said Sarah Swanson, a forkful of food poised in midair, "to think he could have committed such a hideous crime and then come back, assuming his old neighbors would accept him as if nothing had happened."

Mort was picking at his beef tenderloin as if it were unpalatable and not the delicious gourmet treat that Nora had prepared for them. He laid down his fork and said, "You made that quite apparent in there, Sarah. But like it or not, Mike Cunningham's right: the man paid his debt. And no matter what we think, we can only hope that the doctors down there at Western State are bright enough to know whether he is stable enough to be released."

Louise shook her head and exhaled audibly. Then she looked at Mort and saw the attorney rather than the friend. No wonder Mort could accept the man. He was also with Wilson and Sterritt. And he used to manage affairs related to Peter's armament company in Old Town Alexandria. Though it was Cunningham who had defended Peter in the murder trial, Mort might well have helped devise Hoffman's clever legal escape from hard time.

Louise put her fork down. "Mort," she said, "that starts with the whole wrong premise, that the insanity defense was justified. To think that a man who deliberately killed and dismembered a woman is insane is just plain wrong."

Across the table, Hilde raised her head and gasped, her eyes stricken with fright. Louise met her gaze and stopped. What a way for the poor girl to be introduced to the details of Hoffman's crime.

Mort sat back and fussily began to clean his eyeglasses with his handkerchief. He obviously didn't realize the impact his words had on Hilde. "Sounds like an insane act to me. It's far from his normal mode. After all, he was a highly successful businessman."

"Arms dealer," his wife interjected in a sarcastic voice.

Mort slid his glasses back on his nose and gave Sarah a patient look. His gaze then turned to Louise. His expression said that neither his wife nor she could fully under-

stand the situation. "He was not only a businessman," he
continued, "but also a candidate for assistant secretary of
defense of the United States. And ladies, allow me go back
a tick. Manufacturing and selling arms in this country is
perfectly legal. Peter fulfilled many large government
contracts. He's now selling Hoffman Arms Company, a
perfectly honest business, to the man who's Mike Cunningham's house guest. You've met Lee Downing, haven't
you?" He nodded his bald head at the silver-haired man at
the next table. "Now, just because Peter flipped his lid a
few years ago—"

"Oh, my God," Louise exclaimed, sitting forward. Her
pulse was racing. "This was not just one rash act."

Bill put his hand on Louise's arm and said, "Honey,
calm down. Let's not go over all that old ground. We
haven't dwelt on this in years."

Sarah rushed to Louise's defense, but Louise hardly
heard her. Mort Swanson's remarks had awakened a deep
anger in her. She loved Sarah Swanson, who was like a
saint, had Louise believed in saints. But she had trouble
accepting Mort as a good friend. His lawyerly equivoca-
tions made him practically a devil in her eyes, had she believed in devils. But being a pragmatic Presbyterian, she
refrained from judging either of these extremes.

Hilde, sitting across the table, was eating again, her eyes
on the plate. Louise could see why men were attracted to
her. Not only was she a handsome young woman with
tanned, silky skin, but she used her mane of rosy brown
hair like a weapon. It now fell charmingly around her face
as if to shroud her from the harsh realities of the conversation. She brushed it aside as she looked up and said, "I
would never have guessed when Mr. Hoffman walked in,
for he seemed so friendly. An air of the Renaissance man
about him, I thought."

"Renaissance man indeed!" scoffed Sarah. "It takes

more than a mention of Botticelli to make a Renaissance man. This man's an utter scoundrel."

"I see that must be true," amended the earnest Hilde, "if he killed a woman in such a terrible way." Her wide shoulders trembled in a little shudder. "I do not think I would like to meet him again."

Louise nodded. "It would be better for you, Hilde, if you didn't." Then she glanced at Bill, but he'd already set his napkin beside his plate preparatory to leaving. Suddenly, their hostess appeared. Nora slipped into the empty chair beside Louise and leaned over and hugged her, her eyes wet with tears. "Louise, I'm so sorry. I know how that monster hurt you. I had no idea he would show up here, or even hear about our party."

Bill, his face grim, said quietly, "He heard it from Cunningham, no doubt. Nora, we don't blame you and Ron in any way. It only shows how brazen Peter Hoffman is. I intend to keep a close eye on the bastard. There's no way I'm going to let him harm my wife again." He stood up and pulled Louise to her feet. After another around of good-byes, he swept Louise down the patio steps and took her home.

3

Bill and Louise walked down the woodsy path to the street, as the cicadas continued their racket in the sticky night. It was a familiar late-summer sound in Washington. She only wished she could enjoy their cacophony the way she usually did. It reminded her of the powerful natural world surrounding her, more powerful than any that flawed mankind could create.

Bill seemed to pick up the thought from her mind. "A string orchestra," he said, "just for us."

She squeezed her husband's hand. She was grateful for Bill. She was also grateful to be going home, only a short walk across the cul-de-sac. That was why neighborhood parties were so welcome; there was no long car trip home. She imagined cuddling up in bed next to her spouse in the spoon position and drifting off to sleep, forgetting everything, especially Peter Hoffman.

When they reached their front yard, Bill's cell phone rang. He pulled it from his pocket and looked at the unfamiliar local number. "I bet it's Janie," he said. Indeed it was. Their seventeen-year-old, who'd driven to a party in Louise's car, told her father that the car wouldn't start.

"I'll come and get you," he said, and listened to the directions that Janie gave him.

"Humph," grumbled Louise. "That car is only two years old. I wonder if she just flooded it."

"Honey, you can't flood cars anymore. It has to be something else. Probably the battery and it just needs a jump."

They opened the gate to their yard, a tiresome task, but fencing the property had been necessary because of a growing deer population. Moon-shaped and rustic, the gate appeared to stand alone, set as an accent in the landscape. Actually, it was attached to fine mesh fencing that was almost invisible in the random forest shrubbery.

At the garage, Bill veered off so he could get in his car and collect their daughter. Louise continued up the moss-covered flagstone path and passed under the flower- and vine-covered pergola. In the pale moonlight, this overhead bower reminded her of gardens she'd known when they'd been stationed in Israel, though it was not nearly as exotic as those lily-and-rose-filled creations. Gardening in Washington, with its overheated summer nights and high humidity, was a challenge. Not every plant flourished here, as they seemed to do in the Middle East.

She opened the two locks on the front door and went in and switched on the lights, not bothering to relock the door. Bill and Janie would be back soon. Exhausted despite the fact that it was not even midnight, Louise slumped down on the living room couch. She wondered if she would sleep tonight, for bad memories were tumbling through her head. She'd determined not to let Peter Hoffman ruin her life, but now she needed to renew that promise to herself. She knew the answer: a hot bath and a good book. She sprang up, turned off all but the reading light next to the couch and went into the hallway to her bedroom. Then she heard the front door click open. Bill, with Janie.

Her steps slowed. No, it was too soon. Bill and Janie wouldn't be home this quickly.

A wave of cold passed through her body, and she shivered. Maybe it was just her neighbor, Sam Rosen, bringing her something she'd forgotten at the party. "Hello. Who is it?" she called. "Sam?"

There was no answer. For a moment, she allowed herself the luxury of leaning against the wall of the hallway, then chided herself for being so foolish as to think this northern Virginia neighborhood was safe enough that she didn't have to lock the door.

Turning quietly around, Louise tiptoed back into the kitchen. It was lit only with a stove light set on "dim." Every decision she made, she knew, would be important. Stifling a sob, she looked around and considered her options. A knife was too dangerous, for an intruder might be strong enough to pry it away from her and plunge it into her chest. Kitchen scissors held the same danger. Then she found just the thing, something with weight and not too much bulk. She grabbed her new milk pitcher off the counter and held it behind her back. Now the question was, where was the best place to meet the intruder? Certainly not in the hall or the kitchen.

She heard an amused, "What the fuck's this?" and pulled in a quick gasp of air. Was it Peter Hoffman's voice? Whoever it was, he had just bumped into something in the living room. She heard a crash and realized it was her blooming cape primrose, which sat in a corner on a high plant stand. A stab of anger filled her as she realized the intruder had deliberately destroyed the plant. It had to be Peter Hoffman.

A new feeling enveloped her and she gripped the pitcher as she would a billy club. How dare the man come here? A visceral sense of survival grew inside of her. She would not let him harm her; she was going to fight. The crash told her Hoffman was no more than fifteen feet away. She quickly darted from the kitchen into the adjoining dining room, scurrying around the antique pine dining room table as if it were a battlement. Since the living room light was on and the dining room was dark, he didn't see her, at least for an instant. But she saw him and gasped.

Hoffman had changed out of the casual sports attire he wore when he barged into the Radebaugh party. He was dressed now in dark sweat clothes with a balaclava over his face. Images of terrorists flooded her mind, and she wondered if it could be someone else—an Arab extremist, or even a cat burglar.

Then he said, "Louise, my little spitfire," and she was sure.

"You'd better get the hell out of here." She spat it out at him.

"Tut, tut," he sneered, "what language." He pulled off his head covering, stuck it in his pocket and unzipped his sweatshirt top to reveal a white undershirt. His face broke into a big smile, he opened his arms, but he didn't make a move toward her. "That's what I like about you, Louise, that spirit. It's like the spirit of a male pony that hasn't been de-balled."

"Save me your trite rhetoric and go home. Go home to Phyllis, who might appreciate you. Just get out of here, or they'll throw you right back into the mental hospital."

He came into the dining room area and took a few steps around the table. She took the same number of steps away from him. "Oh, no. I came to get you, Louise. I dropped Phyllis off at home and came back. I saw your husband drive off. Wondered where he went. To buy you ice cream or something at the Seven-Eleven?"

"He just went a few blocks." She stopped. She didn't want to bring up their beautiful daughter, Janie, for fear of putting ideas in his head. "He'll be back in an instant, so you'd better get out of here."

Hoffman laughed. "I don't think he'll return that soon. I figure I'll have enough time with you." He moved again toward her. "And I intend to make the most of it, bitch. Pay you back, my dear, for causing me to spend four of the most boring years of my life pretending to be insane."

He moved around the table. Now he was on the side nearest the wall of windows that looked out into the woods. For a big man, he moved like lightning. Louise inched farther away. In a moment he'd pounce, and she'd be a goner.

She had one chance. She threw the pitcher at him. He laughed as he ducked, and the pitcher smashed through a dining room window. "Now what are you going to do since you've emptied your chamber, Louise?" he taunted. "Or do you have an apple parer in your pocket?" Desperate, she realized she was cornered. Behind her was the antique cabinet with pieces of art glass, useless as weaponry. "Peter," she said, willing to deal now, "what is it you want?"

Even in the dimness, she could see his wicked smile and knew he wasn't done with her. He'd only started. "You'll see," he assured her. He feinted, first to the left, then to the right, and she didn't know which way to move. Then he rushed at her like a person possessed. He moved around the pine table and grabbed her with arms of iron and pulled her against him.

Before she could scream, he covered her mouth with one hand and bent her back in an uncomfortable position. What was he going to do—rape her? Or kill her? Her body trembled with rage as she used all her strength in an attempt to slide from under his grasp.

"Now, my dear, you're not so adventurous, are you?" he asked, sneering down at her. His breath was sour and hot, as if it were the physical manifestation of the evil inside him.

Then she heard the voices, and a shudder of relief passed through her body. They came from the patio, not from the front door as she would have expected. Pausing only an instant, Hoffman yanked her upright as if she were a rag doll and shoved her into the living room. Two figures were threading their way through the patio furniture. It was Sam Rosen and Greg Archer. "Sam!" she screamed. "Help!"

Not bothering to flee or even put on his hood to conceal his identity, Hoffman whipped off his sweatshirt, revealing the T-shirt underneath, and tied the dark garment casually by its sleeves around his waist. Stunned, Louise stood and propped herself against the couch as Hoffman switched on a floor lamp and stepped closer to the jagged hole in the broken window. "Hi, guys, it's Peter," he called to the two men. "This Eldridge woman invites me in, then she completely loses it." His eyes widened innocently. "Go figure. I can't. I have to get home now. Otherwise Phyllis is going to get mighty suspicious. I told her I'd only be out a few minutes. I'll leave you two to try to cool Louise down." With that, he hurried through the living room and out the front door.

Pulling in some deep breaths, she went to the patio door and unlocked it. "Thank God you came, Sam. Peter Hoffman broke into my house!"

Sam held her in a quick embrace. "We thought we heard a crash. What happened here?"

Greg added, "Peter told us he was coming to your house."

"What do you mean?" she asked incredulously.

Sam patted her arm. "Just tell us your story first."

She looked warily at the two men and said, "Bill had to drive over to Mount Vernon apartments to pick up Janie. No sooner did he leave than Hoffman walked in my front door, dressed like a burglar!"

Greg said, "Was the door locked?"

"No, actually, it wasn't."

"And you mean you didn't invite him in?"

She gave him a frosty look.

Sam put up his hands. "Hey, hey, let's not argue. What Greg's talking about is that Hoffman told us when we left the party that the two of you were going to be 'talking things over and making peace.' "

"That's an outright lie!" she cried.

Sam nodded his head slowly. "Apparently so. What happened to the window?"

"He was coming at me, Sam. I threw a pitcher at him, but he still grabbed me. He acted as if he'd like to kill me. He wore all dark clothes and he had a hood on, a balaclava."

"*I* didn't see any hood," said Greg. "Did you, Sam?"

Sam reluctantly shook his head.

"What I observed," recalled Greg, "was that he was wearing a pretty innocent-looking t-shirt."

Louise's eyes blazed. "Obviously, he left the party and dropped his wife at home and changed his clothes. Then he snuck back over here and barged into my house."

Greg sighed and rolled his eyes. "One thing sure is true: you've made an enemy out of that guy."

She put her hands on her hips. "You mean because I discovered he murdered a woman?" Louise's eyes blazed with anger.

Sam came over and put an arm around her shoulder. "Louise, sit down on the sofa. You have to calm down. Are you hurt in any way?"

She did as he suggested, wiggling her shoulders and moving her arms around. Then she gazed down at the mess near the smashed dining room window. "But I need to clean up that glass and the pieces of my pitcher."

"Not right now," said Sam. "What you need is a drink. Where's the whisky?"

She slumped back on the couch. "There's some brandy in the cupboard next to the fridge. Glasses are there, too."

Greg sat in the wooden antique chair across from her, the one Louise had inherited from her grandmother. Fortunately for him, he didn't lean back or exhibit any other strenuous behavior, or she would have called him on it. "Face it, Louise, you were talking to this man at the party about an hour ago," he told her.

Stifling all sarcasm, for she had to learn how to get along with this companion of her friend, she replied, "I did not talk to him, or at least not more than a sentence. He talked to me. And you're right. I have made an enemy out of this man. I only hope the police will arrest him."

"Maybe you can get a restraining order."

Sam brought her a little glass of brandy and one for him and Greg as well. She sipped hers slowly. Then the reality sank in. Peter Hoffman didn't necessarily want to hurt her, he just wanted to make trouble. Now she and Bill would have to step up and take the initiative to get a restraining order. Or would they possibly throw him back into the mental hospital?

Greg leaned forward carefully, apparently realizing he was sitting on a relic. "The trouble is, Louise, he could make a case for himself. Your front door was open, right?"

"Not open, unlocked. But that didn't give him the right to come in."

"He said you let him in. That's the story he's going to give the police."

She looked at Sam's new friend. "Greg, you hardly know me at all. If you had any idea of the background here, you'd know I would never let Peter Hoffman in my house, not in my garage, not in my yard, not if I had the means to stop him."

Greg smiled. "That sounds really tough, Louise. What you're saying is, you're not going to take shit from that guy, are you?"

4

Yoga mat before her on the old wooden decked front porch of the rented beach house, Louise completed the sun salutation. Janie, in a high-cut tank suit, sat on the front steps, tucking her long blond hair into a bathing cap. The seventeen-year-old was going with her father into the Atlantic surf for a swim. They invited Louise to join them, but she had pleaded for "quiet time" by herself.

"How much more quiet time do you need on this vacation?" asked Janie. "Are you sure you're all right?" Louise was now doing the upward facing bow, which made her back feel particularly good.

"I'm all right. I really am," said Louise. They'd been at the house in Rehoboth Beach for two days, and her family still fussed over her too much. Martha was arriving soon, which would mean more unwelcome attention.

"Ma, tell me why they didn't arrest Peter Hoffman for breaking into our house."

"It's complicated, Janie," said Louise, now busy executing the cobra. "We tried to press charges, but the police didn't believe me. There were too many witnesses backing up Hoffman's story. But I don't want to talk about it any more."

"Oh, whatever," said her daughter, rebuffed. She flounced to her feet. Arms akimbo, she stood over Louise and gave her a blue-eyed scowl. "Close me out and just keep doing your yoga stuff. Act as if I can't understand anything. Treat me as if I'm still twelve instead of nearly eighteen and will soon be off to college and out of your hair. I'm just trying to be nice. With one day's notice, I get dragged out of town. I have to give up my summer job and time with my boyfriend. Now you won't even discuss with me the fact that some creep is making your life miserable."

Twisting herself into the half-moon position, Louise looked with some difficulty over at her daughter. The girl was annoyed with her, for sure, but part of that was just talk, for Janie was basically happy. Happy in love, Louise feared, smitten with Chris Radebaugh, Nora and Ron's nineteen-year-old son. He'd finished his sophomore year at Princeton, where Janie would enter as a freshman next year. Louise knew Janie cherished every weekend moment she could spend with Chris, who had a summer job in Baltimore. And it was true, Janie's summertime employers at a software firm were not happy to have her suddenly leave for a couple of weeks.

"I'm so sorry, Janie, forgive me. But we had to get away. I'm having a tough time dealing with all this."

"The trouble with you, Ma," said her daughter, crouching down beside her mother, "is that you think you're in this universe alone. You're not a planet out there all by yourself. You're in a constellation." She smiled. "Like that metaphor?"

"Yeah," admitted Louise. "And this constellation?"

"It includes a lot of people. Me, Dad, Martha, and all those nutty friends of yours in the neighborhood and all around the Beltway. Even that funny little Emily Holley in Bethesda is willing to come out and stay with you whenever Dad's away. Did you get that message?"

"No," said Louise, thinking of the handful of pink messages from friends that she'd been too distracted to answer. "I see what you mean, honey. I'll try not to be such a bore."

"Recluse is what you're becoming," amended her daughter.

"Recluse, then. Maybe I'm suffering from post-traumatic stress."

"Maybe you need some couch time." They both laughed, knowing that Louise preferred the counsel of friends and family. She had avoided psychiatrists despite facing traumatic situations more than once in recent years.

And she had been traumatized by Peter Hoffman. His break-in and attack on her Saturday night was insult enough, but the situation grew worse. Bill, angrier than she'd ever seen him, had called the police, and the parties ended up at the Fairfax County sheriff's Mount Vernon substation on Route One, only a mile from the Eldridge home. Detective George Morton had been in charge. He was a policeman who had never appreciated the fact that Louise had solved some perplexing murders that had puzzled the Fairfax sheriff's office. A man who disliked citizen involvement in crimes, he apparently considered her to be no more than a snoopy housewife. Her friend, Detective Mike Geraghty, had also shown up for the long interrogation.

Although Geraghty's blue eyes had been sympathetic and his questions right to the point, Morton had challenged her. "Are you sure you're not paranoid over this guy? All evidence, and these witnesses that Mr. Hoffman has bothered to invite here, indicates you invited the man in."

Louise looked at the big, white-haired Geraghty for help. "You don't believe that, do you, Mike?"

Geraghty had stood solidly and said, "I didn't think you'd

invite Peter Hoffman into your house. But just about everybody, includin' Mrs. Phyllis Hoffman, is corroborating it."

"Yeah," said Morton, a man who would have appeared
handsome had he not sneered so much. "And why would
a guy like that phone us so quickly unless he thought you
were gonna try to get him in trouble? Here's a guy with an
exemplary record during his four years of incarceration,
trying to start his life over again. Then the first thing that
happens is he tangles with you."

Hoffman had apparently met the authorities in the
same casual clothes he'd worn at the Radebaugh's party,
and Louise wondered what had happened to that balaclava. He told his manufactured story: While at the party,
Louise had invited him to come to her house. She told
him she wanted to talk things over with him, "sort of clear
the air. Ask anybody at the party and they'll tell you I'm
right." And they had, and partygoers had backed up his
version of the events. By early Sunday morning, he was
freed to go home.

When she heard this outcome, she realized she was in a
war, like the country's war with terrorists. Her enemy, just
like a terrorist, was unpredictable, ruthless and willing to
sneak about and lie.

Disgusted, Bill informed the police that their lawyer
would appeal for a restraining order after they returned
from their trip.

As for Louise's career, it was slack time in the produc-
tion schedule for her TV show. She'd had only a few appointments to cancel. The watering of her houseplants
was turned over to her reliable housecleaner, Elsebeth
Baumgartner. Sam Rosen promised he'd care for the gardens.

These thoughts raced through Louise's head as she finished her leg extensions. She lay down and assumed the
corpse position to relax completely and wipe her mind

free of all tension. *The corpse position is so right for me,* she thought to herself. *I'll quit being tense once I'm dead.*

She knew her husband was worried about her. He'd been optimistic at first: *I know how you love the water. As soon as you hit the beaches of the Atlantic, you'll come right back to your usual happy self.* But she wasn't recovering the way he thought she should be. It was Wednesday, and she still had nightmares, trembling hands and a fear of going outside. The image she couldn't shake was of a huge man in dark sweats and hood, his fetid breath assaulting her face, his intrusive body pressed against hers . . .

Bill, blond and handsome, came out on the porch, towel slung over his shoulders, dark glasses protecting his eyes from the sun. "Good-bye, darling," he said, bending down to kiss her. "Have a good time by yourself." He and Janie waved and started off.

"You, too," she said absently. She was glad they were going. Bill couldn't help right now, nor could Janie. She needed to be alone to sort out the murky tangles in her own mind.

Her thoughts returned to the Radebaughs' strange dinner party. All their close friends seemed to be having some sort of trouble. The Radebaughs had their perennial marriage problems created by Nora's special needs. Mort Swanson faced grave health issues. Sam Rosen and Greg Archer seemed to be experiencing adjustment problems, though that wasn't surprising, since their relationship was only three months old. And Richard Mougey suffered separation anxiety since he'd left his beloved job of thirty years in the State Department. Now Louise was having emotional problems. As a consequence, her family had troubles as well, big troubles.

It seemed totally wrong to have this murderer put Louise on the defensive and drive her and her family out of town. Just the same, maybe she could be a little more sociable with her fellow castaways. She ran to the porch railing. Her family was halfway down the block. "Hey, you guys," she yelled, "will you wait for me?"

They nodded, and she hurried into the rental house to put on her bathing suit and join her family in the surf.

5

Phyllis Hoffman disliked this unfamiliar role, the role of the little wife serving hot shrimp balls and drinks. For God's sake, she was an independent woman. She had turned herself into one during the past four years. Finding herself with a big problem, namely, a husband who was a murderer, she'd gritted her teeth, gotten a job and learned to live on her own. Most importantly, she'd found a way to anesthetize herself on the matter of Peter's behavior. She simply told herself that if she'd been in his shoes, she'd have done the same thing.

It had been hard, sometimes, to withstand the stares of gawking strangers and keep her head up despite being the wife of the man who committed the most obscene crime in Fairfax County history. A coworker asked her why she didn't divorce Peter. In answer, Phyllis could have replied, "It's the money, stupid." But she wasn't going to describe how divorcing Peter would mean losing her share of that pot of gold all tied up in his multimillion-dollar arms business.

Now, Peter is out of the nuthouse, and like a hausfrau out of the forties, I'm ordered to leave the room so the men can talk in private.

As if her husband read her thoughts, he grabbed her hand as she walked by the couch on which he sat. He smiled fondly at her and said, "Phyllis, you are great. Don't think you aren't." A broad gesture at the shrimp balls, $5.95, frozen, at the nearby Belleview Market. "And these look fantastic. But you know that Mike and I have a lot of business to discuss, and damned quickly."

She wiggled her hand out of her husband's grasp. "There was a time when I used to sit in on your little tête-à-têtes with Mike or with Mort Swanson. I even gave you a little hardheaded business advice from time to time. What the hell are you up to? And why did Mort drop in and then leave before I could even say hello? I know something's up. You've sold the business to Lee Downing. But now what? What's happening to us?"

Mike Cunningham sat there, deceptive as a snake. "Sweetie," he cooed. She thought she'd kill the man if he called her that again. "The deal isn't quite concluded. Seriously, Phyllis, the details are so boring and technical that you'd walk out on us in a minute, anyway. Peter can give you a recap later."

The fact was that she'd appreciate a recap, an explanation by these two allegedly smart men as to the apparent decline in Peter's business while he'd been hospitalized and why the hell that had happened when he used to brag about his brilliant staff. There had to be some reason she was living so low in this creepy little house, when she used to live so high in their architect-designed place of six thousand square feet. Insult of all insults, she'd heard that her beloved former house was on the market again and being considered for purchase by Peter's high-priced lawyer, now sitting there and smiling that Cheshire cat smile at her. Mike's home on Dogwood Court was suddenly too "public" for his tastes.

Despite these thoughts, she didn't want to express too

much interest. She may already have gone too far. There was some reason why their old lawyer, Mort, had ditched this confab. The fact was that she no longer felt she knew her husband. She certainly couldn't figure out Mike Cunningham's influence on him, much less what role Lee Downing, a big shot from Houston, played in the business deal now going on. She also could barely understand why a man who'd just been released from a mental hospital would go and do a number on Louise Eldridge, the woman partly responsible for putting him there. But he'd gotten away with that little ploy without being arrested. . . .

She made a graceful wave with her hand and laughed. "I can't stay, anyway. My favorite reality program is on, and it's a damned sight more interesting than anything you two have to talk about." Leaving them to their private con-versation, she sauntered down the hall to the master bed-room, where she turned on the television set loudly enough for them to hear. Then, first peeking out to be sure they hadn't moved from their seats, she dashed back to the study adjacent to the living room and left the door ajar. It had been her study until Peter had been released from the hospital, and now was being transformed into his office. Several file cabinets lined one wall. All had locking draw-ers, and to her extreme annoyance, Peter was transferring a select few files from Hoffman Arms and then locking the drawers.

Her husband, though clever, did not know everything about her. She'd learned a lot since Peter had gone to the loony bin. She'd had to. She learned how to find a job— not easy in a bad job market—and how to sell. She'd tried like mad to get something in the city of Alexandria, only four miles north of Sylvan Valley and with acres of cutesy shops in its ancient environs, but it was almost as if a cabal was set against her because of what her husband had done. She'd finally gotten a position at Saks in Friendship

Heights. It was on the border between the District of Columbia and Maryland, where the name Phyllis Hoffman rang fewer bells. It was a long drive from northern Virginia, but a job was a job. Helping relieve the stress of the long commute was a nearby gym where she could work out once her shift was over.

At Saks, possibly because of her natural aristocratic bearing, she'd been assigned to sell St. James fashions— understated, tailored and expensive as hell. This meant she got them for herself at a forty-percent discount.

Just months into Peter's hospital stay, she'd learned the designer home she had lived in for six years was to be sold and she was to move to something more modest. With the budget she'd been given, all she could afford was this place. It was practically a hovel when she'd bought it, but she'd had it painted and conjured up some cut-rate designer furniture from a furniture outlet. Her inimitable taste had given the humble abode a makeover that was a hell of a lot better than any on the Home and Garden channel.

Peter assured her that her semi-poverty had an explanation. They'd had to pay millions for his insanity defense. This meant his arms factory in Alexandria eventually had to go. Peter ducked specific questions on the business, but had told her enough for her to infer that the man in the living room with Peter, the obnoxious Mike, was the main recipient of Peter's millions, or at least Wilson and Sterritt was. So why her spouse liked Mike so much she couldn't understand. She would find it impossible to be friends with someone who'd ripped her off. In fact, she'd find every opportunity to break their balls.

This house, though, was not like that quiet mansion where she used to preside as a domestic goddess with a cook and housekeeper, a place where one could discuss anything in absolute privacy. This little house had a drawback that Peter didn't know about. From this room adjacent to the living room, she could hear any conversation, especially with the big furniture placed near the adjoining wall and the heat vent, as she had arranged it.

She sat down quietly on the Herman Miller desk chair she'd purchased for a song because of a stain, rolling it close to the wall.

Mike: "It was not a good move coming to that party. And then following the Eldridge woman home. What the hell were you trying to do, be thrown back in the lockup?"

Her husband's voice now: "You don't understand, pal. I'm doin' a number on that babe. Louise Eldridge is the only thing that stands between me and a lifetime of ease and security. She's so nosy that it wouldn't have taken her any time at all to start snooping into my affairs and maybe even get Phyllis up in arms. After the other night, she's gonna be scared as shit to even think about me, much less pry into my affairs."

Mike again: "I just hope the cops continue to believe your story."

Peter, laughing: "You know how good that story was? The cops, or at least Detective Morton, bought it. Can you believe that? He's got no use for the Eldridge babe. He thinks she's the world's nosiest busybody. He actually believed that Louise told me at the party that she wanted to clear the air. And I gave him the names of witnesses who would prove it."

Mike: "That isn't the way I heard it. I've heard she hates you so much that she won't talk about you, much less to you. The Mougeys told me she acts as if you never existed. And you got the cops to swallow the whole thing."

Peter: "See how good I am at revising reality?" Another one of her husband's annoying laughs.

But why were these men meeting? Certainly not to talk about that asinine Louise Eldridge.

A shuffling, as if papers were brought out. Mike: "Okay, Peter, let's get down to business, get some details ironed out. The monies are in their various places. And we're clear on my cut, right?"

Peter, coughing, or was he laughing: "Forty percent is a huge take for you, Mike. I know what you've done and you've done it well. But for Chrissake, forty? How about thirty-five? I have to live away on this for the rest of my life."

Away? Where away? Phyllis grabbed the arms of the chair. A slow anger began to build inside her. She could feel her body temperature rise.

Mike: "Come on now, you'll be back in business somewhere before I've filed my income tax returns next year. Vienna. Maybe Berlin."

Peter, in a voice so quiet that Phyllis had to strain to hear it: "All right, good buddy. Let's double-check the figures in those offshore accounts. And remember all our cautionary moves. We've got Downing over a barrel and we don't want to let him off it." Then he couldn't resist a good laugh. "The final touch, of course, was phoning the SEC ethics hotline about that industrial spy. The sonofabitch doesn't dare complain about our business deal now. It attracts too much attention to him and his company."

Mike: "When do you think you'll make your move?"

Peter, speaking even more quietly than before: "I'm shootin' for two weeks, maybe sooner. Gotta leave her something, of course, or she'll raise holy hell."

Phyllis wondered if the "her" he referred to was her.

"I've paved a lot of false trails that will make it hard to follow the real me. You and I can work that and the divorce out together. Give her this house plus a stipend."

Phyllis' face grew red. Jesus, they were talking about her and her future as a divorcée. Peter and his lawyer had sold off his businesses, stashed the money and now he intended to run out on her permanently. And after all those promises he'd made as she stood by him. All those tiresome trips down to Staunton, Virginia, to visit him, staying at the Shoney's Inn and eating their putrid food. Keeping him informed with lots of clippings from the Washington papers so that he stayed current on business news and politics.

Phyllis had heard enough.

She could picture the future, for she saw these women every day behind the slick counters at Saks: Phyllis Hoffman, with facelifts and lots of makeup to cover the years, still peddling St. James clothes to rich bitches for decades.

Not for her! Good thing this house had thin walls. Now she had all the information she needed to fuck over the two sons-of-bitches in the next room, who were trying to fuck her over. All she needed were account numbers. Peter was clever at hiding things, but she was even more clever at finding them. Hadn't she found the clue to Peter's hideous crime in his office cubbyhole well before the Eldridge woman had guessed and tipped police? Phyllis'd known her husband was the mulch murderer well before anyone else. The faintest of smells, a horrible smell, had come from his office, and she'd figured out immediately what it was. Though disgusted with the task, she'd secured his dark secret so that it could have remained a secret forever, had not that little lightbulb gone off in Louise Eldridge's head.

She'd always known what Peter was up to in his dealings. He'd told her that was part of her charm—that she was so smart, so canny. That's why she could hardly believe he thought he could run out on her now. She'd outwit the bastard before he or anyone else was the wiser.

As if to confirm all this, and before she got softhearted again and began to invent excuses for the man, Peter's cell phone rang. When he answered, she could tell by the low and insinuating tone of his voice that it was a girl. What girl, she didn't know. Just another of many he'd had during their marriage. He'd lowered his voice to almost a whisper, but apparently turned away from Mike Cunningham and faced the wall, because his voice came clearly through the vent.

"Well, hello there, my dear. Good to hear from you."

How had he found a girl so soon? He only left the hospital five days ago! It must have been someone he contacted while in the damned place!

"And when can we get together? Saturday? No? How about Sunday? Great. See you then."

Phyllis grabbed her head with both hands. It hurt from what must be her blood pressure rising. She felt like getting up and running into the living room and screaming at Peter. He would not get away with this. She took some deep breaths and tried to calm down so she could consider the options. She'd try it one way, by getting hold of the account numbers, or maybe even appealing to Mort Swanson. If she didn't succeed, she'd try it another way.

It was interesting and educational, working as a clerk in a fancy store. Such clerks were a special breed, some of them privileged women like herself who were down on their luck, often because of divorce. Others were up from the bottom. They'd learned from someone how to walk and talk well and had a flair that made them good with upscale customers. Even low-class, foreign-born women, the nervy kind who were determined to reach some level of financial success without necessarily following the rules. Usually, they had good looks that helped them succeed in fashionable boutiques.

These women had lots of murky connections—thieving, drug-taking criminal husbands, sons or brothers, some of them connected with the mob—like her Russian friend Sophie, who fascinated and occasionally repelled her.

Phyllis never told Sophie much about herself, but the woman seemed to sense that life hadn't been fair to Phyllis. More than once, Sophie mentioned to her, in a joking way that Phyllis knew was serious, that if Phyllis ever needed anyone beaten up or otherwise totally removed from circulation, she had just the brother who would do it, for a price.

6

L ouise paced around the living room of the rented beach house, not hungry, for she'd already snacked on cheese crackers and ginger ale, and not sleepy, because she'd napped. She was bored, sated with vacation. She went out on the big wraparound porch and balked for a moment as she stared into pitch darkness. Out there was a lovely white sand beach and beyond it, the world's second largest ocean. Then Europe. But who knew what dangers were on that beach? Normally, she would have fearlessly set out for a walk in bare feet, daring the waves to wash over them. But recent events had spooked her, and she was afraid of darkness.

Seven days at the beach was quite enough for her, but Bill and the girls were still enjoying themselves. They'd all had a new burst of enthusiasm since their twenty-year-old, Martha, had flown home from Chicago and then caught a ride to Rehoboth to join the family.

Louise went back into the living room, catching a glimpse of herself in an old mirror tacked to the door, noting that her arms and her long, bare legs in shorts were a rich brown. Martha, also a brunette, would look like her mother in a matter of days. Bill and Janie, being blond, had turned golden brown. A few more days here and they would all be overexposed to ultraviolet rays. At the moment, Bill and the two girls were out on an overnight charter fishing trip. When Louise announced that she wouldn't join them, Bill had looked down at her with concern. "That's okay, if you still want to be alone. And I know you'll be safe here. But remember, you have to get back to the real world eventually. I have to return to Vienna soon, and you'll soon be due back at the studio."

He was right. Bill would continue his work with the International Atomic Energy Agency, and in two weeks, she'd be on location for one of her television garden shows. Though it was only a two-day trip to the Philadelphia Botanical Gardens, it took lots of prep. And she was behind. She hadn't consulted with the associate producer about logistics yet or even read the script. She shook her long hair, as if trying to shake away the demons of paranoia, but her darkest fear was that if she didn't watch out, her producer, Marty Corbin, might decide that her coanchor, John Bachelder, should take a larger role in the show. She should be spending her vacation time reviewing the script. But she'd left it on the Winthrop desk in their living room in Sylvan Valley.

The thought propelled Louise to grab her purse and take the car keys off a utility shelf in the kitchen. As she stepped outside the beach house and locked the door, she looked at the clear sky with its half-moon and stars shining down on her and saw that it would be a great night for a two-hour road trip.

Nevertheless, she dodged from bush to bush in the scrub-filled yard, like a soldier eluding enemy bullets, as she made her way to the safety of Bill's Camry. A girl couldn't be too careful.

With Caetano Veloso singing in the background, Louise found it a soothing drive back to Washington. There was enough traffic through the pastoral country so that she wasn't afraid, and then she stopped at a crab place, still open at ten-thirty, where she ate two large crabs with butter and vinegar and drank an iced tea. It was an unusual but pleasant experience. Eating alone was something she rarely did. In fact, taking a trip longer than fifty miles without her husband was something she rarely did. But crabs were one of her favorite foods. Messy, but she hardly cared what happened to the old sweatshirt and shorts she wore. She rounded the Beltway and, feeling like a horse anxious to return to the barn, hurried the twelve miles straight south on the George Washington Parkway to her home.

Her trepidation increased as she pulled into Sylvan Valley. The houses were all dark except for the gleam of a dim light through an occasional window and a few backyard floodlights. Still, the night was quiet, and things seemed safe. She focused on the routine of taking the keys out of the ignition and opening and closing the car door, details to fill her mind so she wouldn't think of Peter Hoffman.

Louise went into the house and walked straight to the Winthrop desk. She found the script as she'd left it, on top of a pile of perfectly stacked papers. She was nothing if not neat. Her gaze wandered out through the tall dining room window that she had shattered with her misfired pitcher. In the family's absence, the big pane had been replaced by a glass company. She saw it needed touch-up cleaning to remove the fingerprints of the workmen. Not wanting it in that condition when they returned from vacation, she found her bottle of window cleaner and a rag and rubbed the inside pane until it was spotless.

Her gaze reluctantly turned outward toward the garden, and she could feel her heartbeat quicken. She didn't want to admit that she was scared to walk into her own yard.

"Come on, scaredy-cat," she told herself, and walked over and turned on the patio light. Nothing out there but a lot of innocent-looking garden furniture and her beguiling patio garden filled with peonies, astilbe, cimicifuga and daylilies. Breathing hard, she unlocked the door, went out just a few steps and, keeping her eyes forward, cleaned the other side of the glass. So far, so good. She set down her cleaning supplies, stepped a few paces further onto the patio and stared into the dark woods. One thing concerned her. Since there had been drought this summer and no rain since they left town, she wondered if Sam Rosen had remembered to water her native azaleas. They were in an outlying garden in the deepest part of the woods in an easy-to-forget spot. With her mind now on gardening, her body began to relax.

She made her way down the two timber steps into the darkness of the backyard, treading carefully over the woods floor so that she didn't trip on twigs or downed branches. Through the dark shadows, she could see that the azaleas looked perky and fresh. But who could tell for sure without touching? Crouching down, she burrowed her fingers beneath the piney mulch and made pleasant contact with the soil. It was damp but not sodden. Her good gardening buddy had not forgotten.

She made her way back across the yard and into the house, wandering through the living room, the dining room and then the kitchen, where she stopped and looked around. She straightened the towel with the Grand Hotel logo and looked at the empty spot on the counter where the "Paris" pitcher had stood. When they got back from vacation, she intended to go out and buy another one.

Suddenly Louise felt better, as if she had regained possession of her own property.

She locked the doors, grabbed the script and her purse and left, anxious now to return to the cottage on the beach and her long-suffering family. She'd been a party-pooper on this vacation, but now she intended to go back and enjoy herself.

7

Martha Eldridge sat in the backseat with her mother on the trip home from the beach. "Pretty humdrum scenery, don't you think?" she said, just to make conversation. Her mind was on other, more important things.

"Do you think so?" said her mother, in a surprised voice. "I like the open countryside and these small towns. It's a welcome change from the city."

"Well, you know me, Ma," replied Martha, really meaning *You don't understand me at all*. She was a bit impatient at her parents' lack of understanding of her urban preferences, but of course she and her mother had less contact with each other the past few years, so how was she to know how fiercely Martha espoused a different set of values from the suburban upper-middle-class values of which her parents reeked. "Give me a high-rise any day. I favor cities. Chicago. Zurich. Prague. Rome." She paused, then added, "Paris, of course," and couldn't help chuckling.

Louise looked at Martha over her sunglasses. "You're laughing at me because I bought those French accessories for the kitchen. But that rough tile inspired me. I feel like I'm in a European kitchen now."

Martha couldn't resist the dig. "Maybe so, but I doubt a

Frenchwoman would spread a towel reading 'Grand Hotel' behind her new faucet. Or have a pitcher with 'Paris' written on it sitting on the counter."

Her mother smiled. "I don't care. I love my gadgets, just like you love your cities. That's obviously why you majored in urban studies."

"Anyway," added Martha, ready to end this discussion, "I saw all this countryside on the way here." Behind her sunglasses, she shot a sideways glance at her mother, wondering if this was the time to drop her bombshells. She had to do it soon, because she had a flight back to Chicago the next day. Martha had decided to suspend her studies at Northwestern for a year and marry Jim Daley. She was twenty, almost twenty-one, with her combined B.A.-M.A. degree a year from being finished, while Jim was twenty-five. He already had a bachelor's and a law degree from DePaul University and was working as an assistant district attorney in Chicago. He was straining like a horse in a stall, ready to gallop forth and launch his political career.

Jim had pushed her to tell the folks some time during this unexpected family vacation. "It's the ideal moment," he'd said in a private phone conversation while the rest of her family was out looking for shells on the beach. "Just lay it on 'em. Everybody'll be laid back and just accept it. Anyway, your dad loves me." She told him she'd have to gauge the situation and decide when to break the news. Their plan was for them to marry soon so Martha could help Jim in his campaign for city alderman. After that, win or lose, she'd resume her own university classes.

Each day at the beach house, Martha had waited to see her mother return to normal so she could relate the news. The "normal" Louise Eldridge, her daughter knew, was a feisty, attractive woman who hadn't collapsed just because she'd passed the age of forty-five. Martha was secretly pleased that she resembled her mother so much and liked the idea that she might wear as well as her parent did.

But this parent still wasn't herself after that creep Peter Hoffman had done his damage. Her mother wasn't sleeping well. Martha knew it because she herself was a night reader and she heard her mother prowling the ocean cottage at all hours.

And her hands shook. Today was the first day they appeared to be steady. *When have my mother's hands ever shaken before? Not even those other times when she was in some crazy jam, the kind she always seems to get in.*

Finally, at the beach house, Martha had lassoed Janie to help, and they'd taken over the obvious chores like cooking and setting and clearing the table to spare her mom the embarrassment of fumbling with cooking equipment and silverware.

Now her mother grabbed her arm and pointed out the car window. "Look, Martha, at that flock of birds. There must be thousands of them. I bet you can't see that in the city."

"Pretty cool, I'll admit," said Martha, giving them a fleeting look. Though of course she wanted to help her mother bail out of this funk she was in, she was not totally sympathetic. She knew no man would intimidate her the way this jerk had intimidated her mother. Martha was tougher than that. Her mother was always looking into the fate of every sparrow, anguishing over friends in trouble and obsessing about the future of her career as a TV garden show host. Martha was different, and she was glad. Both she and Jim looked at the bigger picture, at the plight of cities and counties, even nations.

Her thoughts suddenly returned to the birds. "You know what they make me think of? Voters going to the polls."

Her mother laughed. "Do people go to the polls in such

an orderly fashion?" She turned a little in her seat and looked at Martha. "You're working for Jim, aren't you?"

"Of course," said Martha. "What would you expect? We've been engaged for months now; we just haven't bothered with a ring because there were lots more important things to do." She added proudly, "Jim's a great candidate. He'd probably make it without my help, but I want to be there by his side."

"That will make it hard to keep up with your classes."

"Yes."

"So you're dropping them?"

Martha looked at her mother. She was making this almost too easy. "Just for the fall quarter."

"That makes sense. What happens if he wins? Doesn't a politician need a wife?"

Martha's jaw dropped. Was she this transparent, or did her mother have telepathic powers? "He could use one to good advantage. And of course I love him terribly. You already know that."

"Where do you want the wedding, and when?"

Martha reached over and grabbed her mother's well-tanned hand. Maybe it was because of the surprise of her touch, but Martha could feel the slight tremble in the fingers. She clasped it even tighter. "Did I ever tell you you were great? The wedding? Soon, Ma. Low-key. And wherever you think. Here in Washington?"

They received a long look from her sister Janie in the front seat. Had she heard? No, her younger sister couldn't hear over the music that was playing up there, but she knew something important was going on in the backseat.

Her mother said, "I bet you'd rather have it in Chicago where all your political and college friends are."

"Yes, but you and Dad have first choice," said Martha.

Her mother looked deeply into her daughter's eyes.

"My dear, we'll do what's easiest and best for you. It's your life that has to be accommodated."

They rode on in silence for a while. Then Martha stirred and said, "I'm curious. How long did you guess that this was our plan?"

"Oh, I don't know. From the moment you arrived here. You had the look of a woman who had her life all figured out." A nod of approval brought a broad smile from Martha. "I'd say that's pretty good for a twenty-year-old."

At five, the Eldridge car pulled into the family driveway. They stepped from the coolness of the car into the high-nineties heat and stood amidst the pile of luggage and bags of groceries they'd stopped to get at the Belleview Market. Louise strayed for a moment to the edge of the property to look with pleasure at her front garden bed, prospering despite the heat with speckled toad lilies, daylilies in pale rose and mahonia heavy with clusters of blue berries. Her neighbor Sam had done a good job of keeping everything watered.

In the traditional family fashion, Bill began to hand out suitcases and bags to each of them. They had their hands full by the time the neighbors closed in.

Louise was happy to see Mary and Richard Mougey come through the moon gate and stroll slowly up the drive-way, but discomforted to notice that Mike Cunningham had emerged from his house in the far corner of Dogwood Court and was striding across the cul-de-sac.

Mary Mougey embraced first Louise, then Bill, then Martha and Janie. Their neighbor, a fund-raiser for the Children and Families Foundation, had established a link with each member of the family, especially with Martha, whom she often advised on school and career decisions. "My favorite people are home again," said Mary in her melli-fluous voice. "We missed you." The small blond woman, stylish in her pantsuit, looked warily at the approaching Cunningham. "Quickly, let us share the news with you so that you won't be too shocked when Mike gets here with his blunderbuss ways. Peter Hoffman has gone missing. Had you heard?" Her concerned gaze turned on to Louise.

"No," said Louise. "How long has he been missing?"

"Since last Sunday. Poor Phyllis, I have to feel sorry for her. She's been calling me hysterically because the police can find no trace of him." Mary gently urged her husband forward with a slim hand. "But Richard can give you details."

Bill glanced politely at Richard, his colleague at the State Department, and so did Louise and the girls. Louise knew he hardly would have an answer his wife didn't, but Mary was anxious for her depressed husband to get involved in the conversation. He shrugged his narrow shoulders and cocked his long head in a dramatic fashion, stepping right up to the role as neighborhood raconteur. "Peter popped in on that Radebaugh party two Saturdays ago, as you recall. Then, apparently, he lived a normal life for a week. He was missing last Sunday night. Phyllis reported it Monday morning. Cops have been grilling everybody in the neighborhood. Pretty damned hard, too."

Janie, looking unaccountably like a young blond goddess in her sweaty, sandy beach dishabille, stepped over. Richard smiled and took her hands in his for a moment. "My dear Janie," he said.

"Mr. Mougey," said Janie, "why would people around here be expected to know where he disappeared?"

Richard shook his head. "I don't know for sure. Because it's his home base, I guess. If it were someone else, they might have just thought he took a powder and moved to Europe. But this is a little different. He has this murder in his background."

Bill expelled a breath, obviously disgusted. "I'm sure

the police are checking out his other connections as well. I can only hope he isn't up to some new trick. Good, he's gone. Now we won't have to get a restraining order. Maybe we can forget about him."

"Oh, I doubt that," said a loud voice. Mike Cunningham had arrived, looking as if he were straight out of *GQ* in his classic white sport shirt and tan chinos. *Too bad the exterior is so pretty and the interior so defective,* thought Louise. He came up and stood close to her, but cast admiring glances at Martha and Janie. Louise realized that, in the few months he'd lived in Dogwood Court, he had never had the chance to meet them, with Janie busy with her life and Martha away most of the time in Chicago.

"Why don't you introduce me to your daughters, Louise?"

Reluctantly, she did so. The man's eyes lit on Janie, and then, probably realizing she was a little young for him, transferred his gaze to Martha. He said, "I don't think we need worry just yet. It's my theory that Peter will show up just when we've all despaired."

Richard Mougey shook his head. "I'm not so sure about that. The man has a complicated and cloudy business past from what I hear. But then you ought to know all about that, Mike. Aren't you still Hoffman's financial advisor?"

Cunningham flushed under his even tan, and his brown eyes focused on the ground, as if to avoid eye contact with his probing neighbors. "I've advised him, that's right, and defended him in court, but I don't know everything about the man." He chuckled and looked about the group, settling his glance on Louise. "I only hope the guy hasn't run into some woman determined to kill him."

Louise looked up, affronted, though she didn't know why. Yes, she did; Cunningham always went for the stereotypical phrase. It's a wonder he didn't claim that Phyllis, the "little woman," was responsible. As for herself, Louise was sure that some woman somewhere felt like doing Peter

Hoffman in. "What a thought," she said, sarcastically. "Isn't it just as likely to think he's fled the country? He seems the sort who might do that." She leaned down and picked up the luggage to which she'd been assigned. "Anyway, I'm not wasting my time speculating. We need to get in the house." She marched off, calling back to her friends. "Mary and Richard, want to come in for a drink?"

The implied exclusion of Mike Cunningham didn't bother her a bit. Though a boor, Mike was smart enough to know that Louise disliked him.

Richard spoke for the couple. "We'll take a raincheck, Louise."

"Same with me," Cunningham called out. "And nice to meet the girls." He fell in step with the Mougeys and returned to the other side of the cul-de-sac.

As she walked up the flagstone path, Louise gave Bill a weary glance and said, "Some neighbor."

"I agree," said Martha, trudging along while rolling two suitcases. "Why'd he move into this kind of neighborhood? Isn't there some way you could persuade him to leave? Introduce a few big city rats into his garage or something? Otherwise he'll be here forever, ruining your lives." She flipped her long brown hair and sniffed. "That's the beauty of living in a city, Ma. People are not so close—only when it's mutually agreed that they should be."

"Spoken like a true city lover," said Bill, grinning at his eldest daughter. "And now, when we go inside, I guess we'll put in that mysterious call to Chicago, Martha. I can hardly wait."

8

Louise was directing the girls in sorting the laundry, trying not to be too obsessive, but still worried that the casual Martha might try slipping whites in with the colored clothes. Bill was outside on the patio, his cell phone clasped to his ear, pacing back and forth. He was talking to Jim Daley.

Martha heaved a pile of sand-laden shorts and shirts into the washing machine and said, "This is today's equivalent of the suitor visiting the father in his study and asking for her hand in marriage."

Janie gave her older sister a bland look. "Do you think Dad will say yes?"

Martha poked Janie in the ribs and then hugged her, as they both laughed. Louise smiled inwardly. This camaraderie was a good sign, she thought. The sorting done, they went to the kitchen to put away the groceries.

Martha said, "The big question is where will we get married? I have to sort out the possibilities."

"You need a list, Martha," said Janie, at her officious best. Louise wondered if Janie was using the task as a defense against the highly emotional announcement that her sister was to be married. "I have just the thing: a yellow pad. With a yellow pad," she proclaimed, "I can organize your entire life." She opened a kitchen drawer and retrieved a lined legal tablet and a pen. The two sisters settled down at the dining room table, while Louise went and lay down on the living room couch. Looking out the big living room windows, she saw that Bill had collapsed into a patio chair, one leg straddling the arm, and was laughing heartily at something Martha's intended was telling him. A minute or two later, he was through with the call and in the house. He looked at Louise and raised a finger. "That is one helluva guy. He's going to call back in a few minutes, Martha. Wants to talk to you about the wedding plans."

"So I guess that means you gave them your approval," said Janie, in a clipped voice. It had been a surprise to nobody that Bill Eldridge approved of Jim Daley. He'd expressed it every time he saw the young man or even heard of his latest ambitious exploit. Janie turned to Martha, impatience creeping into her voice. "Come on, Martha, that's all settled. Now we have to start planning this wedding, because it all has to happen in a big hurry, and the rest of us have things to plan, too."

Martha gave Louise a quizzical look. Louise answered with a shrug. This wedding news wasn't going down well with Martha's younger sister.

Janie watched her sister rummage in the refrigerator for a couple of sodas. She sat at the dining room table, back straighter than usual, trying valiantly but not too successfully to convince herself to not cry. To not be ruined by Martha's news.

But it was hardly fair. Janie had a serious boyfriend two years before Martha, and now look what had happened! Why did age have to make all the difference, gaining Martha more respect with her parents, especially her father, who admired the way she took everything to heart: cities, poor people, even the refugees that she'd worked on behalf of during one summer internship abroad.

Janie shoved her long blond hair back from her face. It was as if she were just the pretty face in this family, even though she was as book-smart as Martha, maybe even smarter in math and science.

She had been going with Chris Radebaugh for three years. And though they never said it to each other, she was sure that someday they'd marry.

Why had she been born later? Why wasn't she planning her own wedding, now that Chris was halfway through college and she was about to begin?

But no, her parents would balk at that, even though Chris' mom, Nora, was totally cool and would understand. Even his dad, Ron, would accept it. It was her folks who would balk, and Grandpa and Grandma Eldridge, who were so traditional that they couldn't accept anything that was out of their limited suburban Connecticut experience.

She raised her head and stared out into the woods. What if she and Chris just kicked over the traces and ran away and got hitched? After all, they both were adults now. Then she dropped her head to hide a tear that came to her eye. No, she couldn't do that to her sister. It was Martha's moment. She'd be a good sport and help plan the wedding. Even though, knowing Martha, there wouldn't be too much fanfare to it. Maybe they would get married in Chicago's City Hall, for all she knew.

With an effort, she composed her face so that by the time Martha returned with two icy glasses of soda, she looked the picture of sisterly serenity.

Seeing the girls take charge of wedding details, Louise joined her husband in their bedroom, where she began the unpacking of the suitcases. Bill came up behind her and put his arms around her. "How do you feel about our firstborn leaving?" he said. "Come on, tell me the truth."

She turned in his arms and gave him a long look. "Bill, the girl left in body and spirit when she went away to college."

"You're right. With those urban internships and semesters abroad, she hasn't even come home for much more than a week or two."

"I'm worried about how Janie is taking this."

"I don't know, but I can guess—a little jealous and a little sad. She'd probably like to make it a double wedding."

"Heaven forbid," exclaimed Louise. "Janie's only seventeen—"

"Nearly eighteen," amended Bill.

"But I think you're right. She's upset at the news."

"Do you think this Jim Daley is going to be worthy of Martha?"

"I thought you'd already answered that question."

Bill bowed his head until his chin touched her forehead. "Jim's different than the other young men she's dated. He acts much older than his years. I have a suspicion that he's never thought of himself as a child, but only as a man. I hope he has some fun in him. It's always good to have a sense of humor, especially in those moments when your life may be going to hell. Overall, though, I like him very much."

Louise laid her head on Bill's chest. "So do I. And I think she's just as serious as he is. Even when she was very young, she acted like an adult who had some kind of responsibility for the world. My guess is that they'll go through life taking everything very seriously."

"Think of them there in Chicago. They'll be immersed in politics and loving it."

She broke away from his embrace. "You're distracting

me. I'll never get these suitcases emptied. And then I'll never have time before dark to see how the back gardens have fared without us."

"I'm sure Sam tended them just as well as you would have," said Bill.

As she was gathering up a handful of articles meant for the bathroom, they heard the front doorbell. She set the stack down again in the suitcase.

Bill frowned. "More neighbors come over to discuss the missing Peter Hoffman?" He went down the hall to the front door as Louise trailed behind. She hoped her always polite and gregarious husband wouldn't be excessively gregarious, but would plead some excuse such as post-vacation fatigue if it was a neighbor just come to chat.

Instead of a neighbor, though, she heard the resounding voice of Detective Mike Geraghty echoing down the hall. "Bill," said the detective, "George Morton and I came by to have a word with you and Louise."

An unexpected thrill of fear passed through her. But why should she be afraid of the police? This must be a perfunctory visit, just so they could tell their superiors that they'd covered every single person in the cul-de-sac on the matter of Peter Hoffman's disappearance.

When she arrived at the door, however, the expression on Mike Geraghty's red, embarrassed face told her otherwise.

"Coffee?" offered Louise. Mike Geraghty was fond of her strong Chemex-brewed coffee.

"Love it," said the big detective, nodding his white-haired head. "Best coffee in town."

"I know you take it with cream," she said to Mike, looking straight into his marble-like blue eyes. This was the man with whom she had worked on half a dozen crimes, sometimes with his approval, sometimes without. Thanks to her, Geraghty's reputation for solving murders was tops among Fairfax County detectives. Other officers reportedly rewarded him by calling him the "Blue-Eyed Wonder."

George Morton was another matter. Morton, a dark-haired, good-looking man, had an athletic body that unfortunately was set on a pair of short legs. He reminded Louise faintly of a clown in a circus, and each time he reentered her life, she had to get used to his faintly comic appearance, especially since it clashed with his hyper-serious demeanor.

Morton looked somewhere behind Louise, so that she nearly turned around to see if someone were in back of her. But it was merely the self-conscious policeman's way of avoiding eye contact. He said, "I take mine black."

Bill seated the policemen in the living room and asked Janie and Martha in the adjacent dining room if they'd mind moving their wedding planning to Martha's bedroom. Bill, too, must have sensed the two law officers were here for more than a few casual questions.

"I suppose this is about the fact that Peter Hoffman's missing," said Bill.

" 'Fraid so," said Detective Morton. "But let's wait for the coffee before we get into it."

Minutes later, Louise joined the group with the coffee. She sat down and took a big sip of the dark liquid from her own cup, then said, "Well, do tell us what you want to know."

Geraghty glanced quickly over at Morton. "George, please let me handle this," he said. Morton nodded his assent. Mike Geraghty had always been the boss of this two-man team. Why was he acting as if Morton were sharing his command?

The big detective sat forward on the couch, a small pad of paper and pencil clutched in one hand. He tapped the pad against his knee with each pronouncement: "Peter Hoffman's missin', you know that. He's released from the hospital Friday, the third of August. He shows up at the Radebaughs' party on the fourth. He's seen about the neighborhood—"

Morton elaborated: "At the Sylvan Valley Swim Club tennis courts, the grocery store, a restaurant in Old Town Alexandria—"

"—right up until Sunday evening, the twelfth," continued Geraghty. His hand was quiet on his knee. Morton had disturbed his rhythmic tapping. "Phyllis Hoffman forgives him one night, I guess, but reports him missin' Monday noon, August thirteenth. So that means he's been missin' now five days."

Morton turned his brown-eyed stare onto Mike Geraghty. "Tell her about the tip we got today."

Geraghty stared down at the carpeting and heaved a big sigh. He looked over at Louise and said, "We got a phone call today, about how they'd seen you diggin' in your garden last Sunday evenin', the twelfth."

Morton waved an objecting hand. "Not evening, more like midnight."

"Yeah," amended Geraghty, his face flushing an even darker red, "about midnight. Of course, you were at the beach then, so somebody might have identified someone else as you, Louise."

Bill said, "What the hell are you talking about, Louise in the garden at midnight?"

"Bill," said Louise, putting out a restraining hand. "As a matter of fact, I was in the garden that night around midnight. I drove home to get my script. It was one of the nights you and the girls were away on the fishing trip. I wasn't digging, only checking the soil to see if Sam had watered the azalea bed."

"The coincidence sure is significant," said Morton.

"Coincidence?" She laughed. "You can't be implying that I did away with Peter Hoffman and buried him in my garden." She laughed. "No, tell me you don't mean that."

Nevertheless, the thought made her breathless, and she sat back and tried to regain her composure. Her eye caught movement, and she saw her two daughters standing in the living room doorway, listening to everything.

Bill fastened his gaze on Geraghty. "Mike, how could you think that my wife is involved in Hoffman's disappearance? After all that Louise has done for you, it's an insult."

"That's for sure," echoed Janie. She stood, arms akimbo, with her strong, tanned legs wide apart in a defensive stance, looking as if she were ready to throw the detectives out of the house. She caught a rebuking glance from her father and dropped her hands to her sides, but her hands were still curled in fists.

Detective Morton's voice was louder now. "Hey, let's not gang up on me, folks. All Mike and I want to do is to have the right to dig up your garden."

"Which garden?" demanded Louise.

"Specifically, the one that lies out back a ways and a little to the west."

"The azalea bed."

"Yes, I guess so. Is that the one you were digging in that night?"

"I told you I wasn't digging, Detective Morton. I was feeling the ground to see if it was dry or not."

Morton spread his hands and said, "It's a simple request. Gives us permission to go out there and dig a while. If we don't find anything, then you'll be off the hook, and we'll be outta your lives."

Louise thought of her wild azaleas, how they'd had a bad year, and how they wouldn't like being dug up. Not only that, she was hurt, and Geraghty knew it. He looked over at her with remorseful eyes. This had not been his idea.

Bill looked at her. "Louise, what do you think? Maybe we should let them."

Her hurt turned to anger. "I don't want them digging in my garden, Bill. This is pure nonsense." She got to her feet and made a broad gesture with her hand toward the front door, an unmistakable hint that the policemen should leave. "Gentlemen, come back when you have a court order. Without one, you're not messing with my azaleas."

9

Her family clustered around her, as if, like a tender plant, she might fall without their support. "I'm all right. Really, I am," she assured her husband and her daughters.

Martha was standing at the living room windows looking out. "I think we ought to go do a reality check on that garden," she said. "Those guys are coming back with a warrant, or an excavation permit, whatever it takes."

Louise blew out an exasperated breath. "You're right. Let's go out and prove them wrong." She led the way out the patio door and down the timber stairs into the backyard. "I didn't spend more than a minute or two fussing around with that garden last Sunday night. How could anyone possibly think . . ." She hurried over to the azalea bed. Looking down, she pressed a hand to her mouth.

"What's wrong?" asked Bill, standing at her side.

"They don't look right."

Bill cocked his head and stared at the plants as Martha and Janie caught up. "They look fine to me," he said. "What do you think, girls? Maybe they're a little wilted, but not bad. Give 'em a shot of water, and they'll perk right up."

Martha got down on her hands and knees. "Someone could have been digging in these azaleas, Ma. Maybe it was Sam doing a little work with the hoe."

Louise crouched beside her daughter. The edges of the garden, obscured by the loose, leafy mulch on the forest floor, appeared to have been altered recently, though it was hard to detect until she'd scraped away the mulch. The conscientious Sam, knowing she'd been especially concerned about her azaleas, undoubtedly had gotten out here with his spade.

"Those detectives are making me crazy," she said, shaking her head, as if to shake away the whole subject. "I'm sure it was Sam. I'll give him a call to be sure."

Bill put an arm around her shoulder, and they sauntered back to the house. Then Martha's cell phone rang. It was Jim Daley. The girls settled on the patio to have a three-way discussion with him of where and when the union of Martha and Jim would take place.

"I'm feeling frustrated," she told Bill as they returned to the house.

"I know you are," he said. "So am I, for that matter."

"Our daughter announces that she's getting married. Instead of spending our time enjoying the good news, we have to worry about the police coming by to uproot my plants. And that's all because some snoop is telling stories. And I bet I know who that snoop is."

"Louise, please. You're not sure."

"Oh, yes, I am, Bill. Greg Archer is the one who lied about me riding that cart and digging in the garden. I tell you, it will be a cold day in hell before I ever cooperate with the police again."

It was almost midnight. Bill was gently snoring. Louise didn't know which side was the most uncomfortable to lie on, the right, her favorite, or the left. Usually she just cuddled against Bill and went to sleep, but tonight her neck ached and she couldn't get comfortable. She was afraid the ache would soon spread down her back. Then she'd get up in the morning and have to greet the unwelcome police with a throbbing headache. She could just picture an angry-faced George Morton at the door, smugly waving a paper at her that demanded she comply with their order to dig.

The thought made the neck-ache worse. There was no way she was going to let policemen rummage in her azalea bed. She'd rather do it herself. And in her heart of hearts, she knew something was wrong with the azaleas. There was a certain droop to the leathery leaves that was different from a simple lack of water. And this time it wasn't the deer to blame, though those cute-looking animals caused a great deal of damage each time they breached her defensive fences. If only she'd been able to get through to Sam, she could have discovered whether or not he inadvertently did something to set them back. But Sam had not answered the phone.

Slipping out of bed, she groped on the apricot chair near her bed until she felt her bathrobe and shrugged into it. She'd go in the living room and try to think this problem out. By the time she'd crossed the room, she'd changed her mind. She took off the robe and went to the closet. As quietly as possible, she collected a pair of gardening pants, cotton T-shirt and sneakers, forgoing socks.

She dressed in the dark living room, then turned on the small lamp in the interior of the room. Going out the patio doors from the air-conditioned house, she was hit by the steamy night air. She went straight to her toolshed and closed its door behind her, smelling the good earthy odor for a moment before flicking on the overhead light.

She took down her most efficient spade from its roost on the wall, grabbed her flashlight and turned to go, but then glanced back at the contents of the shed. She needed something to hold the plants after she dug them up. Pursing her lips, she considered a stack of large black plastic pots, but instead grabbed a package of heavy-duty yard bags and went outside.

Looking up, she saw the moon. It was almost full now, providing lacy light shadows between the tall trees in the woods. Too bad that she was on this bothersome mission and couldn't enjoy it. Maybe the moon was too bright, and she'd rouse more nosy neighbors to further tattle on her to the cops. Realizing there was nothing to be done about excessive moonlight, she descended the timber stairs of the patio. Using the flashlight only sparingly to guide her way through the forest detritus, she covered the twenty feet to the azalea bed.

Now would come the moment of truth.

Starting with the azalea on the end, she took up the first spadeful of soil. "Oh, no," she groaned. It dismayed her to find how easy it was to dig around the plant. Picking up speed, she laid aside the soil on either edge of the shrub until she was sure she'd caught all the roots. With a grunt, she prodded the loosened plant until it was ready to be moved. Opening one of the big polyethylene bags, she wrestled the azalea into it and pulled it aside. Pausing only briefly to catch her breath in the close air, she went on to the next shrub, quickly prying it from the loose soil. With the second azalea bagged, she had uncovered an area thirty inches wide and five feet long. She quickly dug down, continuing to pile the dirt neatly so she would have an easier time of replanting the disturbed shrubs.

The deeper she dug, the better she felt. With each spadeful, she became more disgusted with the police and their suspicions. Her lip curled as she thought of George Morton, that stiff, robot-like man. Right now, she felt a great satisfaction knowing Morton was wrong. Exhaling a big breath, she stood in the hole and leaned on her spade handle and relaxed. She'd now made a hole more than two feet deep and was about ready to quit. She certainly was sweaty and dirty enough to deserve a shower and bed. On the other hand, it might be prudent to remove a third azalea and one more layer of soil from the existing hole.

Confident now, she was determined to finish the job quickly. Standing at one end of her excavation, she dug straight down and promptly hit something. The pressure from this action sent a tremor of pain coursing all the way up through her arms. "Oh, shit!" she cried, not caring now if anyone heard. She took a step back and felt something embrace her. For a moment she panicked, then realized it was the branches of the undisturbed third azalea bush. She steadied herself and looked down.

It wasn't a rock she'd struck. There were no rocks in this woodsy northern Virginia soil. Something solid but soft was buried down there, like a body. Now that she'd admitted that to herself, Louise fought the desire to vomit. Instead, she took a deep breath and carefully scraped away the layer of soil. She encountered that same sickening soft resistance wherever she dug.

"No," she cried, "this can't be!" She picked up the flashlight lying sideways on the edge of her excavation, aimed it at the bottom of the hole and saw what looked like patches of clear plastic. She dropped to her hands and knees and frantically smoothed the remaining soil away from the rounded object buried beneath it. Then she pointed the flashlight at the cleared area. She saw the outline of an arm, ending with a big hand. There was no more doubt about it. A body was buried under her azaleas.

She set down the flashlight, and like an animal, clawed more soil away from the plastic-wrapped bundle. Grabbing the light once again, she directed it down. Through the plastic, she could now see the man in the white shirt, his face with eyes still open but without the glasses, the gray-blond hair plastered against his forehead, and the horrible movement on his bloodied face that she knew was worms at work.

Dropping the flashlight in horror, she clambered out of the hole and rushed pell-mell through the woods, stumbling and nearly falling as she tripped over fallen forest debris. She sprinted up the patio steps and into the house, not even remembering to close the living room door. Running into the bedroom, she knelt down next to Bill's side of the bed and frantically pulled at his sleeping form. "Oh, God, Bill, wake up. I've found a body in the garden. It's Peter Hoffman." She dropped her head and sobbed in his arms.

10

Friday, August 17

She was walking on that dark, wet street once more—was it *Bonn? It was cold, and she stumbled on the cobblestones. Someone was following her, and her fear was palpable, causing her hands to tremble as she clutched her trench coat close to her throat. She began to run and, turning the corner, saw a telephone booth with its door hanging open. The telephone rang and she reached in to answer it. But someone else got to it before she did, and the ringing stopped—*

Louise was jolted out of her George Smiley dream by someone knocking on the bedroom door. A voice beside her, Bill's, called, "Come in." Seeping slowly back into her mind were the dreadful events of the night before: digging far down under her precious azaleas and finding that body wrapped in plastic. Reluctantly, she opened her eyes on a gray world.

Martha leaned into the room, so that her wavy brown hair hung down by her face. "Sorry to bother you, folks. It's the police again. They called once before. I guess after keeping you up half the night, they think you've slept long enough. They want to come over. They have something new to talk about."

Louise turned her head and looked at her husband,

who'd propped himself up on an elbow. He hadn't shaved in two days, and his blond beard was scraggly, his light hair tousled on his forehead, his pale blue eyes kind and full of concern. He told her, "Even when he's dead, Peter Hoffman's trouble." Then he said to Martha, "Tell them to give us an hour, would you please?"

"Sure, Dad." Martha closed the door.

He looked down at Louise with twinkling eyes. "At least they're coming here and we don't have to go to that godforsaken police station again." The Mount Vernon substation on nearby Route One was familiar territory to Louise, but to those not familiar with it, like Bill, it appeared as it was—drab, tan and depressing, and all the more so at three in the morning.

He slumped down and flung an arm over Louise, who was still prone in bed. His fingers gently played with her upper arm, sending her a message she didn't intend to respond to. Though she admired her husband's enthusiasm for life, who wanted to make love the morning after finding a dead man in the garden?

Bill noted her lack of interest, and his hand became still. "As I said before, that Peter Hoffman sure is trouble."

Louise's eyes were finally wide open and she stared at the skylight in their bedroom ceiling. Through it, she could see a patch of silvery morning light, and the outlines of a serenely swaying Chinese elm tree. "Look at that patch of sky, honey," she said. "It's so peaceful. Would that our lives were that peaceful. But no. We have the police to deal with again while they ask questions, crawl all over the place, paw through my gardens— Oh my God!"

She slipped from under his arm and sprang out of bed.

"What's the matter?"

"I've got to get out there before they do. What do cops know about gardens?"

"Don't get too excited," warned Bill. "They've searched

our house, and they've already taken what they want out of your garden."

"Not necessarily. They're liable to dig up everything, just to be sure nothing else is hidden around the place."

Hurriedly washing her face and brushing her teeth, Louise pulled out a set of fresh pants and shirt. She had them on before Bill had left the bed. "Honey, let's not overdo this," said her husband. He swung his legs onto the floor and headed for the bathroom.

"How can I not?" she said. She shoved her feet into her tennis shoes. "I'm going out there right now."

"Hope they don't kick you right out of the crime scene," he called to her.

"Let them try," she growled. She moved the slats in the blinds on the front bedroom window to see if police had arrived yet, then hurried into the living room and checked the woods. No activity, not yet. The French clock struck seven. Her nose told her that the Chemex coffee pot was on the warmer.

Thank heavens for Martha, she thought. Old enough now not to sleep in, even though she and Janie were up half the night just like Louise and Bill. And mature enough to know her mother's drug of choice.

On hearing the sound of the toaster lever being pressed down in the kitchen, Louise salivated like Pavlov's dog. She hadn't realized how hungry and caffeine-deprived she was. "Martha, I smell coffee. I love you."

"I'm fixing you something to eat," said her older daughter, as Louise entered the kitchen. Clad in a sleeveless white tennis dress, Martha was rummaging in the refrigerator.

"I should wait for your father," said Louise.

"I know you like to do everything with Dad, but you can't always, Ma. The cops are coming, and you'd better start. Your bagel's in the toaster. Where are the lox and cream cheese?" She pulled out two packages, along with a tomato and a big white onion, and clasping them to her bosom, came over and gave her mother a brief kiss. "Go on, sit down. You don't look so well, though I hate to tell you that."

"Morton said they might dig more today. Do you realize what that means, Martha? They could ruin my yard."

"I know," said her daughter comfortingly. "Who'd want cops diggin' in their prize gardens? But one thing at a time. First, you have to eat."

Louise went to the dining room and sank into a chair at the old pine table and stared out the windows into the woods. Except for the yellow police tape, one would never suspect what she'd found out there last night.

Martha brought Louise's breakfast on a round tray.

Louise took a few sips of the strong coffee and sighed. She spread her bagel with cream cheese, layered it with lox, tomato and onion slices, and took a bite. "Yummy," she said. "But you know what's so bad about all this?"

Her older daughter shrugged her bare brown shoulders. "You mean something worse than finding Peter Hoffman buried in our backyard?"

"Almost. I want to talk about weddings instead of talking to police."

Martha patted Louise's hand. "Not to worry, Ma. Janie and I worked some things out last night at the police station while you and Dad were being questioned. And I've cancelled my flight back to Chicago so I can hang around here for a while. We have everything under control, as long as you and Dad don't mind coming to Chicago for an October wedding."

"That'll be fine with us. And it leaves only one set of grandparents to have to make the trip." Louise's parents lived in a Chicago suburb, while Bill's were in Connecticut.

"Aunts and uncles will come, too, of course," added

Martha. "When Jim gets the final okay on the time of the ceremony from the church, I'll call the relatives. That gives them more than six weeks' notice." She looked warily at Louise. "I sure hope everybody understands as well as you and Dad do. Jim and I know this isn't the ideal way to do a wedding, but we do have our reasons."

"What about the gown? And the reception? Can you do all that in six weeks?"

Martha sat back and waved a casual hand. "Bridal clothes are no problem. I'm not wearing white. I want something I can use later."

A piece of bagel caught in Louise's throat. She swallowed with difficulty and put her bagel down on her plate. "You're not wearing white."

Martha glanced up at the ceiling. Louise knew she'd said the wrong thing; Martha had just informed her she wasn't wearing white. After a moment, Martha looked over at Louise and said, "It'll be all right, Ma, really it will. How would it be if I wore a tan knit suit, maybe one of those St. Jarvis or whatever numbers, provided it doesn't cost too much?"

"St. James." How ironic, thought Louise. Maybe Martha could trot up to Saks Fifth Avenue where Peter Hoffman's now-wealthy widow sold those knits. She doubted that Phyllis Hoffman would work any longer than was necessary.

"That kind of thing I could wear for fifty years," said Martha, "and it will look good when I go out on the campaign trail with Jim." She leaned over to peek in her mother's face. "Don't you think so? Tell me you think so."

"If that's what you want, darling, of course it's just fine." Louise turned her attention back to her bagel. She had told herself she wouldn't be the controlling mother, and the first thing she did was to lay a guilt trip on her daughter over the topic of clothes. She had to remember clothes meant nothing to Martha, who was raised in jeans and wore clothes others would give to the Goodwill. *I have to come to grips with this,* she thought. *A girl raised in jeans doesn't want to prance down the aisle in a fancy white gown.*

This thought produced a little twist in Louise's gut. Or was it the bagel and lox?

Martha, who apparently believed she'd settled the wedding gown problem to their mutual satisfaction, was off on another subject. "For the church and the reception hall, I think Jim has a handle on all that. He has lots of ins with the church." She flushed under her tan. "The major problem is to schedule three more pre-wedding sessions with the priest. We've had five already."

"You're converting?"

Martha smiled expansively at her mother. "Yes. We thought it would be better for the children if we were both Catholic."

"*Children.* Oh, my. You don't mean—"

"No," said Martha. "I don't meant that: I'm not pregnant. Children of the future."

"Well." Louise straightened in her chair. "I guess congratulations are in order. It will be quite a change, I daresay, from being a Presbyterian." Even to herself, she sounded like a prig.

Martha grinned, and Louise thought for one surprised moment that her daughter was going to break into a laugh. At what—Louise's brand of reserved Presbyterianism that she'd tried to introduce to her children?

"Ma, your church is great," her daughter reassured her. "Always such terrific people there. I've loved going to the services with you and Dad and Janie. This isn't that big a step. . . ."

Not a big step? Louise felt a little empty, as if she'd somehow let the Presbyterians down. "It isn't?"

"Okay, I take that back. I guess it is a big decision. But

we think unity is important in a family, and Jim's faith is a bit deeper than mine."

Louise gave her a look.

Martha said, "Now wait, Ma, I don't mean anything disparaging by that. In spite of the troubles of the Catholic church, Jim's a devout Catholic, a socially conscious Catholic. Right out of the Dorothy Day school—you know, concern for the working man and woman. I guess you can figure that, since he's running for alderman."

Louise reached out a hand somewhat tainted with remnants of cream cheese and fish and patted Martha's hand. This daughter had been into social change her whole life. She and Bill hadn't thought it unusual that Martha chose someone with the same inclinations.

On to a safer subject, thought Louise. She said, "So what about, oh, let's see, invitations?"

Before Martha could address that issue, the front doorbell rang. Simultaneously, Louise caught the movement of police technicians clad in navy-colored attire entering the backyard. Her pulse quickened. Two men carried shovels and poles and were headed up the steps to her patio garden, straight for her prize tree peonies. "Oh, no, they don't," she said, and bolted straight up out of her chair and strode to the patio door.

11

Martha grabbed her arm. "Ma, you have to ignore those guys. The detectives are at the door. When they called earlier, Morton sounded like they really meant business. You have to talk to them now." She hurried to the front door, with Louise trailing her.

Bill came down the hall and intercepted them, putting both hands up to bar their way. "Hold on a minute," he said, and put an arm around each of them. "My dears, I have something to say. I know we're all exhausted from being up all night, but let's keep calm with these folks. This may take all morning or all day. But then I expect they'll get out of here and let us go on with our lives."

"I'll turn the air conditioning temp down," offered Martha. "That will help keep us cool."

"Great," said Bill, and opened the front door to the police. "Ah, Detective Geraghty, Detective Morton," he said, in a nonchalant voice. "Come in."

Mike Geraghty walked in the front door, then stood aside and said to his companion, "Why don't you go first, George?"

Louise's mouth fell slack. She knew that this order of entry was far from meaningless. What had happened to

Geraghty? Far into the night, all through the hours of questioning at the Mount Vernon substation, it was a Lieutenant Dan Trace who was in charge. Trace was a giant of a man, six-foot-six at least, with a deep voice but a quiet way of speaking, quiet and impressive. He'd posed few questions, but all of them important. But Mike Geraghty had led the interview, as if he were next in command under the lieutenant. Morton had come up with some nasty queries, asking her if she had issues with any of the neighbors "besides" Hoffman. Because she thought he'd learn it from someone else anyway, she'd answered that Mike Cunningham was the only one whom she didn't consider a friend.

"You don't like him?" challenged Morton.

She'd shrugged, trying to minimize it. "Ask the other neighborhood women. He's a bit of a flirt, that's all."

Morton had given her a smirk.

A grim thought hit her. Maybe Lieutenant Trace had decided that Geraghty was too close an acquaintance of Bill and Louise Eldridge to take an important part in this investigation, so by this morning had substituted Morton as lead detective.

Deciding it was best to ignore these bureaucratic details, she led off with her main concern. "Before I offer you coffee, Mike, I want you to promise me that no one is going to disturb my gardens until I'm out there with them. Can we agree on that?"

The detective went to the patio door, opened it and walked out for a brief conference with the technicians standing on the flagstone. They were leaning over and eyeing the flowers. Louise was reminded of thieves who'd just discovered a precious stash of loot.

Geraghty returned to the living room and said, "It's taken care of. As for coffee, Louise, no thanks." He turned to George Morton. "That's right, isn't it, George? You don't need coffee?"

Morton said, "Let's just sit down and get to it." He gave Martha a hard look. "Miss Eldridge, do you want to stay or not?"

"I do," said Martha. "I feel very much a part of this."

They took seats, Louise on the couch with Geraghty next to her and George Morton on the other side in her grandmother's antique chair. Martha and Bill occupied chairs across from them. Geraghty cocked his head toward Morton. "So, George, why don't you start this time?"

Suddenly the room felt close, and she thought she could even smell rancid perspiration on one or other of the detectives, probably Morton. Unlike Mike Geraghty, who had his little worn pad poised on his knee, Morton held only a folded piece of paper in his hand. He raised his big head on his shortened body and addressed her. "Now, Mrs. Eldridge, just a few questions. Here's what we already have. You admit that you hated Peter Hoffman."

"I didn't exactly hate him. I'd say I seriously disliked him."

"But you acknowledge that you had a nasty fight with him in this house on Saturday night, August fourth, following a party at the home of Ron and Nora Radebaugh. During the time of the fight, you threw a heavy pitcher at him that might have killed him if your aim hadn't been off."

"Oh, no. That pitcher wasn't heavy enough to kill him, not unless I'd hit him directly on his head or something—"

"We'll leave that for now. It's thought that you invited him into your house to talk things over."

"Humph," said Louise. "I did not invite him. He broke into my house. That's why we brought charges against him."

Morton bent his head and looked at his notes. "Okay, that's what you say, Mrs. Eldridge. Some of your neighbors and friends say otherwise. Let me continue. Then, after filing charges and petitioning for a restraining order, you and your family set off on a vacation. But you, Mrs. Eldridge, returned to your home and backyard around midnight on Sunday, August twelfth."

"Yes. I told Lieutenant Trace and you and Mike that about six times last night."

"All right." The detective leaned forward and took a deep breath, casting a quick glance at the notes. "Here's what we have. Shortly after midnight on Monday, August thirteenth, someone sighted you, wearing your gardening hat and an old sweatshirt, moving your garden cart from Sam Rosen's side yard into your yard."

"No, no," remonstrated Louise, "I did no such thing."

Morton said, "Hold on and let me finish, Mrs. Eldridge. This same source claims that after that, he heard little noises, maybe like digging noises, way back in the woods where he couldn't see you." He glowered at her. "In other words, in that azalea garden where we found the body."

"I did not dig; I just bent down and felt the soil in that garden. If that person heard me digging, why didn't he come out and see why I was digging in the middle of the night?"

The detective cocked his head, looking amused. "Wonder if our source had decided you were a kind of . . . obsessive gardener who might just do a thing like that."

She released a heavy sigh. "And what's all this about my hat and sweatshirt?"

"The hat was found on a hook in your garden shed. The sweatshirt reads 'Bullfrog Marina.' Sound familiar?"

"It's my old sweatshirt from Lake Powell. I leave it hanging in the toolshed."

"Huh," grunted Morton. "Funny that we found it neatly folded, directly under Mr. Hoffman's body, in the grave you dug for him."

Louise's breath caught, and she thought she'd faint. Bill stood up and came over to where she sat on the couch. He looked down at Mike Geraghty and said, "Let's trade seats." Geraghty moved to her husband's chair, and Bill sat down and took Louise's hand firmly in his.

Morton watched silently. Then he said, "Back to that sweatshirt, Mrs. Eldridge. We've picked up a detail about you—that you're compulsively neat. So this handling of the sweatshirt would be something you'd do, wouldn't it? Sort of your 'signature.' "

"That's bullshit," snapped Bill. "It doesn't prove a damned thing."

"Then maybe the stains will."

Louise's mouth fell open. "It's stained? Stained with what?"

In a gentle tone, Mike Geraghty explained. "The sweatshirt has some dark smears on it. Would you know how they came to be there?"

"I have no idea. You know, this is all wrong. I didn't dig in that garden. I haven't worn that sweatshirt since spring."

"Okay," said Morton, "let's go back a step. Here's what I think happened—here's the big picture. You lured Peter Hoffman into the woods. You hit him on the head a number of times, then wrapped him up in that big plastic tarp. Then you went and got this little garden cart of yours, transported him and buried him under the azaleas."

"I did not do any of that. How did you ever get that idea?"

Morton's brown eyes narrowed as he gave her a long look. "Wait, there's more. In our search of the toolshed early this morning, we found what we think is the weapon. It's a nasty-looking device, and it has your fingerprints on it. It appears to have residual traces of blood in the crevices. We've sent it out for testing, along with the sweat-shirt."

"Where was this tool?" demanded Bill.

"Hanging in this selfsame garden shed, Mr. Eldridge, on a big hook on the pegboard on the north wall."

Louise shook her head in confusion. "About three feet long, right?"

"Thirty-four inches, to be exact," said Morton.

"That's my edging iron. Anyone could have used it and then put it back. But you must realize that."

He turned his brown-eyed gaze on her again. "But how about the tarp?"

"How about it?" she asked.

"Mrs. Eldridge, we've found your fingerprints on the plastic tarp in which Mr. Hoffman's body was wrapped. Yours and only yours, all over it."

She was breathing more quickly now. She'd had plastic tarpaulins stored in the shed for years, using them to cover delicate plants from frost. "Well, well, well," she said, sarcastically. "Look at all this evidence! Why don't you just arrest me for the crime? With my record of helping the Fairfax police solve crimes, surely I must be the perfect suspect for you, Detective Morton."

To her relief, Mike Geraghty spoke up. "We know your record, Louise. Some of us can't believe you did it and think this evidence could have been manufactured. So the Criminal Investigation Bureau will be investigatin' a number of other folks, too." He looked carefully at George Morton. "Isn't that right, George?"

Morton gave Geraghty a sour look. "Naturally, the scope of our investigation will include others, since Mr. Hoffman did not live in a vacuum."

"No, he was living with his wife, wasn't he?" said Bill in a bitter voice. "And his lawyer, who got him off a murder rap with only four years in a mental hospital, now lives across the street from us. And there must be others who might like to have seen the man dead. So why don't you get to it, Detectives?"

Crimson suffused Morton's face as he carefully got up from the chair. Soon, they all were on their feet. Clearing his throat first, he said, "I know how you hate to hear this stuff, Mr. Eldridge, but your wife is a likely candidate to have killed Peter Hoffman." He paused and shrugged his shoulders and turned back to Louise. "I'll concede that maybe it was a crime of passion, a crime of the moment. That much I'll concede. Hoffman was a big man, but I understand you play competitive tennis and do yoga. You're plenty strong enough to have perpetrated the crime, especially with a cart to haul the body."

"Who's your tipster?" asked Louise.

Morton didn't answer her. Instead, he scratched his head, as if his mind were on other things. "By the way, what is it with that little cart?"

"It's a golf cart decked out for gardening purposes," answered Bill. "Sam Rosen had it modified with a metal flatbed on the back."

"We found it parked in your bamboo patch by the side of the house."

"That's my Oriental garden, not a bamboo patch," insisted Louise.

" 'Fraid that's where we found it. And we found dirt removed from the hole, too, near the bamboo. We've taken it away; it might have evidence in it. It appears to have been transported there in your trash can, apparently set on the back of the flatbed."

Bill had moved close to Morton now. His hands were on his hips. "Would you please answer my wife's question? You have a tipster who led you to us. And just who in the hell is it?"

Morton straightened, as if to make himself taller than

Bill, a hopeless task. "I'm not at liberty to say, Mr. Eldridge. But in conclusion, this evidence doesn't paint a very pretty picture about your wife. You're just lucky we haven't hauled her down to the station already. As it is, I intend for us to pursue a few other leads first. If they don't pan out in the next week, we'll know we have our perpetrator"—he sent Louise a somber look—"right here."

Martha, who had listened in attentive silence up until now, said, "This is silly, Detective Morton. My mother has gone out of her way more than once to help you people catch criminals." She flashed a resentful glance at Mike Geraghty. "At least Detective Geraghty has to appreciate that." She stepped close to Morton. Louise noted the red-faced detective was caught in a pincers movement between her husband, her daughter and herself. "Since you're through, why don't you leave?" She put out a hand, as if to take his elbow and escort him out.

For a second, Morton stared at her lithe, tanned figure in tennis costume, then quickly moved across the room. On reaching the front hall, he stopped and turned, studiously avoiding looking at Martha or any of the family. Instead, his gaze was fastened somewhere in middle space. "Mrs. Eldridge," he said, "don't think about leaving home. Remember, right now you're between a rock and a hard place." As an afterthought, he added, "And please don't get any ideas that you're gonna investigate this crime. You're too involved, believe me. If I were you, I wouldn't even talk about it with my friends. Now, c'mon, Mike, we have work to do."

Geraghty silently reached over toward Louise, as if to give her a little comforting pat on her shoulder. But he withdrew his hand before he touched her and followed the lead detective out of the house.

12

Martha was on the patio by herself, slumped in a chair with the cell phone at her ear, her feet propped up on another chair. The woods were loud with birds chirping and insects making a huge racket. She hoped Jim could hear her. When he did, he wouldn't like what she said.

"I'm glad you're coming back this afternoon," he said. "I've missed you so much, Martha."

"I'm not coming, Jim. I've had to cancel the flight. We have trouble here."

"What trouble?"

"You know that big creep, Peter Hoffman, that I told you all about? Well, he was missing for almost a week, and last night my mother found his body in our garden."

"Bummer. I'm sorry, Martha. I'm really sorry. Who put him there?"

"That's the bad part. The cops have been busy snooping around Ma's garden shed, taking fingerprints, et cetera, and they just came over and told her that she's a suspect. I think she's their only suspect."

"I thought she was the police department's best little helper."

"She was. She is."

"Tell me more."

Martha went down the evidence list, piece by piece.

"That sweatshirt's not good, Martha," concluded Jim. "It probably has Hoffman's blood on it. Someone's got it in for her."

"Mike Geraghty probably agrees with you. He's the detective who used to run things at the Mt. Vernon station. It's mainly this George Morton who acts like she belongs in jail. They say they'll arrest her by the end of next week if they can't come up with some evidence that someone else did it."

"Should I come out there?"

"How are you going to run for public office if you're in northern Virginia?"

"It's not a good time, I'll admit. And someone's just attacked me for something my great-uncle did thirty-seven years ago. But I'll come if you need me."

"I'd like to help out here as much as I can. Usually it's Janie who has to help Ma get out of her scrapes. I'll tell you what. Give me a few days. If things don't get straightened out by then, maybe you'd better fly out here and lend your keen Cook County crime nose to saving her."

"I can't believe the police are serious. I sure don't want my future mother-in-law in jail. You'll need to call me every night and tell me how things are going."

"I will, darling."

"Did you tell them about things?"

"Yeah. Ma and I had a chance to talk this morning before the police came and laid their big trip on her. She's accepted my conversion to Catholicism okay. The wedding dress thing was a little harder."

"What did she want, for you to wear a white dress with a train?"

"I think so."

"Is she going to accept the fact that you're wearing jeans?" he said, chuckling.

"Jeans," said Martha, "or a few cuts above that."

Janie came out of her bedroom in her pajamas, surprised to see it was only eight-thirty. She groaned. Five hours' sleep wasn't enough for her. She went into the dining room and stared out into the yard. There was her family in its entirety—father, mother and sister—plus a couple of guys in navy uniforms. More police. But these two looked browbeaten, and she could see why.

Her mother appeared to be scolding the man with a shovel in his hand. The other held what looked like a pole digger. Apparently, they were probing around in other gardens on the theory that her mother was a mass murderer.

In disgust, she went into the kitchen and found the bagels and lox. Though she didn't drink coffee, she looked at the Chemex pot, shaped like a beaker from her chemistry class, sitting on the warmer. A residue of deep brown liquid was in it. She decided to try it. After all, her mother could never exist for a day without her usual allotment of four or five cups. Janie, who didn't drink soda, was tired enough to experiment.

She poured half a cup to start, lacing it with cream just as Louise did. When she thought about her mother, she always thought of her as "Louise," although she still called her "Ma." One of these days, she'd just grow up and call her by her name.

She sat down and found she thoroughly enjoyed this more mature version of breakfast. Heavens knows she needed a boost, for it was déjà vu all over again with that yellow police tape around the yard. Back when they found those gory objects in the bags of leaves, it had embarrassed her practically to tears and made her the object of teasing at school. If she hadn't had Chris Radebaugh as a good friend then, she would have been lost. Though she was too old for tears now, it still was embarrassing.

She wished Chris were here and not in Baltimore. Her boyfriend's summer internship ended soon at Johns Hopkins. It couldn't be soon enough for Janie.

She paused in eating and took another sip of coffee. No wonder her mother loved it so. It had a real kick and an engaging aftertaste. She chuckled. Now that she herself was a coffee-drinker, she was sure she was mature enough to get married.

Her mother was in trouble again, no doubt about it. Janie knew it from sitting around the Mount Vernon sub-station last night with her sister. Louise was a suspect. Why else would they have questioned her for three hours?

Janie knew her mother was innocent, but she also knew that if she had had the gumption to kill anyone, it would have been Peter Hoffman. She'd hated the man, and for good reasons.

Through a haze of half-sleep, she'd heard the detectives arrive this morning and could make out a few things, mainly her mother's exclamations of innocence. It seemed as though they were staying for a long time.

Instead of just helping Martha plan a wedding, Janie would have to see what she could do to get Louise out of this mess. Too bad her sister was bailing out and returning to Chicago today. Maybe the two of them could have fig-ured out how that body got into the azalea garden.

She looked out again and saw Martha hanging right there by her mother's side. Her sister didn't act like some-one heading out for a noon flight to Chicago. Of course, she thought. She's cancelled her trip. As if telepathic, Martha came to the big plate-glass window and peered in at Janie with a sweat-beaded face.

Janie put her coffee cup down and made a ring with her

index finger and thumb. Martha did the same. *Okay,* it meant, in sisterly code, *"let's get on this."*

It was hot and humid on the patio, and Louise knew her long-suffering husband would have much preferred being in the house, checking out the Washington *Post*'s take on the disastrous news from the Middle East rather than out here while she kept the evidence technicians in line.

"Bill, go inside. Believe me, I can handle these two."

"No, darling, I'll stay."

She turned her attention back to the technicians. They were on their knees on the hard flagstone now. She'd handed them each a trowel and told them exactly how to proceed. "Now, officers," she said crisply, "without using those shovels, you can see for yourself that no one has tampered with this garden."

"Yes, ma'am," said one. First, he rummaged around with his hand, encased in a white polyurethane glove, then worked the trowel about, encountering fairly solid soil. "You're right so far, Mrs. Eldridge." Casting her a wary glance, he got up and moved down two few feet and repeated the probes. The other technician was at the far end of the circular garden, coming toward the first man. Intermittently, Louise went to inspect and see that he followed her ground rules as well.

Her husband had collapsed in a patio chair. "Let me know if I can help," he called to her.

Louise looked over at him, her expression distracted. Two weeks ago, Peter Hoffman had entered the house and traumatized her. Now, he'd shown up dead in their garden and, incredibly, she was the police's best and probably only suspect. She was so insulted that she could hardly see straight, much less focus on the worst-case scenario— that she might go to jail and miss her daughter's wedding.

All she could do right now was to be sure that these two officers left her flower beds as sacrosanct as when they found them.

Bill, his head lolling on the back of the chair, called to her. "Honey, why not come and sit down while they finish?"

She apparently surprised him by doing so, for he gave her a big smile. She smiled weakly back at him. "What are you thinking?" she said. She felt anything but relaxed, her body bent forward in the chair, elbows on her knees and hands supporting her head.

"I'm thinking about Phyllis Hoffman," he said. He chuckled. "Though I should be thinking of how I can help ease this international crisis in the Middle East."

She sighed deeply. "Bill, forget the damned Middle East for a minute. Are you saying that Phyllis could have murdered her husband?"

"I'll bet she had plenty of motive."

"But how could Phyllis Hoffman move his body? My cart would have helped her, but it still took strength. Could she have done it?"

"Someone struck him down, then dragged him onto your cart—not an impossible task for a woman. Maybe she's not the one, or maybe she had an accomplice."

Louise slanted a glance at him.

"Okay," said Bill, "you don't buy that. I have a better idea, though. I intend to pursue it as soon as I can break away and go downtown."

"What's that?"

"I'm checking into Hoffman's business dealings. Money's a major motive for murder. The question is, who profits from his death? Mort Swanson might help us, if he isn't too defensive about once being mixed up with Hoffman. Mike Cunningham won't divulge anything; he had a lawyer-client relationship with the sonofabitch."

"Bill," said Louise, "you're great, doing all that work when I know your mind is on other things. One other thought: should you still call Peter a sonofabitch now that he's dead?"

"Damned right. Once a sonofabitch, always a sonof-abitch."

13

The Hoffman murder had landed on Charlie Hurd's desk, and rightly so. He was the *Post's* number one crime reporter. Anyway, it was in his territory.

Now he was trolling. He was keenly aware that with his close-to-bronze suntan, reasonably good looks and red Porsche, he ought to come up with at least one good fish.

He drove slowly down Rebecca Road, one of Sylvan Valley's main drags, and then turned right at the bottom of the hill. Larch Road immediately climbed uphill again. Weird neighborhood, this Sylvan Valley. One hill after another until he got to the flat bottomland where Louise lived. But the Eldridge yard was inaccessible, with cops combing the ground inside that yellow police tape. And Louise wasn't answering the phone, even though he'd left three messages, damned good ones, too, the kind that sometimes pressured her into calling him back: *"Louise, what's the matter—you trapped inside that house? What's the big problem answering the phone? I've heard all about how they found that louse Hoffman tucked in your back garden. Hell, you act like they've charged you with the crime. So, how did he get buried there? You gotta know something. And if you don't know, all the more reason to call me. You can depend on your old friend Charlie to help you find out who did it!"*

While hovering at the mouth of Dogwood Court, Charlie had seen a car pull out of the Eldridges' yard. It was Bill Eldridge's Camry, if memory served him right. When the car passed him with the sunroof open, he did a double take. At the wheel was a young gal with long chestnut hair glinting in the sun. At first he thought it was Louise, and then realized it must be her daughter Martha, a dead ringer for her mother. In the passenger's seat was the blond daughter, Janie, who'd turned into quite a dish.

The two of them had been so preoccupied talking that they hadn't noticed the guy parked in a red sports car. He was sure that if he'd had a chance to talk to them he could have squeezed out good information for a story that was due by seven this evening. So far, he had diddly, nothing much beyond the meager facts divulged by the Fairfax cops: "Body of Peter Hoffman found in yard of the woman who'd tagged him as a killer four years ago."

Poor old Louise, thought Charlie, *she's gotten herself into another mess of trouble. She's really going to need me.*

After bugging the cops for as long as was practical and striking out on reaching Hoffman's wife, he'd resorted to slowly circuiting the neighborhood to see what else he could come up with. His sharp eyes behind his sunglasses had been seeking out prey, and now he spotted one. Charlie, being slighter than other guys and disinclined to sports, had never developed his hunter-fisher instincts. They were latent there inside him, though, because right now every hunter-fisher nerve in his body was tingling.

A lithe young woman wearing the skimpiest sundress he'd ever laid eyes on, thereby exposing a dynamite pair of athletic, tanned legs, was wending her way down a steep, hilly yard filled with plants and trees, looking as if she were out for a jog. *Pretty as a picture,* thought Charlie, then almost laughed at himself for being such a bloody romantic. He slowed the Porsche, then brought it to a stop and lowered his front window all the way. She was coming straight for the sidewalk, after carefully sidestepping a vicious-looking shrub.

"Hi, there," he said. "You make a pretty picture." He decided he'd tell the simple truth and see where it got him.

She liked it and smiled. "Hi, there, yourself," she said. She had an accent, maybe German. She paused momentarily on the sidewalk, then came over, leaned down and put an arm on the open car window. This put the tops of her round golden breasts so close to his face that he could hardly breathe. Or maybe it was the exotic perfume emanating from her lush skin; he couldn't tell which. "I'm Hilde," she said, opening her eyes wide. "And who are you?"

Charlie knew then what it meant to drown in someone's eyes. Hilde's eyes were green, with lots of depth, so they truly were like pools, but with sharply defined small black irises. And they were kind eyes—or was that only a look of patience in them? He decided he'd put his cards on the table right away, so he pulled out his press pass. "Charlie Hurd. Washington *Post*. I cover crime." He didn't add that he covered suburban crime, government and all sorts of screwy feature stories, and had been locked in this goddamned Fairfax county suburban corral for too effing long.

"Oh, a journalist," she said, in a slightly mocking voice. "How exciting." The green eyes narrowed. "Let me guess. You are here with the other media because something terrible has been found in the Eldridges' garden." She was so right. The other media were either parked in Dogwood Court or trolling as he was.

Charlie whipped off his sunglasses and widened his own eyes. "You've heard about the body being found."

"Of course I've heard. The neighbors, we neighbors have been, oh, how do you say, gathering in the street, once we knew police cars had arrived in the middle of the night. Some of us were even interviewed on TV."

"I'd love to talk to you. You probably know the Eldridges. So do you want to hop in the car? I'll even take you out for a cup of coffee, if you like."

She turned her head and looked up at the big glass-fronted house on top of the hill from which she'd exited, as if she might have business up there. Then she smiled, and without saying a thing, slipped around the front of the car. Charlie barely had time to reach over and open the passenger-side door before she arrived there, slid in and fastened her seatbelt across her delightful chest. "Ready, I think," she said, beaming over another smile.

Charlie felt as if he were in hog heaven. Not once since he'd been assigned by the *Post* to the suburbs had he encountered such a beauty. Now he had to remember why he'd picked her up. Oh yes, the Hoffman murder. The package in Louise's garden.

As he drove back up Rebecca Road, the delightful Hilde looked over at him. "I could be hungry, also," she said, laughing, and then spread her hands out. "But I didn't bring a purse. So would you buy me a sandwich for lunch?"

He grinned sappily. "Of course, Hilde. I think we can find a place." But this was a problem for him. Where the hell was there a decent restaurant around here?

His passenger put her hands together with a small clap. "I know a place."

"Sure. Where is it?"

"It's called the Dixie Pig." She pointed a long finger. "It's just the way we're headed right now."

"Yeah, I know," he said, trying not to sound dispirited. The Dixie Pig was the last place he wanted to go. Talk

about lowbrow, the restaurant was Southern trash transported to suburban Washington, D.C.

"I like the barbecue," she explained.

"The barbecued pork sandwich. Sure." The Dixie Pig
was famous for its gross barbecue sandwiches, obviously
fattening, since most people he'd seen exiting the place
were vastly overweight. How could a fantastic beauty like
this, who from the sound of her hadn't been in this country for long, have developed an affinity for northern
Virginia's weirdest restaurant?

Charlie had to admit the barbecued pork wasn't bad. It
was delicious, in fact. He had the red barbecue sauce all
over his hands to prove it. And there were, he was pleased
to see, a few other thin people in the establishment at this
late lunch hour. Maybe, he thought, thin people ate later
because they weren't as hungry as fat people.

"See, you do like it," said Hilde, utterly luminous as she
sat across from him in the red leather booth, the one
clean and shining thing in this place in which all else
seemed sheathed in a thin layer of grease, and where the
air conditioning unit throbbed so noisily it overtook the
country music playing on the kitchen radio.

Hilde was handling her messy sandwich with the flair of
a fine lady, or, in her case, a fine artist. He'd gotten the
lowdown on Hilde. She was interning until October with
Sarah Swanson, a "magnificent" potter of whom he'd
never heard. Hilde picked up the huge pickle in her re-
fined fingers, taking discreet bites, and popped in the
French fries—she'd nearly demolished the huge pile
they'd served her—as if they were little invisible threads.
Such class, he thought. How did she do it?

He paused in mid-sandwich and wiped his hands, finally realizing he couldn't spend this entire lunch hour
trying to make time with this girl. He needed to pry from
her whatever nuggets of gossip she might know, which

probably wasn't much. "So I suppose you've met Louise Eldridge."

"Oh, yes, but only briefly. And her husband—I've also met Bill. And I have caught glimpses of their daughter, who I believe is named Janie." She bent her head and peered up at him with those green eyes. "I also met the dead man."

"Oh-ho," he said hopefully. "You met Peter Hoffman before someone offed him?"

"Yes," she said in a sober voice. "He appeared at a neighborhood party the day after his release from the mental institution that held him."

"So what did you think of Peter?"

"He was very forward, I thought."

"Huh," barked Charlie. "I bet the guy came on to you, didn't he?"

Her gaze dropped demurely to the tan formica table-top. "Oh, yes. Of course, that is not unusual. But he also seemed to be making an appointment, maybe you'd say a date, to meet Louise. We all heard it. Later that very night, he did meet her at her house, and I heard from . . . some-one, that she attacked him."

"Louise? Attacked Peter Hoffman?"

"Rather viciously—or rather, that was what I was told."

"So who told you that?"

"Another neighbor who was at the party. But I don't mean to gossip about anyone."

"Oh, you're not gossiping. You and me, we're friends. Friends can tell each other things. Who was it who told you that Louise attacked Hoffman?"

"Greg Archer." Hilde's face had a guileless expression. This woman, Charlie exulted to himself, was a pure, un-censored font of information. "He lives with Sam Rosen, who is in the corner house next to the Eldridge house. I believe they saw the attack."

"No kiddin'," said Charlie. He mentally filed the name.

Yet the whole thing didn't track. "I can't figure out why Louise would want to meet with Hoffman in the first place. She wouldn't even talk about that guy."

"Maybe she was trying to set her heart at ease," said Hilde, putting her hand on her superb breast in the approximate location of her heart. "Trying to get rid of her hatred or whatever terrible emotions were in here. After all, Peter Hoffman came out of that hospital to rejoin society. She would have to confront that truth some time."

Charlie was very distracted by that hand on Hilde's breast. "So what else do know about these characters? Who else do you know around here?"

She withdrew the hand. "Not very much, Charlie. I recently arrived from Zurich. I've just met the people in the cul-de-sac who came to the party and neighbors on either side of the Swansons. I spend most of my time working very long hours in Sarah's studio, or walking in the neighborhood. We have a large order to fill."

"Order for what?"

Hilde smiled, as if to vanquish all the pettiness in the world. "It is for Hecht's, a department store. Do you know it?"

"Sure," said Charlie.

"You must first know that Sarah is a wonderful artist, and creates beautiful sculptures in clay that win prizes in art shows. What I am working on is Sarah's very popular small vase in the shape of a cat, with big eyes, and to which, on each one, I must attach a set of black whiskers. This is my cross to bear at the moment."

She gave him a look of mock dismay, and he laughed, then signalled to the waitress for the check. "Hilde, you are as refreshing as a day in spring." He could kick himself for lapsing into corny again, but this chick really had him going. He hardly knew what he was saying.

He tried to remember that after he dropped her off, he needed to nail down Greg Archer or Sam Rosen, or both.

After taking Hilde on a pleasant though sweltering walk through a riverside park off George Washington Parkway, Charlie had dropped her back at her apartment above the studio. He got a passing glance at a big workroom with lots of identical cat figures sitting on tables, then a quick look at her sparsely furnished apartment. It was dominated by a queen-sized bed with a pure white comforter, tucked in as if by an Army private. He'd raised his eyebrows suggestively and joked, *Nice bed.* She'd colored delightfully, like a maiden should. Then she had eased him out the door. Although he hated to leave, it was just as well. He was desperate for a hot lead for his Saturday story.

He had cruised the two short blocks back to Dogwood Court, then parked and watched a crew of police technicians pack up and depart in their van. There was one major distraction gone from Louise Eldridge's life. Maybe now if he called, she'd pick up the phone. He pressed her number, which was now on his speed dial, and was cheered when she answered. Nevertheless, he felt compelled to punish her. "Damn!" he burst out. "You finally picked up."

Silence. He'd sounded like the spoiled little boy his mother occasionally reminded him that he was. He decided to soften his approach. "What I mean is, I'm real glad to hear from you, Louise. How ya doin', anyway?"

"Not very well, Charlie. In the first place, the police have told me not to discuss the case. So I should never have answered this call."

"Why can't you discuss it? I've been talking about it with everybody I can get my hands on. In fact, I have an appointment to drop in on Greg Archer in a few minutes. You know, your neighbor."

Louise was silent on the other end of the phone line.

"Hey, wait a minute," said Charlie, finally getting it. "Do the cops suspect you? No, don't tell me!" And he burst into laughter.

"Stop laughing, Charlie. It's not funny. I'm about a week from being thrown in jail. You know the police drill. You find a body buried in a yard, the owner of the yard has a history with the deceased, so naturally the owner must have done it. That's how they think. You're going to talk to that gossipy Greg Archer?"

"Yep, in about fifteen minutes."

"Then you'll find out I allegedly had a fight with Peter Hoffman. That Greg is nothing but a . . . a . . ."

"Scumbag?"

"Yes. Somebody who tells tales that aren't true."

"Someone's already told me some stuff, like the fact that at that neighborhood party you and the newly-sprung-from-the-hospital Peter Hoffman made a date to rendezvous together. So what happened when you met? You didn't kiss and make up?"

"Charlie, when will you stop trying to be funny?" said Louise. "See, that story's part of the lie. Peter Hoffman played out that charade on purpose, talking to me as if we were planning a rendezvous. I spoke hardly a word to him. About forty-five minutes later, he walked into our house, grabbed me and threatened me." He could hear her pull in a breath. "God, he scared me. He wore dark clothes and a hood. He looked like a killer."

"Hey, babe, he *was* a killer."

"That's why he was so frightening. I threw a pitcher at him and a moment later, along came Greg and Sam. Naturally, Hoffman had whipped off his dark sweatshirt and his hood so he looked normal. Greg misinterpreted the whole thing."

"Heaving a weapon at the guy would make it seem as if you were pissed off at Hoffman—a motive to kill, for sure.

When they found him in your garden, there must have been your fingerprints on the plastic used to wrap the body, right?"

"You're good at putting ideas together, Charlie. But you have to verify them with the police. They certainly can't come from me. The good thing is the police haven't arrested me yet. On the other hand, I'm helpless. George Morton's warned me about even talking about the matter."

"Morton's in charge? That's not good for you."

"What an understatement, if it turns out to be true." Louise's voice was glum.

Charlie rested his cell-phone arm on the open window and stared at Louise's low-slung house in the woods. He wondered idly if Louise's two beautiful daughters had gotten back home yet. "Look, don't give up hope. I'm on the case now, and I have lots of ideas on this. I'll be talking with Sam and Greg first. Then I plan to have a go at Phyllis, the wife. And this Hilde who lives in your neighborhood, what a girl! She's smart. She said she might help me check out some of this stuff."

"So you've met Hilde Brunner."

"Yeah, but I also eyeballed your daughter Martha. Looks just like you—not bad. When am I gonna meet her? Your Janie's jailbait, but Martha—wow!"

"Charlie, Martha's engaged. She's about to be married. Hilde Brunner seems like a nice young woman."

"And very sharp. Swiss, you know."

"I know. Go for it, Charlie. We all need to live life to the fullest."

He grinned. His old pal Louise, with whom he'd won some and lost some, whom he'd double-crossed on occasion and at least on one other occasion rescued from certain destruction, understood how it was with Hilde. "She'll be a good helper. You know what they say, two heads are better than one."

* * *

Louise hung up the phone. She had been going rapidly downhill into a complete funk, a headache forming behind her eyes like a dark cloud gathering energy on a stormy day. But Charlie's call made her feel better. Not that she didn't already have her own husband trying to find out what happened to Peter Hoffman, but it was nice to know Charlie was on the case, too. She respected Charlie's stubborness. When it came to crime stories, he was like a dog with a bone. And she didn't know Hilde very well, but she'd liked what she saw of her. If Hilde wanted to help, so much the better. Charlie was right—sometimes two heads were better than one.

14

"Slinging hash, huh?" wisecracked Bill as he walked into the kitchen.

"It's a lot tastier than hash," retorted Martha, as she tended two frying pans accommodating, respectively, eggs and blueberry pancakes. Golden brown bacon strips already lay on a paper towel, ready for serving.

"Gee, a new order of things," he said, staring over her shoulder at the food. "Bagels and lox yesterday, bacon and pancakes today—more breakfast than your mother and I usually eat." He missed Louise, but he'd noted the pills that his wife took last night and realized she would sleep through breakfast and beyond.

"You need food, Dad," Martha advised. "Go sit down. You look stressed out."

"I don't like it that every time I go outdoors, I have to fight off members of the press."

"It will all be over soon," said Martha, blithely. "I just tell them, 'No comment.' In the meantime, these blueberries will be very good for you."

"They will?"

"Absolutely. You and Ma should eat blueberries on a daily basis. They're especially good for retaining the vision in older people's eyes."

Bill had to admit he was stressed out. Still, he didn't feel like "older people," but said nothing to Martha. When the girls called Louise "Ma," he also put on a few years, it seemed, and it might even be worse if they decided to call him "Pa." When he and Louise were older people, it would be nice to have someone like Martha around to be pleasantly bossy and call them whatever she chose. At the moment, he knew his daughter had more than blueberries on her mind.

"So what did you and Jim talk about last night?"

She stood at the doorway of the dining room. "Oh, wedding plans. Don't worry, things are shaping up just fine, except for my dress." She poured a cup of coffee for each of them and then joined him at the table. "But Dad, on to more pressing matters. Jim has a theory about Peter Hoffman that he wants me to tell you about. He thinks the sale of Hoffman's arms business could have motivated someone to murder him. Maybe the wife, maybe the man to whom he sold the business, maybe his partners in the business or people involved in the actual sales deal."

Bill looked at Martha, and as usual saw in her the image of the woman he'd married twenty-two years ago. Martha and Louise had the same hazel eyes, golden skin and brown hair, though Louise's now possessed a streak of gray. The daughter had turned out to be less tentative and more assertive than her mother, almost bossy at times. But insistently curious and smart, also like her mother.

"Jim might be on the right track," said Bill, nodding, expressing his approval again of Martha's fiancé. "Today, though it's not the best day to reach people, I'm going to see what I can find out about the sale of that business. Unfortunately, I'll have little time to help your mother out of this fix. If you heard the news, you know the Middle East is in turmoil once more. The IAEA is right in the middle of it. They want me to leave for Vienna within a week.

I've tried to tell them I don't want to leave the states until Hoffman's death is resolved, but they're putting a helluva lot of pressure on me."

"Poor Dad." Martha patted his hand. "I figured it was something about that. That's all the more reason that Janie and I want to step in and help."

"Hold on," said Bill, putting down his fork. "I don't want you and Janie involved." He gave his daughter a suspicious look. "What're you trying to do, follow in your mother's footsteps? Why can't we give the police a chance to sort it out? Mike Geraghty doesn't believe your mother killed Peter Hoffman, and I can hardly accept that Morton believes it either, even with those unfortunate pieces of so-called 'evidence.' They just haven't had time yet to look into all the angles."

"Dad, it'll be all right. Supposing we just go to Friendship Heights and check out wedding clothes at Saks? Supposing we should run into Phyllis Hoffman? That's no crime."

Bill leaned toward his daughter. "I'm telling you, Martha, I don't want you to put yourself or Janie in danger, hear me? I feel guilty as it is that I don't have much time to check out the facts. I'm already worried enough about your mother. She's not taking this very well. I think she's depressed."

Martha patted her father's hand. "All right, Dad. I promise we'll do nothing to upset her, nothing the least bit dangerous. Just a little schmoozing with neighbors, just a little visit to Saks."

He ignored his pancakes and bacon and the comforting hand that still lay on his. He said, "How can I convince you that you should stay out of it? Just remember that one of the neighbors, or that Hoffman woman herself, could be the murderer."

His daughter slumped back in her chair and slowly spread her arms, as if she were an unfolding flower. "I give up. You know I'm not a child anymore. I'm about to be a married woman—and I'm very competent—yet you won't let me lift a finger to help my own mother, your wife, who right this minute is in a somnolent, sleeping-pill-induced state because she's so worried about being thrown in jail."

Bill shook his head and contemplated his abandoned eggs and pancakes. "Damn," he grumbled, "I hate guilt trips." He turned and faced his older daughter. "Here's the deal. Give the police a few days to do their thing. Who knows, maybe they'll come up with the murderer. If they don't, well, then we can talk this over again and renegotiate."

Martha closed her hand in a fist, shook it and cried, "Yes!"

Louise woke up. The skylight above her head was almost as good as a sundial. It was at least ten o'clock. Thoughts of childhood and her professor father, who never overslept, came back to her. He used to walk back and forth outside her bedroom door until finally she awoke and came downstairs and had breakfast with him in the kitchen of their old house in Wilmette. She smiled at the memory. The old Protestant work ethic had driven both father and daughter, and still did.

A soft knock on the door, and her husband appeared with a tray, like an overly handsome concierge at some fancy foreign hotel.

"I come bearing gifts," he said, walking over and smiling down at her. "Actually, only coffee, because I know how you hate to get crumbs in the bed."

She sat up, straightened her twisted silk charmeuse nightgown, then accepted her husband's kiss on the lips and the tray, which included a copy of the Washington *Post*. She groaned when she saw it. Yesterday's story had been brief, with little detail, since the story had broken during the night. This morning, the story occupied the bottom right of the front page and included, next to a head shot of Peter Hoffman, a picture of her house with policemen prowling through the yard. The headline read:

MULCH MURDERER KILLED, PLANTED
IN GARDEN DIVA'S AZALEA BED

The subhead was even worse.

LOUISE ELDRIDGE WAS INFORMER WHO LED
TO CAPTURE OF ARMS DEALER PETER HOFFMAN

A feature story was headlined:

WAS REVENGE THE MOTIVE
IN BIZARRE GARDEN CRIME?

When the main story jumped inside to page five, she saw a picture of herself—a publicity photo from her studio, WTBA-TV. She was holding a houseplant, smiling at the camera and looking outrageously out of sync with the macabre story that accompanied it.

Louise glanced at her husband. "One could expect no less of Charlie Hurd."

Bill pointed a finger down at her. "Or at the editors. They're the ones who write the headlines."

She bowed her head. "You know our lives will not be normal again until they find the person who killed Peter. And what will Marty Corbin think of that 'revenge' headline? This could even affect my job."

Bill smiled. "I think your producer knows you're incapable of murder, Louise; don't worry about Marty. Just call him Monday morning and let him in on the details. Now drink your coffee, or it'll get cold."

She took a taste. "Delicious, honey. Sorry to sleep so late."

"You needed it. And now we need to talk." He sat on the bed beside her, and she could tell by the frown lines around his mouth that he wasn't happy.

"What's the bad news?" She touched his arm, which was resting nearby.

"I'm sure the man can measure up and be fair."

"Bill, I can't follow you. Who are you talking about?"

"I'm talking about Morton, of course," he said impatiently, as if even a child would know who he was referring to. "You were right, Louise. Lieutenant Dan Trace over at the sheriff's headquarters in Fairfax City called. Though Trace is in charge of the overall investigation, George Morton has taken over as lead detective."

"Poor Mike Geraghty," she said. "They probably thought that he was too good a friend of ours. Do you think this will hurt his career?"

Bill shook his head. "I doubt it. Who knows if Morton even has smarts enough to find this killer? I personally think the man is . . . well, never mind what I think about Morton. I've just finished a few phone calls, and then I promptly passed the information on to our new lead detective."

"What could you learn on a Saturday?"

"Two things that the police didn't know yet," said Bill. "One is that within the past week, which means immediately before he disappeared, Hoffman completed the sale of his arms business to Lee Downing. It may be just a coincidence, but the timing is damned suspicious. And number two, Hoffman apparently still owed his attorney, Mike Cunningham, over a million dollars." He grimaced. "That's only part of what Hoffman paid to save his ass and avoid prison."

"That gives us at least two suspects. But why would Lee

Downing kill the man whose company he just bought? Or why would Mike Cunningham get rid of a man who still owed him a huge amount of money?"

Her husband shrugged. "Beats me. It's a starting point. There could be lots more behind both of those stories. Downing's Texas arms manufacturing company also needs to be looked at. I have some feelers out on him that are promising. In the meantime, I'm hoping the police get right on this line of inquiry. I'm trying to speed up the process."

Standing up suddenly, he bent down to take Louise's coffee tray from her.

"Wait," she said, grabbing the mug. "I have a swallow left. Bill, why are you so fretty?"

He slumped down next to her again, set the tray on the bedside table and put an arm around her. "Leave it to the women in this family to read my mind. Louise, I told Martha and I'll tell you. Things are in terrible shape in the Middle East. The IAEA wants me to go overseas within the week and help. How the hell am I going to be able to help you when all this is coming down at the same time?"

She rested her head on her husband's shoulder for a moment, then turned and looked at him. Her voice was firm. "Go do your work. They need you badly and you know it. Go downtown or wherever you need to go today. I'll be all right. I'm convinced the police will never arrest me. They're going to get to the bottom of this and find out who murdered Peter Hoffman. And then George Morton is going to come over here and personally apologize to me."

He looked into her eyes, and she gazed back at him confidently, a touch of perverse excitement in her eyes.

Louise had just told her husband a big lie. She was sure of nothing regarding George Morton, but Bill needed to be lied to. As for herself, she was tired of being a woman with trembling hands who was so upset at false charges that she resorted to knockout pills to put herself to sleep.

In a vigorous move, she pushed the covers aside and swung her legs over the side of the bed, impatiently pulling the charmeuse nightie straight again. So much for George Morton's warning not to investigate. She intended to pull out all the stops. Nobody was going to frame her for murder and get away with it!

Taking her cue, Bill was already at the bedroom door. She noticed he'd forgotten the tray on the table. He paused before leaving and stared intently at her across the room. "If you say you're going to be all right, honey, I believe you. Now, I've got to head downtown. They're already in a meeting there."

15

As Louise sat in the recreation room and took the last sip of her fourth cup of coffee, she realized she should have stopped at three. She already was so restless that she felt like jumping out of her skin. She had to get out of the house today, even if it meant sneaking out the recreation room door and through the woods to avoid running into nosy press people. Bill had already had sharp words with one TV newsman who had sneaked onto the property last night and demanded an interview. The last thing she wanted to do was tangle with someone else.

She took George Morton's warning seriously not to try and solve the crime on her own, but surely he couldn't object if she merely visited her neighbor Nora. She was the kind of friend who might shed some meaning on this horrible nightmare. For Louise was in a kind of nightmare, an existence dominated by a grisly murder, pushy reporters and suspicious police. Once she'd taken her cup to the kitchen, she returned and carefully opened the recreation room door, peeking both ways to be sure no one was lurking about.

As she stepped out, the August heat folded over her face like a blanket. On this side of the house was the

Oriental garden—a handsome assortment of bamboo, deciduous azaleas, grassy tufts of chartreuse carex and blue-
flowered plumbago. Her gaze was drawn immediately to
the tire marks in the ground. With a little shudder, she realized the killer had done this damage, driving the cartita
straight through the plants, flattening a few low grasses
and plants, and even bending a couple of tough, five-foot-
tall bamboo stalks. But why? It was as if the killer had a
grudge against her.

She knelt down and with dexterous hands pulled the
carex and plumbago back into position, smoothing the
earth around them. She would come back with the loppers to cut down the broken bamboo shoots.

As she worked on neatening the garden, a smile crossed
her face. John Bachelder, her ambitious cohost on
Gardening with Nature, was the only person she could think
of who might bear her a grudge. John wasn't happy that
Marty Corbin kept writing him out of scripts. But ambitious or not, she knew he was not a murderer, just a man
anxious about keeping his job.

She decided to exit the woods by way of her neighbors'
yard, the Kendricks. Wearing tan shorts, an olive drab T-shirt
and old tennis shoes, she blended in perfectly with the
sweet gum, dogwood, oak, wild cherry and sassafras trees
that populated the yard. No news hawk would observe her
here.

She opened the gate in the fence between the two prop-
erties and headed for the street, realizing that this was the
first time she'd shown her face in public since the body
had been discovered Thursday night. No one paid any attention to her, not the evidence technicians still poking
through the front yard nor the patrolmen out at the curb.
Their job was to dissuade nosy people including the press
from prowling inside the yellow police tape that surrounded
the Eldridge yard. Although she could see several strange

cars parked at the entrance to the cul-de-sac, she was a little disappointed to see that Charlie Hurd's red Porsche was not among them.

And here Charlie said he wanted to help solve this murder, she thought. It made sense, though, that he'd be more help looking for clues beyond this cul-de-sac.

Lying before her was the round, sunny asphalt space of Dogwood Court. Emanating from the cul-de-sac were six big pie-shaped yards, the homes themselves shrouded in tall forest and therefore only partially seen from the road. Gardeners like Louise, Nora Radebaugh and Sam Rosen took advantage of this rim of sunshine to plant little front-yard gardens. As she slipped closer to the Radebaugh house, she inspected Nora's tall orange tiger lilies and drifts of small white daisy-flowered *Tanacetum niveum,* accented with fountain-shaped clumps of *Miscanthus sinensis.* She passed the garden and within a few steps had walked from sun into deep shade, where tall pines thriving among the sweet gum and oak attested to the more acidic soil on this side of the cul-de-sac.

She took the shortcut up the slight rise to the house, threading her way through the trees and ending at the big front windows. She peeked in and was not surprised to see Nora. She was sitting on a couch, her bare feet tucked under her, wearing white flowing slacks and a white gauze top. She appeared to be writing in a notebook. The poet at work. No matter what happened in the world, no matter what downswings her personal life with her husband, Ron, took, Nora never stopped writing poetry and had the bylines to prove it in various poetry magazines.

Louise knocked on the window, then realized this was not a good idea after a crime in the neighborhood. But Nora was not fazed. She merely looked up, smiled in recognition and signaled with a cock of the head for Louise to go to the front door.

When she entered the cool house, she heard the low sounds of the stereo playing Brahms and smelled the faintest aroma of furniture oil in this cleanest of houses. Nora enclosed her in a long embrace. "Louise, my dear" was all she said, and it was sufficient. They went to the kitchen, where Nora prepared green tea in a pot that was so streamlined that Louise thought it must have come from an art museum store. They settled in the living room on a big sofa.

Carefully balancing her teacup so as not to spill, Louise relaxed into the softness of the sofa pillows. "Nice teapot. Museum of Modern Art?"

Nora smiled. "Tar-jay."

"Wow, Target?" said Louise, incredulously. She'd missed a large beat in discount store merchandising. "Nora, I came over here because I need your help."

Her friend's gray eyes were all sympathy, but her mouth curved in a smile. "I know the police suspect you of the killing. Do you know I've already been importuned to help by your lovely Martha?"

Louise pursed her lips. "You mean Martha's been here already?" Why did she have the faint feeling that Number One daughter was taking over her and Bill's life?

"Yes," said Nora, and reached a hand over and grasped Louise's. "Martha needs to talk, just like you do. And she's always confided in me, you know . . . and even more so in Mary."

How well Louise knew this, that both Martha and Janie, when facing big decisions, ran across the street to her side-by-side friends Nora and Mary. Of course, she usually discovered this well after the big decisions were made. *Should I take this internship in Guatemala, or would it be better to spend the summer working with the poor in a Chicago ghetto?* Martha would ask. *Would it be a good thing if I dated other boys besides Chris, since he's in college, and I still have another year of high school?* Janie had asked this of Mary Mougey, and Mary had passed it along. The whole situation left Louise feeling that she'd failed as an authority figure. The girls treated her more as a sister than a mother. And she had no clue as to how she could gain more clout with her daughters.

Nora was talking now about their putting their ideas together. "Maybe if we all work together, we can find the person who did this rotten thing." She stared out the front window. "In fact, on the premise that three heads are better than two, let me ring up Mary. She's just pulled into her driveway. I know she fled the house for a while."

"What for?" said Louise.

"My dear," said Nora, shoving her short, dark hair away from her face, "to get a little peace. You mustn't underestimate the impact of this crime on the neighbors. We've all been interrogated by the police, of course, and now the newspaper and TV and radio people are out there like a pack of sharks that smell blood. I personally got rid of them by telling them I had a virus that they wouldn't want to catch."

Louise colored. She thought back on recent years and started to count. What was it, three or four times when murders had encroached on the peace of greater Sylvan Valley? And each time, unfortunately, Louise had been right at the center of the trouble.

"What do we think of Phyllis as a prospect?" said Louise.

Mary Mougey, who had joined them in the living room, crossed her legs, and Louise noted that she wore red Prada sandals. Louise had seen them in a catalog and would have bought a pair herself had they not been so pricey. They went well with Mary's navy-trimmed white pantsuit, a notch down from the elegant clothes she wore for her high-profile Washington job.

"Wait a moment before you start," said Nora, unfolding herself from the sofa and going to a sideboard. She held up a stenographer's pad as she rejoined them. "Martha and I each made notes when we talked earlier this morning."

Mary smiled. "Dear Martha. How is she handling this?"

Nora said, "Very well." She hastened to add, " But of course Louise can tell you better than me."

Louise shrugged. "As Nora says, very well. She has everything including Bill and me under control. Even the wedding plans."

Mary clasped her hands in delight, for she hadn't yet heard the news. Louise had to fill her in on the impending nuptials.

After a few moments, Nora eyed her two companions and said, "Now, let's get to this little list that Martha and I made." She flipped open the notebook. "Your daughter insisted it be alphabetized; she's very well organized. I myself would have just written it in shoddy quatrains."

"Who's on the list?"

"Mike Cunningham, Lee Downing, Phyllis Hoffman and . . . Mort Swanson."

"Mort Swanson?" said Louise. "Don't tell me." Wasn't being faced with his own mortality enough without also being thought of as a possible murder suspect? "I'm not sure I see his motive."

"Louise, this list is just academic," said her friend. "The killer could well be someone we don't even know, but we have to look at the local people, and that includes Mort. I can't believe either that he would do such a horrible thing. But he was Peter's lawyer for a great share of his business affairs. We can't ignore him."

"And how did you and Martha come up with Lee Downing?"

Nora gave Louise a careful look. "Martha said Bill mentioned it to her this morning. Downing just finished buying Hoffman Arms two days before Peter disappeared."

"Oh." Louise hadn't known that her daughter knew as much as she did herself.

"Mike Cunningham's name is here because he defended Peter and seemed to have a close relationship with him as his attorney. Who knows what went on between them over the past few years?"

Mary leaned forward toward Nora and gestured with a graceful hand at the pad. "Why don't you put a name at the top of that list: 'A' for Archer, Greg Archer."

Louise said, "Greg Archer? Did Greg even know Peter Hoffman?"

"I have no knowledge of that, Louise," said Mary. "But what I'm telling you is that darling-looking blond man is terribly aloof when I try to talk to him, possibly because I have a bird's-eye view of him snooping."

"Snooping?" said Louise.

"Yes, and in your yard. He pokes around there when you're away, even rides that little cart around through both yards, though rather awkwardly." Her eyes widened. "I bet he's told police things that might even have helped implicate you, my dear. Just jot the name down, Nora. We'll try later to find a tie between him and the deceased Peter Hoffman."

Nora turned thoughtful eyes toward the woods beyond the living room. In a quiet voice, she said, "I'll put my money on Phyllis right now. If I were Phyllis, I would have killed him long ago."

Silence greeted this statement. Louise looked at her friend and saw it was not meant as a joke, for Nora's face was unsmiling. Louise chuckled as if it were a joke, but the levity sounded a little phony. "It might have been a hard thing to do, since he's been living in a mental hospital. What would you have done, slipped him poison cookies?"

Nora relaxed back in the sofa and said, "I'd like to think I don't mean that. But with his alley-cat ways, Peter demeaned women in public more fiercely than any man I've ever seen. He crassly killed, decapitated and—"

Louise bent her head. "Oh, stop. I agree with you, but don't say any more."

Nora said, "I regret bringing that up, Louise. Forgive me. Let me just say that Phyllis does have a personal motive. Not only did Peter cheat on her time and again, but as soon as he was hospitalized, he put Mike Cunningham in charge of his financial affairs. It changed Phyllis's lifestyle overnight. Mike immediately sold their big house and informed her that she needed to get a job to help support herself. She's had to handle almost everything, including rent on her house, on a sales clerk's salary."

Mary smiled knowingly. "Maybe she thinks she's suffered enough and was anxious to be a rich widow."

"And now she is, I guess," said Louise, "or is she? We don't really know where Peter's money is going, do we?"

"No," said Mary, "but I dearly hope the police find out, or perhaps Phyllis will tell me. She phones me frequently at work, which is quite inconvenient at times. The woman must have no close friends. I am really no more than an acquaintance."

Louise said, "Let's go back to this Lee Downing. Since we'd barely met him before we left on our vacation, I have no idea what he's like."

Nora nodded. "He's another of those men with a wandering eye. I'm sure he has a wife back in west Texas where he came from. But since he arrived on Mike Cunningham's doorstep a month ago, he and Mike have been acting as if they are Washington's most eligible bachelors."

"What do they do?"

"They've had people over to Mike's house several times, which is perfectly fine, of course, but the female guests are a dead giveaway—young-looking, over-painted and over-dressed."

Mary Mougey made a comical wry face. "Ladies of the night, in Sylvan Valley? It adds a new tone to the neighborhood."

"How come I missed all of this?" said Louise. She couldn't imagine Nora peeking out her front window. She was too caught up in her inner world, writing poetry or musing over her difficult marriage, to snoop upon others.

Nora smiled. "Your missed it because your living room faces the woods. I missed it too, but Ron tends to be outside gardening in the early evening. He's seen them arriving in Downing's car. I try to avoid the two of them, for as you two dear friends know, I have my own domestic issues."

"How are you and Ron doing, Nora?" asked Louise. "Um, are you going to that awareness conference in California?"

"Actually, Ron and I are doing much better. Things improved three weeks ago, the night of the party that Peter crashed. I so admired the way that my Ron handled that intrusion." A radiant smile passed over her face, and Louise saw again how beautiful her troubled poet friend was. "I told him that night how I admired him. And it was as if a burden fell off our shoulders. We were able to . . . come together like new lovers."

The three women fell silent in the cool house, and Louise suspected they were all thinking about new love. Her friend Mary, she noticed, had sorrowful lines on both sides of her mouth, despite the expert application of makeup and creams. No wonder: Mary and Richard's lovemaking probably was on hold because of his deep depression.

But it was no better for her and Bill. Things hadn't been quite the same in the bedroom since the night that the loathsome Peter Hoffman had invaded their home.

Louise had to admit that, since then, she had been a distracted and disengaged lover. Unlike Nora, who sometimes told her two friends more than they wanted to hear, neither Louise nor Mary was about to share any of these marital woes.

Louise gave a little laugh, and her friends looked at her as if grateful for the distraction. "Not to change the subject, but it's been two hellish days since Peter Hoffman turned up in my garden. I really need exercise if I'm to stand the least chance for new love. Anyone for a swim at the club?"

16

Martha was sprawled on one end of the living room couch. "I sure do miss Jim."

Janie, propped against pillows at the other end of the couch, put down her book and flipped her long blond hair back from her face. In Martha's opinion, she should have left the hair where it was, for her uncovered face held an unpleasant pout. "What do you think? I miss Chris just as much."

Martha slanted a glance at her younger sister. "Sorry. I didn't mean to say you didn't. Bet you can't wait till he comes home from Baltimore. Talked to him in awhile?"

"No."

Martha laughed. "Why don't you phone him and see if he's cheating on you?"

Janie roused herself from the couch. "Not a bad idea. What're you doing tonight?"

"I need to walk a little after all that shopping we did today." Shopping for hours, and finding nothing, not a wedding suit or a maid of honor dress that the two could agree upon or that wasn't outrageously overpriced. Martha sauntered across the living room and eased out the front door, leaving Janie safely behind.

She'd kept an eye on the neighborhood for the past hour by little walks in the yard and frequent glances out her bedroom window. The Kendricks had departed in dressy clothes for what probably was a dinner party. Sam Rosen and his cute friend Greg Archer had also left. Nora and Ron Radebaugh and Richard and Mary Mougey were spending a quiet evening at their respective homes, as were her own parents.

Unaccounted for were Mike Cunningham and his house guest, Lee Downing. Those were the two people in whom Martha was interested. She was determined to get to know them, but she didn't want her younger sister tagging along. From the stories Nora Radebaugh had told her, Cunningham and Downing were acting like overaged lotharios—not the kind of men to whom the annoyingly attractive Janie should be exposed. In fact, Nora had told her that she was sure Downing was married and just playing the role of a single man during his stay in Washington.

Martha was wearing the skimpiest of clothes, short shorts and T-shirt she'd carefully preserved from her days in junior high school, and well-worn running shoes. People who saw her would guess she was out for an early evening jog in the sultry evening air. She decided to position herself in the Mougeys' plot of woods, which would make it logical to assume she'd just come in from a constitutional on Rebecca Road, a favorite route for joggers.

She hoped the Mougeys wouldn't spot her skulking in their woods. Fortunately, there was a sweet gum stump to sit on. After a few minutes' wait, she saw car lights swing into the cul-de-sac. It was Mike Cunningham's green Jaguar.

By the time he'd maneuvered into his driveway, Martha had jauntily run up the curved sidewalk and right by the front of his house, which sported a new evergreen tree hedge. He stopped the car. His car window slid down, and he called, "Who's that? Come back!" Just about what she'd expected of him when a girl in tight shorts and T-shirt with a really good body bounced by.

She pirouetted, ran back and leaned down to smile at him. Since she'd only met him on the fly two days ago, this was the first good look she'd taken of the man.

She had to admit Cunningham was kind of cute, but in a few years he'd have jowls. And what was with that hair? Did he think he was a game-show host?

She shoved a hand in the car. "Hi. I'm Martha Eldridge, Bill and Louise's daughter from Chicago. I met you when we got home from the beach Thursday night."

"Great to see you again," said Cunningham. "You're lookin' good."

She straightened and looked at his house through the gathering gloom. "So you bought this place. How do you like living in the woods in this naughty liberal neighborhood?

"C'mon now," he said in a scoffing voice, "those old stories about wife-swapping . . . I bet they aren't even true."

"Now don't spoil the image of Sylvan Valley," she said, laughing. "Modern houses plunked in the middle of all of this northern Virginia tradition . . ."

"I'm adding a little tradition to my modern house. I'm having a fountain built in the front yard. It's going to have one of those Aphrodite statues holding a pitcher of water."

Martha smiled. "That should be interesting. There's a dearth of garden statues in Sylvan Valley. No metal bird statues or concrete squirrels or gnomes, no statues of Mary or pagan goddesses." She grinned at him. "What's the next step? Classical columns for the front porch?"

He gave her a long look. She could tell by his shifting expression that he'd decided she was being humorous and not putting him down. "You are your mother's daughter, aren't you?"

Martha shrugged. "Maybe. Is that a good thing?"

"Not always, but, hey, I'm not going to carp. So the neighbors might not like my statue, but I'm not that crazy about pure modern. It's meaningless."

"You think so?" asked Martha. "My guess is that back in the fifties, the people who built a house in Sylvan Valley believed in something, and their beliefs were reflected in the architecture of their homes."

Cunningham cocked his head at her. "You sound like some kind of urban historian."

Martha leaned closer to him. "I am. Urban studies is my specialty at Northwestern. I'm getting a combined degree there—B.A. and master's."

"Oh. We'll have to get together and talk sometime. Actually, this house is just for convenience, a place to sleep when I'm in town. The place I really call home is out on the bay—a big old place on the water. And if you really want to know, the thing I'm doing next on this house is to install a security system, because though you think this is a liberal neighborhood, liberal doesn't equal safe." He looked in his rearview mirror. "But wait, now. Yeah, here comes my . . . friend. I've got to get going. Do you know Hilde Brunner? She's in the neighborhood too." He laughed. "She's more your age than mine, but I'm hoping that doesn't matter."

Approaching them was a figure that Martha couldn't see at first. She came closer to the car. She made out through the gathering darkness a tall, striking young woman with long hair and a brief sleeveless summer dress with complicated diagonal tucks. It was a kind of dress one didn't see often in Washington—or Chicago, for that matter. So this was Hilde. And what, Martha wondered, was she doing here?

Mike answered that. "Hilde," he greeted her, and reached a hand out and grasped hers. "Miss Brunner's come over this evening to visit me and see some of my photos," he explained to Martha. "You could join us if you like. I'm an amateur photographer. But first, do you two know each other?"

After they were introduced, Cunningham excused himself to put his car in the garage. As he did so, a Lincoln town car pulled up, scraping its tires against the curved curb of Dogwood Court. Martha thought she heard swearwords from the confines of the closed vehicle. But by the time the man at the wheel had opened his car door, the nearby streetlight revealed a big smiling face topped by a handsome head of silver hair. This had to be Lee Downing, Cunningham's house guest and the man who'd bought Hoffman's company. The town car was probably a rental.

Downing jumped out, his hands full of what looked like records. Muscular and rather short, he approached the group, greeted Cunningham and Hilde, and looked up at Martha admiringly with his bright blue eyes. "A fella needs an introduction," he said. Cunningham provided it.

Again, Martha recited a bit of her background. "I've been living away ever since the family moved here. College, summer internships in a lot of places, a semester abroad—"

"Oh, and where did you study?" asked Hilde.

"In Rome, primarily," lied Martha. "But being away so much means I'm not acquainted with many people around here. I love tennis, but I haven't found a foursome yet. Now that we know each other, I have an idea. Do any of you play?"

Everyone played. And so they made a date for a doubles game at eleven the next morning, at the Sylvan Valley Swim and Tennis Club.

The club was one of the nice features of the neighborhood, Martha thought, though she'd not had much chance to use it except for a few visits with Janie. It wasn't fancy. Some of the tennis courts showed signs of cracking. But it would do. Nothing like a vigorous tennis game in the Washington heat, followed by a charming little basket lunch complete with wine that she intended to bring with her. People might reveal secrets they might otherwise keep.

As Martha was about to say good night to the three of them, she saw Janie across the cul-de-sac, emerging from the front garden gate. Hurriedly, she said, "See you to-morrow, then," and jogged over to meet her younger sister before Janie walked into the circle of light cast by streetlight.

"What's going on here?" said Janie.

"I was saying good-bye." She reached out and put an arm around Janie's slim shoulders and steered her toward their house. "Janie," she said quietly, "I'm going to play tennis with Mike Cunningham and Lee Downing and Hilde Brunner tomorrow morning."

Janie shook off her sister's arm. "Why are you hustling me away? Why didn't you let me meet Mr. Downing and Hilde? I don't even know those two."

"Oh, you don't want to have anything to do with Cunningham or Downing, believe me. The more I hear about them, the worse it gets."

"You know best about everything, don't you, Martha?"

"Well, not everything. But about this, yes. You know how middle-aged lechers lech after you, Janie—you have to keep your distance."

Janie expelled an exasperated "Oh! What a sister you are. You act just like Ma, as if I am some baby who has to be watched every minute and protected from all things that you guys think are harmful. Where do you think I'm going to live, in a fairy kingdom by the sea, or in the real world?"

"Now, Janie, don't get mad."

"Don't call me Janie, damnit. My name is Jane."

"All right, Jane. Anyway, what do you want? Only four can play tennis at a time. You can meet those people the next time there's a chance."

"The trouble with you, Martha, is that you have a savior complex. 'Messianic,' I think they call it. I guess you both are like that—"

"You mean me and Jim?"

"Yeah," said Janie. "You're into saving the world and all the people in it; I bet you'll have a passel of messianic little brats. But let me ask you: have you ever read *At Play in the Fields of the Lord*?"

"Sure. Peter Matthiessen."

"Just remember the moral of the story. Some people don't think they have to be saved."

17

The men were playing the net. Lee Downing hit the ball viciously at Mike Cunningham. "Those papers yielded nothing!" he hissed. "If I didn't think it was so absurd, I'd say someone was cooking the books."

Cunningham quickly twisted his body and slammed the ball back. "Bull!" he grunted. "It's all there."

Martha ran back to get the ball, but heard Downing say, "There's no 'there' there, goddammit." She sent the ball in Hilde's direction, then ran forward so as not to miss what was said next.

Almost head to head with Downing at the net, Cunningham was red-faced and looking desperate. "For Chrissake," he muttered, "not here."

Downing stopped in his tracks. "Then where?"

Cunningham got in position to lob a ball back in Martha's direction. "Your call."

She returned the ball and hustled back to the net.

"Fine," said Downing. "I'm in New York tonight, but I'm due back Wednesday. Let's meet at your house for a late dinner."

Apparently distracted by her partner, Hilde missed the shot and yelled, "*Mist!*" Martha recognized that as an inoffensive expletive. She herself would have been inclined to say something much worse. Throwing her arms out in a gesture of helplessness, Hilde shook her head and said in a plaintive voice, "I try and try . . ."

Cunningham came over to her and put an arm on her shoulder. "So sorry, Hilde. We lost it there for a minute." He turned back to Lee Downing. "Ready to finish this game and call it quits?"

"Sure am," said the unsmiling Downing.

This tennis game was more fruitful than Martha could have imagined. The tension between the two men had grown noticeably since the four of them had met in the cul-de-sac last night. This morning, Cunningham had exclaimed, "What a picture we make! But that's mainly because we have two of the best-looking gals in metro Washington with us." Hilde, in her skimpily cut tennis dress, had smiled shyly at the compliment.

Downing had sourly rejoined, "Let's cut the talk and get going. It's too damned hot already to play tennis." Because of Martha's heavy picnic basket, they had driven the short distance to the Sylvan Valley Swim and Tennis Club in Downing's Lincoln.

And now, after an hour, the match was abandoned and they decided to eat. Threading through the woods, they found an open picnic table. Apparently few club members were braving the midday heat. Martha set out a cloth, paper plates and the food, and Downing opened the wine. On the nearby path, people passed on their way to and from the swimming pool and the courts. Martha was impressed to note that Hilde knew quite a few of the passersby: Sam Rosen and Greg Archer, the Kendricks, and other Sylvan Valley residents whom she herself had never met. She warned her companions, "Any moment now, my family may come down the path. They attended the ten o'clock services at the Presbyterian Church. It's just two blocks away."

"Good to know someone could be praying for us besides my mother," said Downing brusquely. "Hope it does us some good."

Cold chicken, gourmet salads and wine mellowed the men's moods. Lee Downing turned his attention to Martha, prodding her for details of her university major and her intern work in the inner cities of America.

In effect, he shunned Mike Cunningham and Hilde, who eventually left the table and took a stroll down the path. It startled Martha to see that the two looked like lovers. Yet she could not believe Hilde would get involved so quickly with this man who was twice her age. From what she'd heard, Hilde had arrived in Sylvan Valley only six weeks ago. Cunningham had moved into his house a month or so before. Yes, she decided, time enough to start a relationship, even if it was, in her opinion, a foolish liaison.

Their absence gave Martha a good opportunity to find out more from Lee Downing.

"Now tell me something, Lee."

"What do you want to know, my dear?"

"About your buyout of Peter Hoffman's company."

Lee Downing flinched, but quickly covered it with a cough. "Now, would a lovely girl like you really be interested in those details?" Martha had her elbow on the table and her arm casually upraised. He reached over and took her hand and laced it in his.

"Oh," she said, surprised, and he immediately released it.

"Sorry. I—"

She quickly returned to the subject of their conversation. "Don't forget, Lee, I have a double major: urban studies and economics. Of course I'm interested in your buying Hoffman Arms. I'm always interested in the business world and how deals are made."

He gazed at her, his blue eyes full of admiration. "Well, honey, this buyout just took place. His arms manufacturing setup dovetails nicely with the other military products we manufacture. The business media has commented a lot on how good a match it is. And understandably, our stock has taken quite a boost." His mouth twisted down, and she suspected she might learn what the trouble was between him and Mike Cunningham. "That's not to say there aren't problems. There are always problems getting full disclosure when you pull off something of this magnitude."

"I'll bet," said Martha, all sympathy. She laid her hand close to his on the table to indicate there were no hard feelings about the previous hand incident. "I gathered maybe there was some unfinished business when you were talking to Mike during the game."

"Yeah." His voice was hard, on the edge of brutal. "But don't think it won't be worked out to my satisfaction. If people thought Hoffman was tough, they hadn't met me. You see, Martha, I'm not just one man, I'm one man with"—he spread his arms out wide—"a helluva lot of resources, all sorts of resources. I don't mean to be threatening, but no man in my position can afford not to have a little muscle—uh, intellectual muscle, I mean—on the side."

She turned and gave him a close-up look. Very cold blue eyes, square-jawed face damp with sweat, and thin lips that had a capacity to indicate displeasure and even cruelty. "I bet that's true. You are a tough man. A rugged American entrepreneur who understands that growth is not only good, it's obligatory if we are to survive. It's what's made this country great." Martha nearly choked on these clichés. But Downing positively glowed at her words.

"My God, girl," he said, "are you sure I can't hold your hand?"

She smiled the kind of smile that gave men promise. "I'm sorry, Lee. But you and I both know it's not the right time."

Sam Rosen and Louise were going to work on the new vegetable garden. It lay in a fortuitous patch of bright afternoon sun on the border between Sam's yard and hers. A couple of weeks ago, they did the hard work of removing the extant soil and replacing it with compost-rich garden dirt. Sam phoned this morning to remind her that they needed to plant crops. He also volunteered to help her replant the wild azaleas, which languished now in plastic bags near the abandoned garden bed in the woods where the body was found.

He was waiting out in the yard for her, looking garden-ready in jeans and matching jeans shirt. "Sam, hello," she said. "I need to get my gardening hat and shovel," she said.

"I have two shovels right here," said her neighbor. She headed for the toolshed for the hat, then remembered it was still with the police being analyzed, no doubt, for hairs, fibers and maybe even cooties. She had no idea if or when she would get it back. She turned and joined Sam at the edge of the property. He had a sweet face, the kind a mother could love, and the smile on it right now as she approached made her glad he was her friend.

"Let's do the azaleas first," he said. "I've been looking at them and worrying they'd die." A faint rebuke that she hadn't had the fortitude to come out and replant them yet?

The three big shrubs were encased in black polyurethane bags and sat where she'd left them the night she found Peter Hoffman's body. "They look different," she said.

"That's because I watered them thoroughly, then slipped another bag over the top of each one. Otherwise, I didn't think they'd make it."

"Sam, thank you," she said. They uncovered the plants, which were in surprisingly good shape, and quickly restored them to their spot in the garden.

"Now for the fun part," said Sam, as they moved their operations to the vegetable garden. "I bought a lot of onion sets. And it's not too late for a crop of green beans. At least it's worth a shot." The garden was exceptionally deep, built on a natural crevice in the land and supported on its two ends with timbers Sam had patiently sawed.

It wasn't until they were actually planting that Sam brought up the crime that was obsessing the neighborhood. "What do you think happened, my friend?" said Sam.

She told him about the manner of the crime and how the evidence pointed to her. "It's sure to be Hoffman's blood on my sweatshirt," she said. "The question is, who's done this to me and why?"

"Well, who?" asked Sam, intent on his digging.

"Mike Cunningham, Lee Downing, Phyllis Hoffman or maybe Mort Swanson." She laughed. "I'm being facetious. I'm not accusing anyone. Those are just the names that my friends have put on a suspect list." She neglected to say that Mary Mougey insisted that Greg also be on the list. "This leaves out, of course, all the business people who may have had a grudge against Peter Hoffman."

Sam said, "I saw your daughter Martha over at the tennis courts this morning with Hilde Brunner. You could always include Hilde on the list. She's all over the neighborhood like a blanket. On the other hand, she may be too vacuous. She asked me the other day who my favorite rock star was, as if at age forty-eight I have a favorite rock star. But maybe Peter Hoffman tried to make time with her. That could be a motive."

Louise laughed. "Don't you have to know a person longer than two weeks before you murder them? Who else could we pin this on?"

"There's alway the iron-handed Sarah Swanson."

"Oh, please, Sam, she's my friend."

"Think about it. Ever notice that strong body and those strong hands? I remember how that woman hated Hoffman. She practically had a hissy fit when he broke into the party at the Radebaughs. If Ron hadn't thrown him out, Sarah Swanson would have."

"She's strong, I'll concede that, but not violent, not murderous. My friend Sarah could never have done this."

"Well then," blithely answered Sam, "knock her off the list. I'm just wildly speculating. Knowing nothing that the police know—"

"Same here. They've told Bill and me nothing."

"Trouble with me is that I'm not home much, so I'm not well-acquainted with the likes of Messrs. Cunningham and Downing. But my favorite candidate is Phyllis Hoffman, with help from a guy."

"Hmm. Hadn't thought of a conspiracy, but if you think about murders, and how they take planning and execution, I bet a lot of the unsolved cases are conspiracies."

"Sure," said Sam, "two children, anxious to have the grandmother die so that they can inherit, two partners pissed off at a third one who's givin' them trouble . . ."

Louise had finished her rows of onions and got to her feet. There now were neat little rows of green onion tops before her. She leaned down and brushed the dark brown compost-rich soil from her gardening pants, then straightened to see someone peering at her through the woods.

It was Greg Archer, just barely visible through the leaves as he stood behind the high brick wall on Sam's patio. Only his head was visible. He stood in silence and stared her way. She was sure he was the one who had spied the killer riding off in the cartita and who later heard the sounds of quiet digging. Greg had thought it was Louise . . . or did he know quite well that it wasn't her but someone else wearing her garden hat and sweatshirt?

At the very least, the man was devious. Why hadn't he been decent enough to talk to Louise about all this?

Sam looked up from his work, which was now done, and from her expression must have guessed she saw something or someone she didn't like.

"What, Louise? Is Greg home?" He smiled and waved at the younger blond man. "We're just getting done in time then. He's been out all afternoon at an antiques show, and I promised to have dinner on the stove."

"I hope it didn't burn. We've been out here for more than an hour."

"Oh, no," said Sam confidently. "I put everything in a crock pot. It'll be done perfectly."

"Crock pot. I've never owned one." If Sam used it, it must be good. The man had once won a cooking competition among Congressional legal aides on Capitol Hill.

Her neighbor gave her a fond look. "Maybe it's time, Louise. Tell you what. I'll loan you mine and you can see if you like it. If you do, you can use it to prepare that gourmet dinner you promised the neighbors."

Dinner party! She'd forgotten that rash promise. A sensation of vertigo overcame her, and she had to plant her feet wider apart so she didn't fall. Too much heat, too much bending, too little lunch, too many promises to the neighbors. "Oh, Sam, I'll never be able to have that dinner until I get this albatross from around my neck."

He gave her a little pat on the back. "Don't panic about

the dinner. I'll help you cook. Maybe even Greg will pitch in. As for this Hoffman thing, you'll be vindicated any day now. How you could be a serious suspect, I'll never know."

Louise wanted to retort, *Ask your roommate.*

18

After coming home from the tennis game, Martha had a shower and a nap and felt totally refreshed. Janie's bedroom door was open, and Martha went in and settled in a chair. Her sister was lying on the bed, reading *Moll Flanders*. "Cute bedroom," said Martha. Her gaze swept over the drapes, the bedspread and the carpeting, all in different shades of the same color. "Of course, you have to like blue."

"Very funny," said Janie through narrowed eyes. "Did you come in here for something?"

"Sure did." Martha gave her what she thought was an intriguing summary of the tennis game and picnic.

Janie murmured, "That's interesting," and went back to her book.

Martha was silent for a while. Then she said, "Maybe it's something about being Swiss."

"You mean the reason she appears to have fallen for Mike Cunningham? Maybe it has to do with being horny."

"Really, Janie."

Janie shrugged her slim shoulders. "I only see her once in a while walking around the neighborhood. She doesn't really walk; she strides like a model."

"I wonder if she's that sophisticated," said Martha. "Maybe she doesn't know where a man like Mike Cunningham is coming from."

Janie giggled. "Where's he coming from—Iowa?"

"Don't be silly. Mike Cunningham is not someone for a young girl like Hilde to get mixed up with."

Janie glanced slyly at her sister. "You always think that. Are you sure she's as young as you think she is?"

"Why? What do you mean?"

"It's the way she walks. She knows what she's doing when she swings her bootie like that—"

"Janie, girls pick that up early. Just because you're kind of . . . never mind."

"Kind of what?"

"Kind of . . . gracefully gawky and ingenuous—"

"Hey. That's enough of that unless you want a fight. Maybe you'd better leave my room. Or else apologize."

"All right, I apologize. Janie, I didn't mean anything negative. In fact, that slight gawkiness of yours—"

"What!?!"

"Unselfconsciousness of yours, I mean. It makes you all the more attractive." Martha was thinking fast to get out of this. She hardly needed her younger sister mad at her at this point. "Let's get off that subject. What I really want to talk about is Hilde. I think she should meet someone closer to her age. If I knew anyone around here, I'd introduce her."

Janie gave her a sour look. "You needn't introduce her to Chris when he gets home next week—remember that."

"I will."

"So I suppose you told your tennis foursome that you spent three months at the University of Berne. That gives you a special link with Hilde."

"Actually, I told them I studied mostly in Rome."

"What for? Since when did you get so closemouthed?

You only toured Rome. You studied in Switzerland for at least half a semester."

Martha leaned forward. "Janie, when you're detecting, it's about them, not you. They don't have to know particulars about me or the fact that I'm getting married in October. Get it?"

"Actually, I do," said Janie. "Not that I haven't done a little detecting myself in the past."

"I know. You were a great help to Ma a couple of times. So I picked up a few tidbits, which of course I'm going to pass on to Dad. And who knows how many more I might pick up from Hilde. I've invited her over for lunch tomorrow. Can you stand still for that? Besides the fact that she might know stuff about Mike Cunningham, she could use other influences in her life besides those—"

"Yeah, I know—those two lechers across the street." Janie stuck her nose back in her book, and Martha left her and went into her own room to read her own book.

She had to watch what she said to Janie. She didn't want to lose her maid of honor six weeks before the wedding.

Louise was grateful when Charlie Hurd phoned. She'd been feeling lonesome since she came in from gardening. Granted, her friends Nora and Mary and even Sam said they'd keep in close touch. But her family was gone; Bill was still downtown in meetings. She was sure they would absorb most of his time until he left on a plane for Vienna. What an inopportune time it was, she thought, for an international crisis demanding the IAEA's help. The girls weren't around much, and when they were, they had their minds on the wedding. This afternoon they'd gone off to a movie and promised to be back by nine o'clock.

"Good time to call, Charlie. I'm totally alone."

"So am I," said the reporter.

"What have you found out?" she asked, trying to mask the hope in her voice.

"I'm on the computer right now, tryin' to dig up something on Peter Hoffman's business. So far, I've come up with diddly."

"You're good, Charlie. You'll find something."

"I dunno. It sucks when I can't find things I'm tryin' to find." His voice was discouraged. Or was it that he was trying to discourage her, kill the hope she had that he'd unravel this murder? "I'll tell you, Louise, the truth is I'm busy with some other stories, too. I got the whole county to cover, you know, and it's a damned big county, Fairfax. And it's not like the usual shtick, where I can spend all my spare time working on a favorite story. I've got someone in my life."

Louise repressed a laugh. It sounded so corny, coming from Charlie, who was usually so hip. *Someone in my life.*

"Do you mean Hilde? Want to tell me about it?"

"Naw," he drawled, "it would be bad luck. I gotta get better acquainted. And I'm gonna do that in about half an hour when I close down this program. I just called to warn you that I don't have any real time to help you out of this scrape."

"I understand," she said. She suddenly felt weak, as if she'd been abandoned by everyone. *You have no time to help me, Charlie, and neither does my husband,* she wanted to tell him. But that would only make Charlie feel guilty, and besides, it was disloyal to Bill. "I'm sure the *Post* only wants you to work forty hours a week, anyway."

Charlie laughed. "You got it. My boss gets pissed off when I dog a story too hard. Doesn't want to pay the overtime."

"I see. Well, you go out and have a good time tonight. And keep in touch if you learn anything."

"Sure will, Louise. I'm just sayin', don't count on me for too much."

Louise hung up the phone. The empty feeling persisted, even though she'd just had a sandwich for supper.

19

Bill reached over and found her hand under the covers. "Hi," he said.

"Hi, " said Louise.

He gave her hand a squeeze. "I think you're back with us."

She turned and his face was beside hers. She kissed the soft lips in his whiskery face. For two weeks, she'd been a trembling neurotic, disinterested in making love to her husband. Last night, they'd pursued their sexual pleasure as if it had been years, and not weeks.

"I'm curious," said Bill. "What happened?"

"It could have been the swimming yesterday afternoon," said Louise. "But more likely it was because you brought me a snack at bedtime."

Bill pulled his head up and looked at her closely. His blue eyes twinkled. "You mean . . . the snack did it?"

"For women, it's the little things that count the most. Or wait . . . maybe it was hearing Nora's inspirational talk about 'new love.' "

"Nora's found new love? Damn. What happened to her former love? Ron's waited for her to settle down for years." Ron and Bill were poker buddies. No closer link than that, reflected Louise. The poker group, which she named the "Giggling Men" because the games were one of the few times she heard grown men giggle, met religiously every two weeks. She knew her husband secretly took Ron's side in the marital battles over at the Radebaugh house.

"Oh no, she hasn't found *a* new love. She's just found new love with Ron."

He knit his eyebrows. "Glad you cleared that up."

"She liked the way he handled Peter Hoffman the night of the party at their house. It made her realize what a masterful man he is."

Bill chuckled. "That means the neighborhood gossip's going to be pretty tame. We won't be hearing about Nora's love troubles anymore, because she won't have any love troubles."

"Bill, I wouldn't call it neighborhood gossip. She only very discreetly confided in Mary and me. I just passed things on to you because you're my buddy."

"Point well taken," he said with a smile. He got out of bed and stood looking thoughtfully down at her. "Now, honey, enough of this romantic stuff. Let's talk schedules. I need to grab a bite and leave soon. I'll be working late tonight and . . ."

Her mind wandered as her husband talked. Romantic stuff, indeed. Making jokes about their neighbors' tumultuous love life might be his idea of romantic talk, but not hers. Bill, though as affectionate a partner as a woman could have, had little romantic talk in him and, in fact, rarely sent her flowers or presented her with candy. With Bill, romance came in the form of doing kind deeds and being an intelligent and caring husband. So unlike, for instance, Peter Hoffman. One of the last things she'd heard the murdered man say was to young Hilde was *You are like a dream.* Or had he said, *You are as beautiful as a dream?*

Hoffman, whom Louise knew to be a ruthless man, had uttered these empty blandishments to lots of women. No wonder they had responded to his charms.

Bill was still talking about his schedule. "As you might expect, I'll have this same heavy schedule all week. I'm worried about you, hoping you aren't plagued with calls from the papers and TV. Maybe it's best if you leave the house. What will you be doing today, something with the girls?"

"I don't know. They're busy a lot of the time, playing tennis when they're not shopping for wedding finery. Maybe I'll have lunch with Sarah Swanson. I'll get up and fix breakfast for you." She started to pull back the covers.

"Don't bother. Get a couple more winks of sleep. You know that Martha loves to feed me in the morning. I can smell that the coffee's made already."

Louise propped herself on her elbow. "I think you enjoy breakfasts with just you and Martha. That's nice."

"Enjoy? Not quite the word, honey. Martha's . . . challenging. Sometimes she's even annoying. But she's ours, and she's great."

Tears came to Louise's eyes. "And it's probably the last time she'll be around to fix our breakfasts. She'll be busy with Jim, and then with her babies."

"Yep, Martha's nearly out the door for good. Our nest is getting emptier."

A new rush of moisture formed in Louise's eyes, and for an instant she was tempted to lie back in bed and wallow in the misery of being a mother without a brood. Then she did a quick reality check. She was the target of a police investigation. This was no time to languish in bed, for her husband, her main defender, had been swallowed up by this latest international crisis and wouldn't have time to help her. Even Charlie Hurd was useless, totally absorbed by the beautiful Hilde. The once hyperactively nosy reporter sounded almost bored with Peter Hoffman's murder. *Peter Hoffman's murder. The body in Louise's garden.* How many times did she have to hear those nightmarish phrases? She decided to call it something else. Perhaps the "yard murder" would do. That description removed the crime from her and Bill's property, and it eliminated the need for using Peter Hoffman's name.

With a sigh, she threw the covers off, went to her closet and picked out a neat skirt and blouse. She would take a long shower, giving Bill and Martha time for their morning tête-à-tête, and then she'd join them.

The first thing on her agenda was to call Marty Corbin, to reassure herself that her job was secure. She also should straighten the house in preparation for the arrival of her housecleaner. After that, she hoped to persuade Sarah to go out to lunch with her, since her older daughter had invited Hilde to their house for lunch, adding, "I'll give her a tour of your gardens, too. She'll be impressed."

Thinking of Marty Corbin gave Louise an uncomfortable twinge in her chest. She hadn't been in contact with her producer at WTBA-TV since the news of finding Hoffman's body was splashed all over the TV and newspapers. Strangely enough, he hadn't phoned her with a word of comfort. Until now, she'd had solid support from both Marty and the station's general manager. That was because *Gardening with Nature* was earning top ratings, unhurt by the other "scandals" that had clung to Louise over the past few years.

She didn't want to be a worry-wart, and was almost one-hundred percent sure that Hoffman's murder would have no effect on her career. Still, like that slogan for Ivory Soap—"ninety-nine and forty-four one-hundredths'-percent pure"—there was that tiny percentage left to fret about. And there also was that twinge in her chest she had to deal with . . .

The twinge was a harbinger of the annoying heart palpitations that sometimes overcame her. Harmless, according to her doctor, who'd checked Louise out thoroughly. He said they were due either to too much stress or too much coffee, and airily suggested avoiding both. But avoiding stress was easier said than done right now, when her job and even her freedom could be in jeopardy. The same was true of coffee: how could she get along without caffeine in her hour of need? She smelled its delicious odor wafting through the house right now, and could hardly wait to go and have a cup.

Louise's little glass collection was easy to clean. She simply brought the pieces out of the glass-front wall cabinet and placed them on the dining room table. Then she wiped them with a damp cloth and replaced them. Possibly once a year, she hauled them off to the kitchen and doused them with hot, soapy water.

Today, she'd make short work of it, for she had to get over to see her friend Sarah. Sarah Swanson, married to the difficult and inscrutable Mort, represented Louise's last untapped resource in the neighborhood. If she couldn't help, then Louise didn't know where she would turn next.

Swinging open the glass door of the curio cabinet, she looked in on her collection and pulled in a quick breath. Things were out of place. How could that be, since everyone in the Eldridge family knew there was a special place for each object. The small Satsuma cachepot was now on the top shelf, not the bottom; the powder jar with the jasper cameo top was shoved far to the back; the Tiffany-like bowl with the green glass flower was on the bottom shelf instead of the top; the Lalique perfume bottle with dancing nude was turned illogically to the back instead of facing front; and finally, the cobalt blue jar with the sterling silver top was jammed in a far corner.

Louise's forehead creased in a frown. This was no accident, nor was it a playful daughter at work. They wouldn't
be that unkind. Who had done this?

She put a thoughtful hand on her chin. There was no
harm done, actually, and Bill might call her a fussbudget if
she were to tell him about it. Still, she knew an intruder
had been in her cabinet, and she didn't like it much. She
carefully dusted the cabinet shelves, then wiped each glass
object free of dust before putting it back in its proper
place.

She walked quickly through the other rooms of the house,
inspecting to be sure everything was in order and ready
for Elsebeth to clean. There was little to do, because other
family members had been forewarned of the housecleaner's
arrival and had picked up after themselves.

Then her eye was caught by something out of place on
the patio. It was easy to see through the floor-to-ceiling
patio doors: a big, transparent tarpaulin folded into a two-
foot square. It was identical to the one used as a burial
shroud for Peter Hoffman. The police technicians must
have forgotten to put it away. She strode out onto the
patio, grabbed the tarp and went to the nearby toolshed.
It was locked, which was the way she'd asked the police to
leave it. She groped in her pockets for the key.

Due to moisture, the door was stuck, and she gave it a
good pull. As it opened, there was a rush of movement
above her head, and she instinctively leaped back. And
just in time, for a heavy pickax clattered noisily down on
the flagstone at her feet. Louise pressed a hand against
her chest and took some gasping breaths. Then anger suffused her, because she realized the police were responsible for this. In the process of their murder investigation,
those evidence technicians had nearly killed her!

She walked into the toolshed and looked at the inside
of the door. The technicians had set her pickax on two

supports over door. But why, when she normally stored it upright in the corner of the shed? *Probably thought it made it less likely that the murderer would use it for another victim,* she thought. She replaced the ax in the corner where it belonged. Then she returned the tarp to the shelf, which contained one other, also neatly folded.

Still shaken by her close call with the ax, she knew it was time to get out of this nerve-racking house. But first, she had to make an important phone call.

20

"WTBA-TV, good morning."

"Hi, Shirley. This is—"

"I know: Louise. I suppose you want to talk to Marty."

"In fact, I do."

"Sorry. He isn't available until one."

"I see. Would you be kind enough to leave a message that I called?"

"Of course."

"And how are you, Shirley?"

"Doin' all right, Louise. Except the switchboard's busy. Gotta go."

Was the switchboard really that busy? Or was Shirley, the friendly receptionist at the station, giving her the cold treatment?

Looking at her watch, she realized it was close to lunchtime. She'd told Sarah she'd drive today and hurried out the front door to pick her up. This was a moment in her life when she had no other choice but to turn to friends. Nora and Mary were eager to help and had promised to see her again tomorrow to talk over things. Sandy Stern was on vacation. The only wise mind left to probe was Sarah Swanson's.

Louise preferred not to dwell on the fact that her older daughter might also be snooping into the crime in spite of her father forbidding her to do such a thing. If Martha was detecting, Louise tried to convince herself, it probably amounted to little more than list-making with Nora and Mary, or talking with Hilde over lunch.

As she made her way down the front walk, she was relieved to see the press was nowhere in evidence. The yellow police tape around the yard was gone, but not the police. The large person just shoving his body out of an unmarked police car at her front curb was Mike Geraghty. After the scare in the toolshed, she was glad to see him. The detective was wearing a white shirt with the sleeves rolled up, his limp jacket slung over his shoulder. He ambled to the front gate; every movement expressed weariness.

"Hi, Mike," she said, and opened the gate for him.

"Louise, how ya doin'? You look like you're on your way somewhere." He nodded at a nearby bench in the front woods, which Bill had constructed for her out of two old tree stumps and a long piece of flagstone. "Can we hunker down there for a minute? Darned hot this morning, and it looks cooler in the woods."

They strolled to the bench. "It's about five degrees cooler in here," said Louise, "which makes it only ninety-two. You look tired, Mike."

"I am." He grinned at her. "I've been real busy investigatin' a murder."

"Do you know anything new? Am I out from under this yet?"

It was a four-foot-long bench, tight quarters for a large man and a tall woman. She could smell the detective's stale body odor. He turned his bright marble-blue eyes toward her. "We found the blood on the sweatshirt was Peter Hoffman's."

"I'm not surprised. Bill and I already thought that would be the case." Her mouth turned down in a grimace. "If you're going to frame someone, blood evidence sure helps."

Geraghty was silent. She glanced over at his big, slouched figure and found he was the picture of remorse. "I'm truly sorry, Louise, but we're still investigatin' lots of other angles. Among them is a proposed time study of your trip back home on Sunday night, August twelfth. I need to know the name of the crab house where you stopped to eat on your way back from the beach."

"Let's see, it was something catchy, something alliterative: 'Charlie's Crab House' . . . no, 'Carl's Crab House.' It was east of the town of Helton."

"All right," said the detective. "That's progress."

"You mean you're going to go over the route I took and try to figure out a time line?"

"Yep. Try to dovetail it with the time our source said they saw someone in the woods, movin' the cart and diggin'."

"That'll help, provided your source is telling the truth." She sighed in frustration. "As if the source is a secret. I know it was Greg Archer who thought he caught a glimpse of me in the woods that night. But who knows if he's telling the truth about it, even the time he saw me?"

"Louise, why do you mistrust him?"

"The man dislikes me, that's why. And that's why I doubt your time line is going to mean much." She shrugged. "Okay, so I've said enough about that. You can't blame me for being grumpy. Now tell me what's new in the investigation. Or wouldn't George Morton approve of that?"

He gave her a troubled look, then gazed down at the safety of his notepad. "We got lots of lines out on Hoffman's business contacts, which includes Lee Downing, of course, and Michael Cunningham. We're questioning Mrs. Hoffman, of course."

"Of course," said Louise.

Moving slowly, he got up from the bench. "Louise, uh, I hope you do what Morton suggested and don't get involved, okay? Please just stay home and keep out of trouble. Things should improve pretty soon."

"You think so?"

"I can't promise you anything, you know that."

"One thing you could promise me is that your evidence technicians put things back in the proper place."

"You mean they didn't?"

"No, and I was nearly hit with a pickax they stashed on a rack above the doorway. Furthermore, they left a tarp on the patio."

Geraghty frowned. "That's odd. Let me get back to you on that, Louise."

She hopped up from the bench. "You do that," she said in a cool voice. "And now I have to go. I have a friend waiting for me."

As she made her way to the garage, she could feel the red in her face, and it was not from heat or embarrassment, but from anger. Mike Geraghty and the Fairfax County police wouldn't have nearly as good a reputation had Louise not helped them time and again in their investigations. And now they had her dangling, proposing that she was a murder suspect. Not only that, their sloppy technicians had imperiled her life!

She got in her PT Cruiser and revved the engine. *Let him arrest me for that!* She sped out of the cul-de-sac, not able to feel the full satisfaction that a speeding car gave the human psyche. After all, Rebecca Road wasn't the autobahn and Sarah Swanson's house was only two blocks away. She got there in less than a minute, slammed out of the car and realized she was panting as if she'd run a mile. She took a few deep breaths and paused to look around her. Before Louise was one of the most beautiful natural gardens in the Washington, D.C., area—Sarah Swanson's front yard. It was featured last year in one of her TV gardening shows. She'd called it "The Wild Suburban Garden." Its only trouble was that it was on a steep hill. She took another deep breath and started upward.

Admiring the prize dwarf hawthorn tree, *Crataegus crusgalli*, at the base of the yard, she ascended through clusters of native grasses and oakleaf hydrangeas interspersed with low-growing specimen evergreens and deciduous small trees. By the time she'd reached the top of the hill, the frights and frustrations of the morning were dissipated, her composure almost restored.

She tucked her blouse in her skirt and headed for Sarah's studio. Talking to Sarah was a more sensitive matter than chewing over the facts with her friends Nora and Mary. Mort Swanson had close ties with Peter Hoffman that apparently went back for years. Still, Louise had to do it, for the potter was one of her shrewdest friends, with an artist's eye for detail. She had learned more than once that it was the details that counted when one was trying to find a killer.

As she was about to knock on the studio door, it was opened by Hilde Brunner, and Louise stepped back with a little cry of surprise. The potter's beautiful intern was obviously in the middle of her work, her apron and her hands smeared with clay. A strand of rosy-tinted hair had escaped from her bun and fallen across her unusual catlike green eyes.

"Mrs. Eldridge, what's the matter?" She approached Louise and lightly touched her shoulder. "Did I frighten you? I am so sorry."

"Don't be sorry, Hilde, it's me who's jumpy. I've had a sorely trying morning at home."

"Oh," said the girl, as if soothing a hurt child. "If you're looking for Sarah, she's in the house."

"You look busy."

"I am," the young woman said, flashing a radiant smile. "I'm hurrying to get my work done so that I can go to your house."

"I know. That's why I came here. Sarah and I are going out for a bite. That way, you young people can have the house to yourselves." She laughed ruefully. "At least the two of you won't disturb things in the house."

Hilde said, "Disturb things? Oh, no, of course not. I wanted to express how sorry I am about what happened. It must have been such a terrible shock to find a body."

Louise flinched involuntarily. She'd been so busy fretting about the pickax incident that she'd forgotten for a while about that dratted body in the garden. Life was one shock after another, and nearly being bonked on the head by twenty pounds of steel was only the latest. Now she had the sense that nothing was quite right about her house or her yard.

She pulled in a deep breath, hoping the girl didn't notice how rattled she was. "It was a horrible thing, Hilde. I'm just trying to recover from it."

"I hope you do, and soon. So, today, Martha and I will lunch, and I get the pleasure of meeting Janie. That means I can say that I am now friends with everyone in the . . ."—she put her arms up to form a circle—"what do you say? Immediate neighborhood."

Louise smiled back. "And in such a short time. Quite an accomplishment. In fact, I hear you've met Charlie Hurd, too, though he's not a neighborhood person except when he's around covering a story."

The expression in Hilde's eyes became noticeably noncommittal, and Louise could see that while Hilde might be the new love of Charlie's life, the reverse was not necessarily true. "Yes, Charlie. He is such a fun person. I introduced him to your Martha the other night. It seems she had never met him."

"That's because Martha's seldom home. So nice of you to do that."

Louise walked thoughtfully to the side door of the Swanson's house and suddenly felt that, unlike Hilde, she didn't really have a clue as to what was going on in this neighborhood, or even in her own house.

Over a sandwich at the Coffee Pub in the Belleview Shopping Center, Louise could see how unhappy her friend was. Sarah Swanson's handsome countenance seemed to have aged by years, and even the usually curly strands of gray hair around her face were limp and cheerless.

"Sarah, tell me what's troubling you. Is it the medical problems?"

"No, it's not Mort's diagnosis, or rather lack of a diagnosis," said Sarah, "although that is the shadow that fills our lives. But there's something else, too. Sylvan Valley, where we have lived so happily for thirty-five years, seems to be in mourning over the disgraceful fact of finding the body of that man in your garden." Her tired, red-rimmed gray eyes turned to Louise. "But why am I sorrowing over this, when you must feel it more than any of us?"

"We can't avoid it, Sarah," she answered. "What we have to do is try and dig ourselves out of it. Somebody did this, and it wasn't me."

Tears formed in Sarah's large eyes. Quietly, she said, "I'll only share this with you, Louise. Please don't let it go further. I'm terribly frightened over the role that Mort might have played in this—"

"Oh, no, he couldn't have—"

"I don't mean the murder. Of course he wouldn't kill anyone. I'm referring to the events that could have precipitated it: the sale of Hoffman Arms. I'm so afraid he knows something of that and has unwittingly contributed to someone else's motive for murder. I know there was a meeting after Peter was released from the hospital. . . ."

Louise could hardly restrain a smile. At last, her chats with neighborhood friends had hit pay dirt. "A meeting," she said, cautiously, without appearing overly interested, "with Peter and Mike Cunningham?"

"Yes. But I have no idea what it was about. My husband doesn't confide in me like he used to, and he already feels terrible because of his physical ailments. So what can I do, beg him for information that implicates him?"

"I'm so sorry you're in this quandary. I had the impression that Mike Cunningham handled the sale of Hoffman Arms all on his own. Maybe you shouldn't worry if Mort only played a peripheral role."

Sarah shook her head hopelessly. "He's been with Wilson and Sterritt for almost thirty years. Mike Cunningham's their flashy newcomer hired in as a partner; he's only been there six years. I don't know what this will do to Mike's career, but I'm afraid it will tarnish Mort's—and after all he's given to that firm, poor man. Furthermore, he shouldn't have to think about these things right now."

"I'm sorry," repeated Louise. Her potter friend stared unseeing out the restaurant window. She let the silence restore them for a few moments, then said, "I have to go downtown this afternoon. I, uh, cracked a tooth and have to see my dentist in DuPont Circle. Would it be all right with you if I just dropped in on Mort?"

She smiled at Louise. "Dental appointment downtown? I bet. You could try. I know his workload is lighter these days, and he probably'd have time to see you. Something has to be done; we can't go on this way. The more I think about it, it would be nice of you to talk to him, to try to get through to him. I know you and Mort haven't always seen eye to eye, but he likes you—and he's a good man at heart."

"I know."

After a companionable silence, Sarah said, "Do you know something funny? We ought to be scared, living in a neighborhood where there's an unsolved crime. But I'm not spooked at all, are you?"

Louise had just been upset by a series of small household mishaps, that didn't have anything to do with Peter's murder. "Why aren't you scared?" she asked her friend.

"Whoever did it was someone Peter knew, someone who hated him viscerally." Sarah clenched her strong potter's hands into fists. "I have to admit that I knew Peter for at least six years and hated him from the first time I met him. I hated having Mort represent him."

Louise didn't know how to respond.

Sarah continued. "Someone was after just him. Whether it was that wife of his or some business associate he cheated, the killer's not going to come after anyone else."

Louise laughed and decided to share her story. Then she said, "But almost anything can scare me these days," she said. "Probably the only thing I should be scared of is being thrown into jail for murder."

The potter laughed—a big, deep laugh. "That'll be the day. My dear Louise, if that ever happens, I'll personally organize the neighborhood to come by the jail and picket the place."

"I only wish I could help you in some way. I'll try today, if I get a chance to talk to Mort."

Sarah reached out a rough-skinned hand and clutched Louise's. "I wish the same thing—that I could help you. And if I find anything out about this, I'll call you immediately. At least Mort and I have Hilde. She's so helpful, and it's a pleasure having a young person around who's like the daughter we never had. You're used to it, with your charming Janie and Martha. What I'm most pleased with is that she's become Martha's buddy. They were out together last night with some young man named Charlie, and they're together again today, having lunch."

Louise was unsure whether she was pleased with that or not. Hilde, Martha and Charlie Hurd could be a powerful combination. She knew that two of the three, Martha and Charlie, were real operators, though she didn't want to go so far as to call them devious. Yet she had no reason to worry. Martha was so busy with plans for her own wedding that she hardly had time to get in trouble.

21

Martha had never seen anyone more enthusiastic about a mere house than Hilde Brunner. She strode through the rooms exclaiming and touching. "So many things!" she cried. "Such delightful appointments! The plants, the antiques, the books and, oh yes, the charming art glass . . ." Martha looked around through new eyes and realized her mother had packed the place with stuff. It did look interesting, almost like an antique shop in training. But Martha pictured Hilde living in much simpler, more Spartan surroundings in some house in Europe.

Strolling casually after her guest, Martha tried to analyze why Hilde looked different from the rear. She'd noticed it first while they were playing tennis yesterday. And then she got it. Janie was right. Hilde, wearing that stylish, sleeveless dress, walked like a model, with a pelvic thrust and self-conscious pivoting of her fine legs, as if to show them to best advantage. Perhaps it was the European in her, mused Martha. Or maybe Hilde had at one time been trained for the runway.

Hilde had been just as enthusiastic during the garden tour and was fascinated when Martha led her into the deep woods and showed her the garden under which Peter Hoffman's body was buried. "Maybe this will become a local tourist attraction," Martha had said with a laugh. Actually, it made her a little nervous to stomp around a site where someone killed and buried a man. She continued the joke. "I know! My mother can erect a sign: 'The garden plot where they found the body.' "

Hilde gave her a puzzled look. "Should you joke about that?"

Martha sighed. "Why not? It's what we call a sick joke." She chuckled, incapable of stopping herself. "Of course, it won't do to put up the sign until after the police let her off the hook as a suspect."

Hilde seemed shocked. "Martha!" Then she changed the subject. "The poor plants in this garden—they suffered, didn't they, by being dug up?"

"Yes. You can see they're still kind of droopy. But my mother's hoping they'll survive. Azaleas apparently are hardy."

"They suffered, just as she suffered."

"How sympathetic you are, Hilde," said Martha, giving her guest a quick glance.

As much as Hilde enjoyed the tour, Martha decided it had gone on long enough. "I don't know about you, but I'm hungry. Also, we need to get lunch organized and take it onto the patio before Mrs. Baumgartner gets here to clean. She is terribly nice, but she appreciates it when people stay out of her way so she can get her work done."

"Your housekeeper, I expect?"

"Not exactly. She comes every two weeks and bails Ma out by digging in all the corners we miss. To put it crudely, Mrs. Baumgartner saves my mother's ass." Martha knew Hilde well enough to know she'd understand this expression. "She also teaches me the occasional German phrase."

"Let me help you, then."

"It's salad, and the ingredients are prepared."

They stood at the counter and assembled the dish together, Martha handing off the greens for Hilde to arrange on two plates.

"Ah, the *Vogerlsalat*," said Hilde.

They heard a knock, and Elsebeth Baumgartner came in the front door. She embraced Martha and said, "I feel so sorry for what has happened. It is a terrible thing to plant a body in the garden of a woman as nice as your mother."

"Thank you, Mrs. Baumgartner," said Martha. She introduced Hilde. "Hilde's from Switzerland, and is living and working in Sylvan Valley for a while."

Elsebeth smiled at the girl. "And I am originally from Vienna." She turned to Martha with a concerned look. "You, dear, you must do what your sister does and call me Elsebeth. You make me feel very old otherwise," said the woman, who was not much older than fifty or so.

"We're assembling our *Vogerlsalat* and crabmeat salad."

"But you'd call it '*Nüsslisalat*,'" said Elsebeth, turning to Hilde.

Hilde shrugged her bronzed shoulders. "I call it *Vogerlsalat*," she abruptly said.

Martha glanced at Elsebeth and watched the woman's face darken with displeasure. At her side, the indifferent Hilde was still busy arranging greens. It wouldn't do to have the irreplaceable Elsebeth ticked off by an outspoken luncheon guest, though what was wrong with Hilde's remark, Martha couldn't fathom. Could Elsebeth be jealous because there was another German speaker in the house?

She touched Elsebeth's arm and gave her a wink. Elsebeth smiled back at Martha. The tense moment passed.

Martha returned to Hilde's side and unceremoniously plopped the crabmeat in the center of the greens. "There," she said. "Now we're getting out of your way, Elsebeth, and I know you'll be glad of that."

"I am, Martha," said Elsebeth. "I can stay only three hours today. So, Hilde, '*Servus.*' "

Hilde smiled. "*Servus.*"

Martha and her guest carried the trays to the patio. As they sat down at the glass table, Hilde said, "I thought your sister was to be here, too."

"Me, too," said Martha. "But I left the crabmeat and, uh, *Vogerlsalat* in the fridge, and Janie can assemble her own salad if and when she arrives. Now, Hilde, tell me more about Charlie Hurd. It's nice that you've become friends. I've heard stories about him for years from Ma."

Hilde smiled. "I called my mother 'Mama.' "

"That's nicer than just 'Ma.' Is your mother—"

Hilde had a stoic expression on her face. "She died two years ago. My father died the previous year."

"I am so sorry," said Martha. "You are so young to have lost both of your parents."

"There's little to be done when people die, except to mourn them properly."

There was a long moment of silence, during which Martha thanked her lucky stars that she still had her loving—though sometimes annoying—parents. Then she said, "So, getting back to Charlie. Do you think he's a smart man?"

Hilde suspended her fork over her plate. "He is quite intelligent, I think, but naive in certain ways." She gave Martha a knowing look. "Do you have a sense of what I mean?"

Last night, when the three of them went to a bar in Georgetown, their drinking, talking and taking turns on the dance floor was not an opportunity to get to know someone in depth. She did notice that Charlie was absolutely gaga over this luscious female. Yet Martha guessed that if she'd come onto the reporter the way Hilde came onto him, he'd probably have fallen in love with her, too.

Her final assessment of Charlie: egocentric, vulnerable and probably decent at the core. She didn't share this opinion with Hilde, on the theory that the less she shared of her own opinions, the better.

"I know he did some brilliant detective work in the past," said Martha. "Yet he is a little kiddish—maybe that's what you mean."

"Kiddish is a good word for it," said Hilde, and took a small, elegant bite of French bread. "I hope I do not hurt him."

Martha waved a hand casually. "Sometimes it's hard, isn't it, not to hurt men? I had the impression he'd like nothing better than to have you, or maybe you and me, trot around with him and help him find Hoffman's killer—just so he'd have a good story. I had to tell him I was busy with wedding preparations, but there's nothing to stop you. It might be fun to do a little detective work, wouldn't it?"

Hilde shrugged. "Maybe. It would be a new thing for me." She slanted a gaze at Martha. "Like you, I have other friends as well—"

"Yes, Mike Cunningham, for instance."

"Yes, Mike. I do not have all my time for driving around with Charlie."

"Mike seems like an interesting man," offered Martha. This young woman might know just how interesting.

"Mr. Cunningham is very intriguing." A shy smile passed her face. "I really know nothing about him except he seems willing to advise young people like me with their careers."

"Does he talk about his business?"

Hilde seemed almost shocked. "Oh, no. I think he's too professional to do that."

This conversation is yielding nothing about Mike Cunningham, thought Martha. She dropped her detecting mode and decided to relax and enjoy lunch. Diving into her crabmeat salad, she said, "On to another topic, and Europe is always one of my favorite topics. Tell me about what you've studied. We never got a word in about such things last night. I know you've been specializing in more than pottery, although pottery is certainly a, uh, wonderful thing."

Hilde giggled charmingly. "Yes, last night there was too much talk about deadlines not met, and a country editor furious with Charlie—"

"I think it's a city editor who'd get furious with Charlie."

"Yes, yes. You want to know about my major. This might sound . . . inbred, perhaps, but I studied European cultural history, specializing on the years 1933 through 1945."

"I guess that means focusing on Hitler and the Holocaust, and all his works."

"Yes," said Hilde, eyes narrowing. "Some of us are trying very hard to see it straight."

"That's a good thing." Martha realized, despite the fact that she looked and walked like an international model, that Hilde was very serious-minded, apparently part of the European students, most of them German, who wanted to see history through a clear lens. This made her feel warmly toward her new acquaintance. Some acquaintances remained just that: passing acquaintances. She had a feeling Hilde was more than that. Hilde was a keeper.

Hilde said, "Tell me more about your life, Martha. Your fiancé is with the government? And if so, why?"

"He's an assistant district attorney at the moment, but he's running for public office—the job of alderman in the city of Chicago. And why does he do this? I guess it's because both of us love the urban environment. We have this ridiculous sense of pursuing justice. You know, of trying to make better cities, and better lives for people in cities."

Hilde casually plucked a cherry from the fruit bowl. "Pursuing justice. In many ways, that is what I've been doing. Men are okay, aren't they, Martha? But pursuing justice is much more important."

Martha laughed. "All the more reason for you to go out with Charlie and try and get a line on Hoffman's killer."

22

L ouise's cell phone rang as she was driving home from Sarah's. It was Marty Corbin, returning her call.

"Hi, Marty. Thanks for getting back to me."

"Hey, Lou. I've been keeping track of you through the TV and the newspapers. You and Bill must be feeling pretty low. Bad luck to find that guy, of all people, buried in your garden."

"Definitely bad luck. But here it is, three days later and I'm getting used to the bad news. I'm sure they'll clear me in short order." She pulled the car into the driveway and was glad that she was off the road, for she didn't like the tone of her producer's voice. It was too cool, too removed. Marty, a big man with curly brown hair and warm brown eyes, most of the time was one of the friendliest people she'd ever known.

"Look, Lou, we've got some considerations here. According to the GM, it's not exactly the best publicity in the world for our station when you get in these scrapes."

She sat stunned. "Sorry about besmirching WTBA-TV. But I had no control over the fact that some murderer left a body in our yard."

"No, no," he hurriedly said, "I'm not accusing you of

anything. You're not to blame, of course, not at all. I'm just saying there's quite a bit of notoriety left over from some past things you've gotten yourself into. . . ."

Louise slumped in the front seat. "And now this, huh? Well what do you want to do about it, Marty?"

"I thought of a solution. It'll ease the pressure on you, too. You probably don't feel like traveling out on location anyway right now. In ten days, we tape the first of four fall shows—"

"I know the schedule, Marty, and I have input for that show, and the ones following—"

"I thought we'd get your sidekick to step in and host at least the first two of 'em."

"John will love how this is working out."

"John's been very nice about it," said her producer. "He understands the situation."

Louise could picture her cohost John Bachelder, he with his dark-fringed brown eyes, handsome face and athletic thirty-six-year-old body perfected with the help of a personal trainer, positively gloating over the chance of doing two shows on his own after a season of being cut from show after show. The fact that John was younger than she was no longer insignificant. Now it was she who would be left on the cutting room floor. No, it was worse than that. She wouldn't even be in the tape. Obviously, Marty had talked with John, and John had agreed. The deal was done.

"The deal is done."

"Essentially, yes." Then he returned to his more familiar tone. "Forgive me for this, Lou. I feel real bad about it, but there's pressure from on high. The GM, that is. Now, if you want to drop by some day and give me your input on those shows . . ."

The air in the closed car was getting intolerable, so she opened the car door to let in some air from the overheated garage and held it open with a sandaled foot. "What will you do when the police discover who the killer is?"

"Then all the pressure will be off, Lou. You can climb right back in the saddle and get back to work. Is that detective friend of yours helping much?"

"You mean Mike Geraghty? He's not heading the investigation, but he's doing what he can. In fact, he's probably the only reason I'm not already in jail. Lots of evidence points to me as the killer."

"Damn!" said Marty Corbin. "I'm sorry to hear that. The papers haven't said that, though the suggestion is there because of your past link with the guy."

"Don't I know it. The whole sordid story of the mulch murder, how Hoffman attacked me back then, how he copped an insanity plea and got four years, how we had a fight after a neighborhood party . . . All the viewers and readers have to do is draw their own logical conclusion: 'That woman had plenty of reason to kill him.' "

Marty's voice was low and solemn. "You did have a lot of reason, Lou. I wouldn't blame you if you'd buried that guy in your garden."

She could hardly believe her ears. Her producer wasn't totally convinced of her innocence. She wondered how many other people felt the same way—neighbors, friends, maybe even relatives, like Bill's mother. Her mother-in-law's imagination—or was it lack of imagination?— had always made her suspicious of Louise's detecting adventures. When Bill phoned his parents and told them of this recent discovery in the Eldridge garden, his mother, Jean, had been horrified. In contrast, Louise had been gratified at the way her own dad and mom had not only believed in her, but even offered to come to Washington and offer their support in person. She'd declined the offer, saying that she and Bill would be in the Chicago area soon enough for Martha and Jim's wedding activities.

Marty was saying something. She could hardly process it. He was trying to retrench, adding words to soften his harsh message. Now he was saying good-bye to her. "Just get some rest for a week or so, Lou."

"Good-bye, Marty," she responded, pressed the "end" button and got him out of her life.

It was urgent now. She had to do something to get herself out of this mess. Her job was in jeopardy, and the world was beginning to believe that Louise Eldridge, TV garden show host and fierce protector of all things organic in gardening, was a cool, calculating murderer. What was almost worse was that people would believe that she'd screw up her wild azalea garden by stashing a body underneath it!

Because Louise's mind was so overloaded with thoughts, her drive downtown was on automatic pilot—up GW Parkway through a hoard of cars, into the curving wave of traffic that led to the bridge over the Potomac, into the white-knuckled driving competition in the District of Columbia. It hardly registered. On a couple of occasions, when she had swerved out of her lane, she noticed fellow drivers looking anxious and tacking away from her, like sailboats flitting out of the way of a predatory powerboat. In what seemed like only a few minutes, she was at her destination, parked in a lot a few blocks from Wilson and Sterritt. Her dentist was in the neighborhood too, but there was nothing wrong with her teeth; she had no intention of stopping there.

Mort Swanson's office was where she was heading, but if she was lucky, she might also look in on Mike Cunningham. Knowing these were two men who would rather not talk to her at all, she'd taken pains to at least look good. She'd worn a pale green linen pantsuit that brought out the hazel in her eyes, put on her makeup with great care and brushed her hair into a gleaming pageboy. Granted, the suit was wrinkled already, but that was impossible to avoid on such a hot day. She blended perfectly with the other people, men in summer suits, women in stylish cottons, in this low-key but exclusive part of the nation's capital.

The tenth floor opened to the quiet splendor of Washington's top law firm. Summoned by the receptionist, Mort Swanson walked into the reception lobby in shirt sleeves, busily rubbing at his horn-rimmed glasses with his handkerchief. He smiled at her. Other than the dark circles under his eyes, he looked quite in charge, like a partner of the firm should. "What a pleasant surprise," he said. "Of course I have time to talk to you, dear friend—a little time, at least." He squired her past an administrative assistant opening mail and into his corner office. He seated her facing him across a big desk, so that she looked through slim blinds into the sunshine of the nation's capital.

Mort's glasses were halfway down his nose, and from over them he sent her an avuncular look. "I'm guessing you're here because you need legal representation."

Of course he would guess that, thought Louise, with deep relief. It took a load off her shoulders, for she hadn't known how she would approach Mort Swanson without offending him mightily. She couldn't have come in and announced: *Your wife Sarah is desperately worried that you might be mixed up in Peter Hoffman's murder.*

"I— I might need a lawyer," responded Louise. "I thought I'd wait until I was actually charged. But one must be prepared."

"Louise, if you need me, I'll be there for you."

"Thanks, Mort. In the meantime, what do you think of all this? Knowing Peter Hoffman as well as you did, have you any idea who could have actually killed him?"

Mort leaned back in his executive chair and swung halfway around, so that he could see the Capitol Building and the Washington Memorial in the distance. "I was his close associate for some years, during those expansion years of Hoffman Arms. But that changed, Louise . . ."

"You mean after he murdered Kristina Weeren?"

Swinging around again to face her, he said, "Absolutely. That's when Cunningham took over the criminal case. Peter thought it would be simpler if Mike did everything for him from that time on. Oh, I'll admit that occasionally I was asked for my input on various decisions—"

"Such as?"

The attorney stopped and looked at her in surprise. "Come on, Louise, you're expecting too much of me."

"I need information. In case you hadn't heard, the police think I might have been the one who killed Peter Hoffman. Unless other evidence turns up, they intend to arrest me at the end of the week."

"I'm sorry." Louise could see his tired eyes reassessing her, finally figuring out that she hadn't come here to hire him as her lawyer. He sighed. "Louise, this is turning into another of our verbal sparring matches. Of course my sympathies are with you, but all that attorney-client information is confidential. You should know that."

She flipped her hand in a careless gesture. "Don't mind me, Mort. I don't know the etiquette of lawyers at all. Not to be repetitive, but do you know anything specifically about the sale of Hoffman Arms? Bill and I've been thinking that the sale might be related to the murder."

Mort Swanson was now at attention, sitting straight in his chair, looking a bit impatient, as if this unexpected visitor had taken up her allotted time. "I will repeat that attorney-client communications are—"

"Come on, Mort, give me something that isn't sacrosanct."

"I do know some details, but not all of them. The sale was pretty standard. Hoffman took half the proceeds in stock in Lee Downing's corporation, the other half in cash."

"Who inherits from Peter—Phyllis?"

"Damnit, Louise. Again, it's Mike who handled all that—Peter's business, Peter's estate. The police can find out all about it. The sale of the business is in the public record, you know. You could dig out the information yourself, if that's how you want to spend your time." He made a point of looking at his watch. "Speaking of time, I really should get back to these." He patted a pile of tan folders sitting on his desk.

"Of course. It's good to know that you'd represent me if worse comes to worst."

"I'd do that, because I have great respect for you and Bill."

Louise rose from her chair. "I had lunch with Sarah today."

"That's great."

"Your wife's a little worried about you."

"I know. This liver stuff . . ."

"No, besides your liver. She's worried about whatever else is bothering you, Mort."

She could hear him breathing heavily. Looking down at the thick gray carpeting instead of at her, he said, "I know you and Sarah are good friends, Louise, so I forgive you for your forwardness. But you should let this alone. I swear there is nothing I am able to tell you about Hoffman's demise. If I could, I would."

He escorted her back out to the lobby, and instead of the cool handshake she'd expected, he put his arms around her and gave her a hug. She hadn't realized what a big man he was, and how strong. His arms felt like iron bands. The hug was not just a hug, but almost a warning. Without another word, he turned and went back to his corner office.

*   *   *

Louise stood in the lobby of Wilson and Sterritt, wishing she could just cruise down the halls and find an office marked with the name of "Michael Cunningham" and barge in. She gave the smooth-looking young receptionist a glance and decided that was not a good idea. Instead, she said, "Is Mike here, by any chance?"

"Mike—" the young woman prompted. "There are two 'Mikes' here."

"Mike Cunningham."

"Oh, downstairs at the moment in the sweet shop, probably having a sundae." She smiled. "Go down and join him. He loves company when he's blowing his diet."

"I don't mind if I do," said Louise. "Thanks."

Cunningham sat at the sweet shop counter, his sundae almost consumed. Louise had arrived just in time to catch the man. "Doesn't that look tasty," she said, sliding onto the counter stool beside him. "I'll have what he had," she told the waitress.

"Well, well, Mrs. Eldridge." Mike Cunningham looked down on her with an air of suspicion, his big but attractive face made a little less attractive because of the sneer on his lips.

"Hi, Mike. My dentist is in the building next door. Once through there, I found I had time to drop in on Mort. I just got through talking with him."

"And then they told you where I was."

"That's right." She smiled in a friendly but not intimate way. It did not behoove anyone to encourage Mike Cunningham.

"I betcha you're trying to work out who killed Peter Hoffman."

"Maybe. Can you help me? I want to know about the company sale. Mort told me it was standard: half cash, half payment in Downing Corporation stock."

"Mort told you right," said Cunningham. None of the flirty, forward behavior he'd exhibited with Louise in previous meetings. "Not that it will help you, but Peter sold the Downing stock as soon as he received it. If you check the market, you'll see Downing stock gained after the sale. So actually he might have held it longer to good advantage."

"Oh." Louise tried to digest that, but couldn't, so she filed it for future reference. "Is it fair to ask about Peter Hoffman's will?"

"You can ask. But I'm not in a position right now to answer you, since all interested parties are not privy to it yet. It's safe to say that Phyllis Hoffman will be comfortably well off."

"Sounds like she's not the sole inheritor, or whatever you call it."

"Nope." He wiped his lips with his paper napkin, pulled out a pocket comb and quickly ran it through his programmed hair, which looked exactly the same as before he combed it. He then extracted a five-dollar bill from his wallet and put it on the counter.

"And that, my dear lady"—he lapsed into a pronounced drawl, as if he was a southerner or perhaps a cowboy—"is about all I intend to reveal to you at this time." There was no smile on his face, no attempt to impress her. His eyes were as blank and cold as a shark's. Mike Cunningham was being honest now. He disliked her just as much as she disliked him.

23

Just to be safe, Louise had picked up a big frozen pizza to feed whatever hungry family members were at home and waiting for dinner. But she'd forgotten her Number One daughter was in the house. When she arrived, the delightful aromas from the kitchen told her Martha had dinner in progress.

Louise entered the kitchen and saw that something that had been missing was back in its place. The Paris pitcher. She turned to Martha with a questioning look.

Martha shrugged and grinned. "I bought you a new one."

Louise gave her daughter a hug. Then she went to the stove and stuck a spoon in a saucepan to taste some golden substance gently bubbling under the heat. "Yum!" she said.

"That's freshly made butterscotch sauce," said Martha. Her daughter was in shorts, sleeveless top and bare feet, and she had a big apron wrapped around her middle. Despite her casual attire, she looked very much in command.

This also was evident when Janie sauntered into the kitchen, also with an apron covering her shorts. Her moody expression reminded Louise of the character Ruby in the British TV series *Upstairs, Downstairs*. She gave her mother a hug and needlessly explained, "I'm helping."

"Wonderful, darling." Louise leaned over and looked at the alien-looking food in the frying pan.

"Chicken piccata," said Martha.

"Chicken piccata? What a treat."

"It's easy," said Janie. "I watched."

"You'd make it yourself if you knew how easy it was," added Martha. "Dad would love it. I'll show you before I leave. By the way, he won't be home until late."

Dinner was delicious. Afterward, since no one had plans to go out, the three of them took the opportunity to discuss the wedding. Martha pulled out her tabbed notebook. "You won't believe it, but almost everything is set."

"And you did it all by phone?"

"Jim handled some stuff at his end. Attendants, cake—he ordered it from a bakery we know in Chicago—church, flowers, honeymoon—Jim's taken care of that, too—invitations, organist, phone calls to relatives, reception, soloist—"

"You forgot 'clothes,' " said Louise, "wedding dress, et cetera."

Martha gave her a guileless look. "It's an alphabetical list. Clothes come next: 'togs.' "

"Oh. So, have you found some togs?"

"No." Martha looked at her mother purposefully and then at her sister Janie, bent over her plate and finishing her butterscotch sundae. "And some people I know aren't too helpful."

Janie looked up languidly. "I'm not about to wear some of the dresses you liked, Martha."

Martha shrugged her bare shoulders. "We've only looked in two places. They didn't have a very good selection, and everything was outrageously priced."

Janie looked at Louise and gave her head a little shake. *My sister has awful taste in clothes* was the message.

"And," said Martha, "I'm not known for my taste in clothes, so Janie's suggested we go to Friendship Heights tomorrow to hit some of the shops there and tap the brains of fashion experts."

Louise and Janie exchanged a jubilant look. Louise said, "Good idea." She thought for a moment. Friendship Heights aroused some alarm in her mind. "Are you going to Saks?"

"Maybe," said Martha. "I've never been there. Do you think we should?"

Louise sat well back in her chair. "I think you should stay away from Phyllis Hoffman. You know that she works there."

Janie rushed in where her sister feared to tread. "We thought we'd go and scope her out. After all, she could be our murderess, you know."

Martha put up a hand in a gesture that was supposed to be reassuring. "Not to worry, Ma. I'll see that our brave Janie is kept out of harm's way. The most we'd do is sail by the St. James department and see if she's still working there. I mean, maybe she isn't, since she probably inherited Peter Hoffman's money." Louise saw her direct a dark look at her younger sister.

"Fine," said Louise. "Just do as your father said and refrain from getting involved in this yard murder."

"Yard murder!?!" Martha broke in loud guffaws. "Ma, you are so funny. Talk about euphemisms! That's an absolute denial of the fact that we found a dead body in *your* azalea bed in *your* backyard." She kept on laughing until Janie began chuckling, and Louise broke into a smile herself.

" 'Yard murder' is a dumb expression," Louise admitted. "I just got so tired of saying that man's name. But enough ridicule of your mother, dear. Remember, you'll be a mother yourself one of these days, and then you'll regret treating me badly. Tell me about your lunch with Hilde."

"Lunch with Hilde," mulled Janie. "It sounds like a PBS play. I got tied up and missed lunch, but I would have liked to meet this girl everybody talks about."

"We had a nice lunch and a nice talk," said Martha. "She's a pretty serious person. She lost both of her parents in the past few years. Too bad I won't be around Sylvan Valley for long. She might make a nice friend. Of course, Elsebeth wasn't enthusiastic about her. They had a little quibble over language, but I didn't get it, being a little fuzzy on the niceties of German."

Louise frowned. "Not a serious quibble, I hope?"

"Just a semantic argument, Ma. I know you don't want anyone to offend Elsebeth. What would you do without her?"

"I'll be around," said Janie.

"You'll be around?" asked Martha.

"So I can get to know Hilde."

Martha looked at her younger sister. "Jane, Hilde would not be a proper friend for you."

"And just why not?" snapped Janie.

"For one thing, she's older. I think she's at least twenty-four, though she avoids telling me exactly how old she is. And she's Swiss. That means she's worlds more sophisticated than you are. Europeans grow up faster. They're way ahead of Americans in maturity. I mean, Hilde likes Mike Cunningham; did you know that? She thinks Charlie Hurd is too immature for her."

"Hmm," said Louise, "Charlie Hurd, immature?"

"He is a little immature, I agree with her on that. But I don't think a woman who enjoys an uncultured individual like Mike Cunningham is going to be any kind of a friend for you, Jane."

Louise could see that Janie was growing angry, her blond hair thrown back from her face, her cheeks flushed with the humiliation of being categorized so thoroughly by her elder sibling. Janie said, "I hate it when you— oh, never mind!" She ran from the table.

Martha called after her. "After you get over your hissy fit, don't forget we're doing the dishes." She looked at the figure of her retreating sister and heard the slamming bedroom door. "On second thought, Janie," she yelled, "never mind. I'll do them alone."

After a moment, Louise said, "You shouldn't treat her like the younger kid anymore, Martha. She has very adult feelings. She's soon going off to college. And she's in love, just like you are. Only she knows she's too young to do anything about it. Do you realize that?"

"She and Chris Radebaugh, you mean?"

"They're in love, as I said, just like you and Jim. There's not that much difference between being twenty and being almost eighteen."

Martha stared out the big dining room windows into the woods. "I guess I haven't thought about Janie that much, period. Maybe I ought to pay better attention and listen to her. I've been so obsessed with my own life and my own wedding."

Louise reached over and patted her daughter's hand. "That would be nice. The two of you have always been good friends. I'm sure she'll share a lot with you if you start to listen. Now let me tell you about my day. It was a humdinger."

By eleven o'clock, it was totally dark, and Janie knew stray neighborhood kids had headed home to their beds. The night and the neighborhood now belonged to her. For the five years they'd lived here, she'd made Sylvan Valley her nighttime dominion, prowling quietly through every backyard, block and park. Not that she was a Peeping Tom. She never lingered to stare long into uncurtained houses. First, it was to relieve her loneliness when she was a newcomer to the neighborhood. Then Chris Radebaugh became her friend, and they roamed together in the dark. Since Chris had left for college, she seldom went out at night for walks, perhaps having outgrown the need to peer into lit houses and invent stories of the lives people were leading within them.

It was sheer frustration that drove her out tonight. She had no trouble slipping out of the recreation room door without being seen by her mother and sister. Why would they notice anything since they were deep in conversation about the details of Martha's wedding? But she wouldn't come back in through the rec room. As she had done many times before when younger, she'd loosened the screen of her bedroom window and would reenter that way.

She moved soundlessly around the outside of the house and through the back woods, passing the garden where her mother had found Peter Hoffman's plastic-wrapped body four nights ago. She closed her eyes for a brief moment and sighed. What would it be like to be the daughter of a more ordinary woman who didn't constantly get involved in embarrassing situations?

As she moved skillfully down the wooded path, she thought, *More to the point, what would it be like to have an older sister who wasn't judgmental, who didn't treat me like a hothouse flower, a girl too "naive" to befriend a person like Hilde and too immature to come along and play tennis with the older neighbor guys? Heaven forbid that Mike Cunningham or his house guest even looked at her!*

What irritated her most was the way Martha had practically taken over the family. Martha caught more fish on the charter boat, winning her father's frank approval. Martha was getting married. Martha was helping her fiancé in a political campaign. And Martha had become the family's self-anointed savior, the one who would save her mother from being arrested for Peter Hoffman's murder.

That was the unkindest cut of all. As the one who had personally saved her mother's skin not once but twice, Janie was crushed. The thing that hurt the most was that she'd always loved and looked up to her older sister. Until this summer. Now she realized she could live without her sister very well. Martha thought Janie had been born yesterday!

She didn't really know why she was veering toward the east end of the neighborhood. She hadn't come out tonight to snoop on prospective murderers. But this was where Phyllis Hoffman lived, in the last cul-de-sac before Sylvan Valley ended not with a bang but a whimper—a pair of empty fields.

In the family's random discussion of suspects, it struck Janie that no one had better cause to kill Peter Hoffman than that weird wife of his. Traveling through the backyards of houses, she reached the one that she'd heard belonged to the brassy-haired Phyllis. As usual, there were a number of uncurtained windows, but disappointingly no one appeared to be home.

In fact, a car was coming into the cul-de-sac. Janie dodged even deeper into the backyard and barely missed being revealed by headlights when the car nosed straight into the garage, which was a mere carport and not a genuine garage.

A little nervous over this near-miss, Janie watched the small but sturdy Phyllis unload herself and a lot of brown bags from the car and enter the front door of the house. Lights only went on in a back room, probably the kitchen. She was not about to peek at Phyllis while the woman boringly put away groceries. Janie headed for home.

She walked on the edges of front yards, avoiding street-lights as much as possible, until she got to the swim and tennis club. With its gates open and welcoming as always but dark as a dungeon, the club grounds were a handy shortcut to her home. As she passed the pool, she looked in at the big black surface of the water, bereft even of the reflection of the moon, which was hidden behind clouds. It was the place where she'd had so many good times with Chris and other friends. The tennis courts were a few hundred yards farther on and set even deeper in the woods. It was then that she felt someone was following her.

A quick look back, but no one was there. She speeded up anyway, just for good measure. Not that she intended to get paranoid. One of the rules of night prowls was that you couldn't get paranoid. After all, she had taken this path many dozens of times in her life and knew every inch of it.

Once past the tennis courts, Janie got that feeling again. This time when she glanced back, she caught a movement. Her heart felt as if it were bursting. Suddenly, the import of the body in her mother's garden struck home. A murderer was still on the loose around here. And it could be the person who was now following her down this wooded path.

With a huge twist of regret inside her chest, she begged forgiveness for being a snot to her sister, for being ungenerous and not giving Martha some slack. For rudeness to her father and mother. For . . .

Janie ran like the wind, taking every curve in the irregular path with knowledge and grace. Now she could hear the footsteps behind her and, to her horror, realized they were striking the dirt path more quickly than hers! She had to get away, for if someone attacked her here in this big woods, no one would find her until the morning.

There was a side path ahead, not the surest route to her house, but perhaps not as well-known to her pursuer.

Chancing another look behind her, she could barely distinguish a figure in dark clothes. Then came the turn onto the side path, and she took it fast, narrowly avoiding a root sticking up from the raw dirt. The person followed, and Janie heard a cry as her assailant stumbled on the obstacle and crashed into the bushes at the side of the path.

Giving a wordless prayer of thanks, Janie reached the road and crossed through the patch of woods that was part of their back neighbors' property. To get home, she had to barge through the plantings near their house. She thanked her lucky stars that she could distinguish the roses, with which she didn't want to tangle. Soon she was almost home free, running through the woods in back of her house, rounding the corner and slipping by the bamboo garden until she'd reached the front of the house and her bedroom window. Though breathless, she dared not rest. She gathered up a stump that lay nearby as part of the forest detritus, set it beneath her window and climbed up. Never had her neat blue bedroom been so welcoming.

With shaking hands, she replaced the screen in the window, then shut the window and locked it. For long minutes, she stood in the dark, breathing heavily and staring out the glass pane, waiting for someone to come around the house. No one came. Finally, Janie went into the bathroom and got herself a glass of water. Returning to her bedroom, she slipped under the sheet, groaned once, and fell into an exhausted sleep.

24

George Morton stood in the doorway of Mike Geraghty's office. Mike noticed the specks of glazed sugar that clung to one side of his mouth, a leftover from a stop at the Krispy Kreme doughnut shop a block up Route One. Mike, who was on the South Beach diet at the behest of his heart doctor, avoided the place these days, but looked enviously at his colleague. How well he could remember the gratifying combination of a good cup of coffee and hot, fresh, greasy, sweet doughnuts.

"Did the lieutenant call while I was gone?" asked Morton.

Mike leaned back in his chair. "Yeah, with big news. The Securities and Exchange Commission is starting a probe of Lee Downing."

"Oh, is that your big news?" Morton asked. "Isn't he the guy we interviewed and then let make a trip to New York? Who gave the lieutenant the tip, Bill Eldridge?"

Mike was determined to keep his temper with this difficult fellow officer, once his subordinate but now the one in charge of the portion of the Hoffman murder investigation handled by the Mount Vernon substation.

"As a matter of fact, it was Bill Eldridge who found out about this and passed it on to Dan Trace. The investigation's still at the private stage, apparently, but about to become public information. This Lee Downing's quite an operator. Seems he's a master at industrial spying."

"Oh, yeah?" said Morton.

"That's according to Bill Eldridge, but Dan is confirming it. The charge is that Downing has paid big money to spies who've come in and stolen other company's weapons secrets. He took the ideas and used them himself. Made big profits, apparently millions, off an initial investment of, say, three hundred thousand to some clever industrial thief."

"So. Now let's see where we're at," said Detective Morton, shuffling uncomfortably, as if he wished that he were sitting and Mike were standing. "Downing had a pretty straight deal with Hoffman to buy Hoffman Arms—"

"We haven't all the details of that yet. They still need to sit down and talk to Downing again. Seems he's been a little hard to schedule in. That happens tomorrow."

"Just assume the Hoffman Arms sale was a straight deal. What would Downing's motive be to kill the guy whose company he'd just taken over?"

When Mike Geraghty leaned farther back in his chair, it announced it had reached its outer limits by squeaking in protest. He thought for a long moment. "Because I've heard somethin' that makes me think it wasn't a straight deal."

"What's that?"

Geraghty had received that phone call from Martha Eldridge yesterday regarding the angry exchanges at the tennis game between Cunningham and Downing. He'd passed the information on to Dan Trace, but he had a feeling that if he told this to Morton, George would pooh-pooh it just because it came from the Eldridges. So he phrased it differently. "Everything I know about Peter Hoffman leads me to believe he could have hoodwinked

Lee Downing, somehow shortchanged him. That would be a plenty good enough reason to murder the guy."

"Why couldn't Downing just renege on the deal if it wasn't to his liking?"

Ignoring the squeaks, Geraghty leaned back farther and closed his eyes. "What if Hoffman had found out Downing was facing a federal investigation? Then if he stiffed him in a sales deal, Downing might be reluctant to make a fuss."

Morton shook his head. "You mean two crooked guys screwing each other?"

Mike nodded. "Yeah. Something's becoming clear to me. Hoffman had a reason for crashing that party and setting Louise Eldridge up. You know why?"

"No, why?" said Morton.

"Say that Hoffman was swindling Lee Downing. He'd figure the only one that might snoop into his shady business affairs would be Louise Eldridge. That's why he made a preemptive strike, to frighten her away."

Morton's lip faintly curled down. "You sure do shine the best light on that woman. Anything else? They got details on Hoffman's will yet?"

"They're s'posed to have, pretty soon. In the meantime, we're s'posed to, quote, 'hold down the home front.' "

"Yeah," said Morton, his sneer deepening, "we know what that means—controlling the busy Mrs. Louise Eldridge. You gotta call her, Mike. She's gone over the line again."

"Call her and tell her what?"

"To stay home and stop nosing around." Morton's big face, Mike noticed, colored as soon as the subject of Louise Eldridge was brought up. He'd never been able to understand the other detective's antipathy for Louise. On the other hand, Louise could be difficult.

Morton said, "I hear that yesterday, besides whatever

else she did, she went and talked to Mort Swanson and, more importantly, Michael Cunningham."

"Two people of interest."

"Yeah. Go figure. I told her to stay out of this. You've gotta remember, Mike, that despite how you might feel about Mrs. Eldridge, she's our best prospect. We've got more evidence on her than we get in most murder cases: a sighting of a perp wearing her hat, the victim's blood on her clothes, the victim's blood on the weapon, her prints on the tarp—"

"Did you ever think that it could be a frame?"

Morton withheld a sneer. "Did you ever think she left stuff around because she didn't think we'd ever link the crime to her? Hell, we should have her in jail right now."

Mike Geraghty shook his head. "Lieutenant Trace doesn't want to do that yet, George. It could really embarrass us. Let's let him get more information on Hoffman's business deals and the will. Meantime, I'll give Louise a phone call. She probably didn't do any harm."

Morton shuffled impatiently. "How are we sure of that? She might have put either one of those guys on guard so that we'll never get useful information out of 'em."

"Like I say," said Mike, "I'll call and tell her to cool it."

Morton turned from the door and wheeled back again for final shot. "Just remind that woman that it's only because of our good natures that she isn't already in jail on suspicion of murder."

When Morton left for good, Geraghty got up and closed his office door. In the old days, when he used to drink and smoke, he might have pulled a hidden flask from underneath papers in his bottom drawer. Or at least lit up a cigarette. Or gone out for doughnuts and coffee. He swung his big arms around in a circle to give them a little exercise, then went down the hall and drew himself a cup of stale black coffee. Once he'd drunk that, he went back to his desk to face calling Louise, a woman who was already pissed at him, and for good reason.

Mike Geraghty spent more than an hour chewing out Louise for straying off the plantation. Not that she didn't expect it. From the moment yesterday that she headed her car north toward the District of Columbia, she knew she might get in trouble with the police.

After the initial embarrassment faded, she found herself filled with the same restless energy that had driven her yesterday. Only now she'd been absolutely forbidden to do more investigating. She paced up and down the living room until she'd calmed down. She realized that her detecting efforts had yielded nothing. All they did was worry her family and outrage the police. The only thing left to do was to read a book.

She slumped down onto the living room couch and opened her novel. It was hard to get into at first, and she had to reread the first few pages. But then something clicked, and soon she was immersed in T. Coraghessan Boyle's writing, forgetting about the Hoffman murder and Geraghty's threat that she was about an inch from being arrested.

When she heard a ringing, she turned her body a little and wrestled the cell phone out of her pants pocket. It was Charlie Hurd.

"Louise, good news!"

"I could use some good news, Charlie. What's up?"

"I'm getting into this murder now. I just wanted you to know."

"Glad to hear it," she said, wishing the reporter would hang up so she could get back to her book.

"You don't sound too curious. But I've got some lines out on Lee Downing. He's a very big fish in the military-industrial complex, y'know. And there's something seriously wrong about him. I can tell when a guy sounds really crooked. And *he's* really crooked."

"You don't say so." Louise's detective antenna, which had relaxed, was now humming again. She lay her book down in her lap.

"Mind you, this is just my instinct talkin'. Have you met Downing? He's hangin' out in your neighborhood. I haven't caught up with him yet."

"I only met him once, Charlie. He's been staying at Cunningham's place across the cul-de-sac. Martha's played tennis with him. Why don't you talk to her? She might know more about him than most people around here."

"Martha. You don't say. Uh, who else played tennis with him?"

"I believe it was Hilde and Mike Cunningham."

"Son of a gun. Hilde, huh? Well, I'll ask her what she thought of him. Hell, either Downing or Cunningham could be the killer."

"I know that."

"I don't like the idea that she's socializing with them."

"Who, Martha?"

"No, Hilde. But I don't think Martha should hang with him either, and I'll tell her."

Louise smiled. No one had ever been able to tell Martha who to hang with. Just let Charlie try.

"Listen, I can tell you're bored."

"No, I'm not bored at all. I'm so glad you're getting into this."

"What're ya doing right now?"

"Reading a really great book, or rather, trying to. My heart wasn't really in it, but you know how good writing comes out and grabs you."

"You can't get into it because you're a feisty broad who doesn't like to be caught in a police trap like this. I think it's crazy of them to suspect you of a murder."

"So do I. And it's making me jumpy. It's almost as if Peter Hoffman has put a hex on me. I get spooked by things. Altogether, Charlie, life sucks."

"Whoa, Louise, I didn't think you used that kind of language."

"I don't. I picked it up from you. Well, at least I have my book for comfort."

His sigh came across loud and clear. "Wish I had time for things like that. I'll ring you back as soon as I know more, okay? And meantime, I'll debrief Hilde on that tennis game I never heard about."

Martha and Janie had just arrived in the sleek, cool world of St. James clothes, an enclave on the third floor of Saks Fifth Avenue that was totally devoted to high fashion. Most of the clothes were hidden behind walls, except for a silk cream-colored suit hanging in splendid isolation on a rack. She turned over the price tag and winced. Then she noticed Janie frowning at her. This gave Martha pause, for they'd been getting on well this morning, better than for days, and Martha didn't want to ruin a good thing.

Janie murmured, "First things first, Martha dear. We have to figure out what we're going to say to Mrs. Hoffman if we run into her."

"How about telling her, 'I'm getting married and I need an outfit.' "

"Just like that, huh?" said Janie. "I don't think so." Looking deceptively girlish in her wide-skirted lawn dress with blue sash, Janie proceeded to take charge. She strolled across the room as elegantly as a queen and approached a woman who appeared behind a counter. The woman was about forty, with a fashionable but tangled mass of blond hair. Janie said, "Excuse me. We're looking for Phyllis Hoffman."

Through mascara-laden eyelashes and lens-enhanced

blue eyes, the saleswoman spoke with a Russian accent. Her tone was skeptical. "You are customers of hers?"

Janie gave a little shake of her head.

"Friends?" When Janie nodded assent, she revealed, "You have missed her by seconds. She just left the floor to go to lunch. She won't be back, I'm afraid, for an hour or more."

Martha dashed up beside her sister and said, "Thanks so much," grabbed Janie and hurried her out of the big room and onto the down escalator. "C'mon, we can catch her."

Janie groaned and made a face. "There goes our chance to look at some good clothes and get a little advice. Don't tell me we're going to tail her!"

Martha shrugged and said, "Those clothes are way too expensive for me. I'd never buy them. And why not tail her? That's part of why we're here. Anyway, look."

Having scrambled down the last few escalator steps, they had a view of the nearby exit, where a small blond woman stood.

"She looks like she's waiting for a taxi."

Janie said, "We'll never get the car out of the lot in time to follow her."

"I'm betting there aren't that many taxis around here. Folks out this way must average four cars per family, so why do they need taxis? I think we can make it to the car in time." They raced out the doorway, avoiding the woman at the curb, and into the adjacent lot. Martha gunned the motor of the PT Cruiser and sped up to the store entrance just as a yellow cab departed with its passenger.

She turned an excited glance at her sister. "Are you havin' fun now, Janie?"

"Oh, God, Martha," said Janie, "I see you're just like Ma. You love chasing people. I got over that by the time I was sixteen."

Martha laughed. "You mean last year." Being a Chicago driver, she had no trouble keeping the cab only one car-length away. They were racing downtown. The cab made a soft right and stopped, dropping Phyllis Hoffman off in front of a restaurant, La Delice. Without waiting to watch her go in, Martha sped away and found a nearby parking lot for the car.

As they sprinted back to the restaurant, Janie breath-lessly said, "I hope we guessed right. We're going to feel real funny if she isn't here."

Entering the dimly lit place, the sisters could hardly see. When Janie whipped off her sunglasses, Martha mut-tered, "Put them back on. We don't want her to recog-nize us. And get out from underneath that directional light."

"I've seen that woman, but that woman's probably never seen me," grumbled Janie. "And for sure she's never seen you, so why should we worry?"

"Just being cautious, that's all," said Martha. She stretched her neck and gradually identified the golden-blond head of Phyllis Hoffman in a booth not far from where they stood. With a little prodding she got the maître d' to seat them nearby. With faces averted, they passed Phyllis and settled in the booth across the aisle and down one.

Janie sighed again. "Thank heavens we can relax for a minute. I'm not up to this anymore."

"Janie! You sound like an old woman." From behind her menu she surveyed the surroundings. A man had now arrived and seated himself opposite Peter Hoffman's widow. "Can't you get excited about the fact that Phyllis is having lunch with Mort Swanson?"

"Mr. Swanson, our neighbor? I like Mr. Swanson. So what? Is that the end of the world?"

Martha leaned forward confidentially. "I forget you're

not up to speed on this. That's what lovesickness can do for you."

Janie frowned at her sister. "Who says I'm lovesick?"

Martha grinned. "I've known you for seventeen years. I can tell. You're gaga over that Chris Radebaugh. Lovesickness makes you dreamy and distracted. It makes you blind to other people's problems."

Janie rolled her eyes and listened.

"Jim and I," continued Martha, "are in a more mature stage of our relationship, and so I'm better able to function and pay attention to things like Ma's problems with the police. I've talked to Nora Radebaugh about the murder. We made a list of potential murder suspects, and Mort Swanson is definitely on the list." She nodded over to the booth in which the man sat.

Janie bent her head and slanted a glance at her older sister. "For what, pray tell? The way I heard it, Mr. Swanson used to be Peter Hoffman's attorney, but he isn't anymore."

"Even though Mike Cunningham took over Hoffman's legal matters, who says Mort wasn't in there advising or something? I hear Hoffman and Mort go way back."

"Too bad we can't eavesdrop," said Janie.

"No, but we can read their body language. Fortunately, we have a superb view, and between the two of us, we ought to be able to decipher everything that's going on."

Janie shoved her blond hair away from her face. "Wow," she said, "are you ever an optimist."

Martha watched their quarry and noted that Phyllis's entire focus was on her male companion and nowhere else. She felt comfortable enough now to lower the menu from her face and read it. "Hey, they have good food here. While we're spying, let's enjoy lunch."

Janie wasn't studying the menu, but instead was staring speculatively at Martha. "Look, I approve of what you're doing, checking out the possible neighborhood perps. Phyllis Hoffman is a good place to start." Janie leaned a little farther in, as if afraid a passing customer or waiter might hear. "And I know for a fact that the killer lives in our neighborhood. Let me tell you what happened last night."

25

Louise's friends sat on the patio with her and sipped iced tea. Mary Mougey waved a hand in the air, as if the motion of her slim fingers could relieve the afternoon heat. "We promised we'd try to help you, Louise. And here we are, with a few bits of information."

She smiled. It was late afternoon, and Mary obviously had just come home from her office downtown, wearing a slightly crushed linen suit in a pale pink shade. Nora and Louise were in shorts and T-shirts. "When have you had time to be a detective?" asked Louise.

"It's as I predicted," Mary said. "Phyllis phoned again, and it was very interesting. She overheard Peter and Mike Cunningham talking a few days before Peter disappeared. From this, she learned that Peter tattled on his buyer, Lee Downing, to the SEC about some illegal activities of Downing's." Mary's bright eyes shone with excitement. "I told Phyllis that she had to tell this to the police, and if she didn't, I would."

"Go, Mary," said Nora, grinning.

"She also told me that Peter and Mike used subterfuge when arranging the sale of Peter's company."

"Yes, I—" started Louise.

"You may already know some of this, Louise," said Mary, barely pausing in her story, "but what you might not know is that she heard Peter saying he was going to flee the country and divorce her!"

"Oh, my," said Nora, dismay in her voice. "That didn't go over well, I'm sure."

In a low voice, Mary said, "Then there's the last thing she complained about: Peter's will."

"What about Peter's will?"

"She wouldn't tell me, damnit, just that something about it didn't suit her. I failed to wring that out of her, Louise."

"You did well, though," said Louise. "The police need to know all of this."

"They will, because I put the fear of God into Phyllis."

Nora said, "Maybe I'm a cynic, but how handy, how self-serving for Phyllis to tell this to the police. It throws all the suspicion on other people. Why would you trust Phyllis to tell the truth?"

Mary shook her head. "I don't know, Nora. You're quite right. Why should we believe her? She's buttered up to me for no good reason that I know."

Nora stared off into the woods, where the light was beginning to fade among the tall trees. "Although I've had my mind on other things, I tried to do my small part in this investigation. I deliberately went out and talked to Mike Cunningham this morning as he left for work." She took a sip of tea. "It was interesting."

"What was interesting?" asked Louise.

"His demeanor. He was bouncing along, hopping along his front walk like a pleased pubescent boy. The phrase 'the cat that ate the canary' came to mind. He's very happy and unworried about anything regarding Peter Hoffman's horrible death."

Louise shrugged her shoulders. "You could interpret that a couple of different ways."

"Could Cunningham have profited from Peter's death?" suggested Mary.

"Or maybe," said Nora, "it's just that Mike Cunningham is an insensitive wretch who never gave a care for his so-called friend from whom he earned millions of dollars."

Louise broke out in a big smile. "You two are good, do you know that? Too bad you don't have more time to give to this."

"Where are my girls?" asked Bill. "They're missing a decent dinner."

"Gone for the evening. But they'll be home at a decent hour, they said."

Another person might have concluded his description of her meal was damning with faint praise, but Louise read her husband's remark as an indication that her cooking was on the upswing. She'd thrown away the twenty-minute-dinner cookbook and was now operating out of *The Joy of Cooking,* a gift from Sandy Stern. Sandy said she'd buy her a more sophisticated one once Louise mastered some basics. Frozen puff pastries filled with chicken à la king had not been that much trouble, especially as Martha had poached the chicken for her early this morning in some complex broth.

Her husband gave her a quick glance. "I can see you're rather pensive. Good day?"

"Not very. Mike Geraghty called and chewed me out for talking to a few people."

"I heard about that. Morton called me and warned me. Louise—"

"Bill, I took what he said to heart. I spent the rest of the day reading. After a few hours, I have to admit I got very jumpy. Thank heavens my friends dropped over to see me." She related what Phyllis Hoffman had told to Mary Mougey about her husband informing on Lee Downing to the SEC and also cheating him in the sales deal of Hoffman Arms. "She also said that Peter was ready to flee the country, leaving her behind." She mentioned what Nora Radebaugh had said about Mike Cunningham's demeanor, but Bill seemed uninterested, as if it were too subjective to be of value.

He thought for a moment. "The police need to know about Hoffman being the one to inform the SEC about Downing. I'll mention it to Dan Trace when I talk to him tomorrow."

"Do you talk to him every day, Bill?"

"I call him or he calls me. I tell him everything I learn about the case. Maybe I'm wrong, but I figure that the more I can do for him, the less they'll consider you a murder suspect."

"If they don't find another suspect by Friday, I might be arrested."

Bill shook his head. "George Morton just won't let go, even though God knows I've given him a strong lead in another direction. If Lee Downing knew that Peter Hoffman outed him to the SEC, that gives him an even stronger reason to kill."

He turned to her with a warm, blue-eyed smile. "I'm sorry you got chewed out by Geraghty. On the other hand, you are pretty aggressive for one who has so much evidence pointing to her." He shook his head a little and took another bite of his dinner.

"What are you trying to tell me?"

"You must realize that we're limited in what we can do. We can listen. We can talk to friends. But we can hardly charge ahead with the investigation, because it could be that a Chicago hit man did it, and not one of our neighbors."

"So you want me to cease and desist, just like the police."

"No, but your direct approach may not be the best. How would you like to do it another way and see what information we can pick up?"

She put her hand on his arm. "You mean surveillance?"

He laughed. "Just a little walk in the neighborhood after dark. We've done it before, haven't we? Not too long ago we found some good information that way."

"Yes, when Madeleine Doering's killer was out there. So you do mean surveillance. All right!"

"Eat up," said Bill. "Then we'll change into some clothes that will help us disappear into the night."

It was ten-thirty, and only night owls were still up in Sylvan Valley on this week night, for tomorrow was a work day for most adults. The evening was hot and moist, but a trace of a breeze came and went and relieved the steam room effect. The furtive moon dodged behind a fat lid of clouds. Louise realized the Washington monsoon season would soon be at hand with its big soaking rains. The cloud cover produced utter darkness, so that she and Bill could hardly see their hands in front of them. They walked in the street, lest the aged sidewalks with their jagged edges trip them up and send them flying.

They headed first to Phyllis Hoffman's house, which lay almost a mile down the road at the edge of the neighborhood. Here, trees were not the soaring, 110-footers as in the central part of the neighborhood, but sparse and small.

"Do these houses remind you of something?" asked Louise.

"No," said Bill. "What are they supposed to remind me of?"

"The outlying slave houses near a plantation."

"Huh," said Bill, chuckling. "That's a bit of a stretch, considering that people have to pay a few hundred thousand for them."

"They're so much plainer than the houses closer in."

"It's the relative lack of trees. Sylvan Valley is a strange place. It's not every neighborhood where prestige is measured by how many trees crowd your yard."

She gave his arm a gentle tug. "We turn down this cul-de-sac. Phyllis lives in the third house on the left, I hear."

"Let's be careful now," murmured Bill. "Peter Hoffman lived here after leaving the mental hospital. He could have put in an alarm system. And keep your scarf ready to pull up over your face in case anyone approaches." She'd worn the only dark scarf she owned, a silk one embroidered with her initials. Her husband wore a jaunty visored dark cap.

As they entered the yard, Bill used a pinpoint flashlight in short bursts, so its light could have been mistaken for a firefly's. He whispered in Louise's ear, "I think we can approach the house without fear. Just don't touch anything."

They eased up to the side of the house, where a light was shining, and pushed their way cautiously through a row of hemlocks that Phyllis must have planted for privacy, or to get more into the original spirit of Sylvan Valley. Peeking through open blinds, they saw a small study lined with file cabinets. Standing in front of an open file cabinet were two harried-looking people.

"Bingo," whispered Louise.

Bill grabbed her arm and pulled her back a few steps. "We don't want them to hear us. There they are—Phyllis and Mort Swanson." Phyllis, in shorts and sleeveless blouse, was busy rummaging through the files. The tall, slim Mort stood beside her. On a desk near them was a ring containing a dozen or more keys. "God, Bill, Mort looks so tired."

"Yes, he does, but the search is on nevertheless. What do you suppose they're looking for?"

"Maybe an alternative will," she said. "Mary mentioned that Phyllis was grumbling about the will—"

"Phyllis undoubtedly knows now how it reads. Maybe they're looking for one that gives her a better deal."

"Wow," said Louise, taking another step back. "That would be something." Her foot landed on a branch, and to their horror they heard its loud crack as it broke from her weight. Nearly losing her balance, she started to fall into the scratchy arms of the hemlock, until Bill pulled her straight. They saw Phyllis and Mort start at the noise and approach the window.

Bill held her close to him in the hemlocks. Louise pulled her black scarf over her face. "Hold still and they won't see us," he said. They froze in place while Phyllis and Mort stared out the window straight at them. When they turned away, Bill hissed, "Let's get the hell out of here." He guided her carefully away from the house and across the yard. They sprinted out of the cul-de-sac and onto the main road. Not until they were blocks away and under the safe cover of the deep woods did Bill slow down.

"Louise," he said, "we've got to be more careful than that if we're going to case the neighborhood."

"Sorry, darling."

"Maybe it wasn't enough noise to make them deeply suspicious. I hope not, because that scene inside Phyllis's house could be significant."

"How so?"

"Maybe Mort is more than a legal counselor. . . ."

"Could Mort have helped Phyllis arrange to have her husband killed?" finished Louise. "He's always been one of the most unreadable men I've ever met."

"He bears watching. What's our next destination, the Swansons'?"

"Yes," said Louise. "Let's see what Sarah, and for that

matter her visiting intern Hilde, does when Mort's out spending his time with Phyllis Hoffman."

Avoiding the tentacles of the pricklier trees and shrubs, they made their way through the thick plantings until they reached the house. Though they peeked in several windows, they saw no sign of Sarah or Hilde. "I bet Sarah's reading in bed," said Louise. "Hilde could be anywhere."

Bill sighed, and she sensed her husband had had enough window peeping. He said, "Now where to?"

"Back to our own Dogwood Court. We'll see what the locals are up to."

Once they'd breached a thick cluster of scrub trees, it was easy to see into Sam Rosen's house. A wall of windows would reveal the domestic scene within, but set in front of it was an array of cedars, not a difficult barrier to get around. "Isn't it strange," said Louise, "that Sylvan Valley folks think a clump of trees is as good as a drawn blind?"

Bill laughed. "How wrong they are." They stood and looked at their neighbors. Sam and Greg were sitting on separate couches in the dimly lit living room watching a large high-definition TV screen. Each held a drink in his hand and was studiously drinking it. Greg Archer was a man of considerable beauty, with his chiseled features and his blond hair glinting in the lamplight. Louise realized then why he was so attractive. He looked the way Bill had looked ten years ago. Sam and Greg exchanged only the most desultory conversation. It was as if they had been forced to sit there together.

"Not a happy pair these days, are they?" said Bill. "Though they probably don't look any different than other couples sitting in front of mindless television, not connecting, zoning out . . ."

Louise felt a twinge of guilt about the two men, as if she were responsible for the cooling of their relationship.

"Let's move on. We can go through the backyards of the Mougeys and the Radebaughs."

As they made their way through the Mougey yard, Louise couldn't help but peek at their friends Richard and Mary. The view here was obscured only by a little grove of see-through amelanchiar trees. They were cuddled on a couch in the family room, Richard's morose head in Mary's lap, watching a rerun of *Law and Order*.

"They look like newlyweds," murmured Bill.

"They know how to do it," said Louise.

"Do what?"

"Do marriage."

"So, don't we?"

She squeezed his hand. "Of course. That's taken for granted."

"Just don't take me for granted."

She drew closer to him, pushed his cap back on his head and gave him a soft kiss. "I try not to, honey."

"Mmm," said Bill, nuzzling her neck. They approached the Radebaugh backyard, but there was no sign of the occupants, Ron and Nora. Louise pointed to a dim light in a room whose draperies had been drawn. "That's the master bedroom."

"Damned good sign," said Bill. "Keep your fingers crossed for my friend Ron."

"We can skip the Kendricks, I think," said Louise. "I saw Roger and Laurie go out for the evening. They're probably not home yet."

"Fine. Then that just leaves your quarry—Mike Cunningham and Lee Downing."

She aimed an elbow at him as they continued through the woods. "It's annoying sometimes how well you can see through me. But I also thought it was good that we looked in on Phyllis Hoffman."

"Indeed," said Bill in a droll voice, and she couldn't tell

whether or not he meant to tease her. "We snooped in on a woman consulting a lawyer."

"And rifling through files. Don't forget the files."

"So, here we are at Cunningham's house. Which way d'you want to go in?"

"Let's stay in back," said Louise. "It's safer. Head for that light. It's faint, but it's a light." With Bill again using the small flashlight, they carefully approached the house.

They slid their way through some thick scrub brush until they were ten feet away from the room with the light. They could just barely make out the shapes on the couch, turning, writhing. Suddenly, one shape sat up and turned up the dimmer switch on a nearby table lamp. Now the couple was in plain sight. Hilde Brunner's long hair was strewn carelessly around her face, her bronzed legs in short shorts intertwined with the legs of Mike Cunningham. Cunningham's hair, too, was disheveled, and his shirt halfway out of his pants. Hilde leaned against Cunningham, ruffled his hair further and appeared to be laughing at him. The attorney made a move with his hand toward Hilde's breasts, at which point she leaped from the couch and threw her hands up in dismay—the classic damsel-in-distress pose.

"We've seen enough," said Louise.

Her husband mumbled. "Let's go home."

Louise realized later what a mistake it was, but at the time it seemed logical to continue around the back of Cunningham's house and exit through the front yard. When they got there, they heard the front door slam and saw Hilde run down Cunningham's front walk, apparently heading for her studio apartment at the Swansons'.

Unfortunately, Louise hadn't known what was going on behind Cunningham's newly installed Leyland cypress hedge at the front of the house. She and Bill were making their way through the darkness and had only twenty feet to go before reaching the sidewalk when Louise bumped into something hard. The whole world appeared to be falling, including her. She could feel the black scarf ripping away from her neck as Bill grabbed her before she toppled over with a concrete object.

It stood almost as tall as Louise and Bill on top of a pedestal of some kind and fell to the ground with a crash. Bill dared a quick glimpse with the pinpoint flashlight. "We've totaled a classical statue of a lady in loose garments."

"Oh, no," said Louise, "it's a fountain."

Bill turned the light on the broken statue once more. "I think we'd better get out of here. We can settle up later with Cunningham, maybe make an anonymous donation to pay for the thing."

They scuttled across the cul-de-sac and into the confines of their own deep woods. Putting her hand to her throat, she realized her scarf had been torn off. She decided not to tell her husband.

Once safe in the tall sweet gums, they turned and looked across the street. The noise had brought Mike Cunningham to attention. His front porch light was on, and although they couldn't see him through the trees, Louise guessed he was standing there viewing the damage to his concrete work of art.

A little voice inside her said, *Serves him right for bringing such a tacky ornament into our neighborhood.* To Bill, she said, "Let's go in and not worry about it tonight. He'll be calmed down by morning. I doubt he'll recognize the scarf."

"The scarf?" They made their way up the flagstone path to the front door.

"Um, yeah, it was torn off back there at his house."

"Louise, that has your initials on it. I know. I gave it to you."

"Sorry, honey." They slipped into the house and went to the kitchen, where Louise poured each of them a glass of cold water and handed one to Bill. "Or would you rather have sherry?"

"Yeah. Sherry would be good." He reached down into a cupboard and got the bottle, and she handed him a small glass. Slumping against the kitchen counter, he took a sip, then ran a tired hand through his blond hair. He pursed his lips as if thinking carefully about what he wanted to say next. "Louise, the idea of surveillance is to slip quietly through the neighborhood without people knowing you are there, not to knock things down. I have a real problem now. I hate to pull rank, but I've just been elevated to a higher position at State: special U.S. liaison with the IAEA." He grinned and shook his head. "You might say there's a certain discrepancy between the dignity of my professional life and the degradation of my personal life at the present time."

"Bill, that sounds stuffy."

"Then how can I make it plainer? That guy's going to find that scarf, and it won't take him long to figure out who 'L.E.' is. He's going to come after us, and you know it. How the hell can I explain at the State Department why I was out at midnight vandalizing a statue in my neighbor's front yard?"

26

A couple of sherries and Bill was ready for bed, joining Louise, who was already in her nightgown. When they heard the girls coming in the front door, she said, "Do you think we should check with them and see what they've been doing?"

Bill nodded. "That's a good idea." She opened their bedroom door and called to them.

Martha came to their bedroom door. "Hi, guys. Want to come out and talk for a minute?"

They settled in the living room. Janie was flopped on the couch and looking worn out. Her pretty white cotton dress was rumpled and grass-stained from whatever the day's activities had been, her blue sash dragging. Louise noted how lovely she was, even in this state of dishabille. Their equally handsome older daughter, wearing jeans and tan blouse, looked as fresh and wide awake as she'd been this morning. She sat in the antique straight-backed chair, looking like a professor conducting a late-night seminar. Her straight back and high chin said it all: *I'm in charge.*

Martha said, "Janie and I've been all over the place, and in fact we saw the two of you a little while ago skulking in the woods."

Louise, tucked into a corner of the couch, looked amazed. "You mean you and Janie were out there too?"

Janie shrugged. "Sure. Just checking out the neighborhood."

Bill bowed his head. "We all have to remember that this murderer could be some distant business connection of Hoffman's, or it could be someone local. Martha, I thought I told you to not get Janie involved in something dangerous."

"Dad, tonight is the first time Janie's come along."

Janie gave her sister a cold look. "Thanks. Why are you all being so careful of me, when I'm more experienced than Martha is?"

Bill put up a cautionary hand. "Are we talking or just bickering? So where did you go tonight, and did you notice anything at Mike Cunningham's house?"

Janie said, "We circled his house, then camped out back when we saw Hilde come visit. A very insect-heavy experience. Then they started making out on the couch. And then you two came along, and we retreated into the forest, so to speak. Didn't want to upset you, Ma."

"We saw you leave," continued Martha. "They we saw Hilde leave. Then we heard a big crash out front. We were afraid to move at that point. Mike Cunningham was cussing up a storm, yelling something about how he'd get even 'with the asshole who did this.' What did you do, break his statue?"

"Yeah," said Louise. "I bumped into it. I couldn't believe it would break so easily."

"Good," said Janie. "It was a horrible statue." She giggled.

"Janie," Bill admonished, "this isn't funny. Your mother's initialed scarf was torn off. He's going to know we were there."

Their younger daughter found it hard to keep the smile

off her face. "Well, Ma, maybe you'll get the death penalty for that."

"Very funny," said Louise.

Martha said, "Cunningham sounded apoplectic. We hunkered down for a long time before we dared sneak home."

"Okay," said Louise, "can we get off the topic of Mike Cunningham? You were headed downtown today. Did you go shopping?"

Martha briefly recounted their trip to Saks and subsequent lunch at the same restaurant as Phyllis Hoffman and Mort Swanson. "I think he's her lawyer," said Martha.

"And," said Janie, "she's not a happy camper. In fact, she's frantic." Her big blue eyes grew bigger as she related the tale. "Maybe she's not getting any money from Peter Hoffman's will or something. So if she offed her old man, it's not been worthwhile."

"Janie." Louise's rebuke was gentle but firm. "Don't be too rough."

"Ma," said Janie, "I know murder's hell and you don't like it and the violence that surrounds it. But I'm only describing to you what I saw." She smiled. "I got all that just from reading Mort and Phyllis's body language, which your fine older daughter told me I should do. Of course, I knew all about that already."

"How remarkable," said Louise. "Your father and I peeked in Phyllis's window about an hour ago, and she and Mort were busy looking in file cabinets. Bill, maybe it is a will they're after."

Bill stroked his chin, rubbing the day-end whiskers gently with his fingers. "Could be. Okay. Now let's think about any significance to the fact that Mike Cunningham is involved with a young woman like Hilde Brunner. Do you think there's any more to it than—"

"Than what," asked Martha, "lust?"

"Yeah," said Janie, "he's even got a pot belly. Why doesn't she go with someone her own age?"

Martha paused for a moment to gather her audience's attention. "I think it's a power trip for Hilde. An older, prestigious Washington lawyer takes a fancy to her and she thinks she's succeeded in this country. I don't know if you heard this, Dad, but Ma's reporter friend Charlie Hurd is nuts over our Swiss Miss. So it isn't as if she hasn't had some younger man's attentions paid to her. But Charlie doesn't turn her on at all. Maybe she likes older men, just like older men like younger women."

Louise noticed that Martha had the grace to blush.

"For instance, when we played our tennis foursome on Sunday, I found it quite easy to, um, flirt with that silver-haired devil Lee Downing. He must be fifty if he's a day. He would have been game for anything."

"You told him you were getting married, didn't you?" asked Louise.

"No."

"And why not?"

"Because, Ma, a good investigator doesn't go around talking about herself. The less people know, the better."

Janie nodded in agreement. Louise was happy the two girls appeared to be getting along better than previously.

"Okay," said Bill, "now let's talk about Lee Downing. What did you learn about him?"

Martha stifled a yawn, now unable to disguise her fatigue, which meant she was catching up with the rest of her family. "To put it mildly, he has issues with Mike Cunningham. Talked about someone 'cooking the books.' It must be over the sales deal of Hoffman Arms—what else could it be? He had a mess of files with him the night I first met him. Then Sunday, the day after that, he complained to our neighbor lawyer that he couldn't find some information he wanted from the files. Alas, I didn't pick up any details, only that the two of them seem seriously pissed with each other."

"Martha," admonished Louise.

"Sorry, Ma, it's late, and I've been associating with Chicago politicians. But anyway, lots of people say 'pissed.' "

"Martha," said Bill, "the police should have been told."

"They have been. I phoned Mike Geraghty and told him my little tennis gossip right after the game. I would have told you, too, but we haven't crossed paths for a day or so."

"Okay," said Bill, " point taken. Today your mother heard that Hoffman was the one who reported to the SEC about Lee Downing's industrial spying."

Martha's eyes shone. "That's an even stronger motive, isn't it? Mr. Downing seems to be between a rock and a hard place." She turned to Louise. "There, see, I said it poetically, instead of just saying he's being screwed from both sides."

"Never mind, Martha," said Bill. "Well, girls, I congratulate you on your observational powers. What else are your mother and I missing out on?"

Martha ticked off the items. "As of today, we know Mort Swanson is trying to help the anxious and troubled Phyllis Hoffman—"

"Probably signed on as her lawyer," said Bill. "Sorry. Continue."

Martha went on, "As of two days ago, we know Mike Cunningham and Lee Downing are arguing over the lack of papers, possibly headed for a lawsuit or at least a fistfight."

"As of tonight," said Janie, "we saw that Sam Rosen and Greg Archer have had a serious falling out. Yet Greg has no motive to kill, or does he?"

Bill said, "I don't think he does."

Martha continued. "On the lighter side, the *Entertainment Tonight* segment of our investigation, we know Mike Cunningham and Hilde are fooling around, and she's teasing him and not wanting to go the whole way. Right, Janie?"

"Right," said Janie. "I interpreted that couch scene the same way. She's what I believe one would call a cockteaser."

"Janie," said Louise, "you don't need to say everything you're thinking. So, I guess everybody admires Hilde a lot."

"Everybody except Elsebeth," rejoined Martha.

Bill raised an eyebrow. "Elsebeth met Hilde and didn't like her?"

"Yes," said Martha. "She met her when she came over for lunch. Elsebeth was a little annoyed at Hilde—some minor flap over language."

"So that's your report."

"Yes," said Martha, "and you are free to share any of this with the cops, of course. But now I think I need to leave for Chicago. I talked to Jim earlier today, and he's stressed out over the wedding. Can't seem to find time to handle all that detail about the church and the reception and still campaign for alderman. He needs me there." She turned to her younger sister. "And I think I need Janie."

Louise heard this and sat up. "Yes, you both should go. Janie will be a big help."

Their younger daughter perked up. "I'd love to go. I'm the perfect wedding planner. Does that mean we drive together to Chicago?"

Martha looked at her sister. "There's no other way unless we pay a fortune to the airlines. It'll give us a chance to get, uh, you know, in sync."

"Yeah," said Janie, relaxing back on a sofa pillow, "or else kill each other."

Ignoring this remark, Martha said, "Once in Chicago, we can hit a lot of discount stores and buy clothes. As for flowers, Ma, I've decided I'm going to carry fall crocuses. You know, those pale lilac flowers."

"*Colchicum autumnale*," said Louise.

"Won't that be fab?" said Martha.

Louise looked benignly at her daughter. "What a wonderful idea. I can just picture it."

"There's just one shadow on the wedding plans, Ma," said Martha.

"What's that?" asked Louise.

"The question is, will you be there or will you be in jail? Nobody's going to care what I wear as a bride if my mother's in prison for murder."

Bill jerked his head up and glared at his older daughter. "Martha, your mother's not going to be imprisoned for murder. I'll see to that. We love you very much, and you're a fine person. But it's just as well that the two of you leave. I think it will be a relief for all of us. You get the wedding planned, and we'll resolve things with the police."

"If you really think you can do without us," said Janie, her blue eyes wide with concern.

"We can, Janie," said Louise. "But don't think we aren't grateful to you for all that you and Martha have done."

"Just one more thing," said their younger daughter. "Be careful, because the murderer is someone who lives in the neighborhood, not some distant business connection."

Bill frowned. "How can you be so sure of that?"

"Just say it's a premonition," said Janie.

Louise gave the girls a good-night hug, then turned to her husband. "Come, darling. We both need some rest."

Louise wished she were as sure as Bill was about her future. Although she probably would never be convicted, it would be heartbreaking to be arrested by the Fairfax sheriff's department, the beneficiary of so many of her intuitions.

27

Under the ever-watchful eye of a still-lingering TV crew, Louise helped Martha and Janie load their suitcases into her car and drove them to the rental car lot in Alexandria. Her last words were to urge them to find Martha a wedding gown.

"You mean a proper wedding gown," teased Martha. "I bet you want me to change my mind and wear white."

"No, I don't," Louise said. "Any gown will do, darling." And she embraced each of them. Once she'd picked up a few groceries in town, Louise had little interest in doing anything but return home. She'd thought of a gardening project to keep her busy for the day. She headed south again on the GW Parkway.

The irises in the front sorely needed dividing and resetting, as did the *Cimicifuga purpurea* in the patio garden. Snakeroot, with its pure white snaky tasseled flowers on purple stems, was one of her favorite plants. But she didn't want to work where newspeople could see her and decide to intrude on her privacy. Instead, she was going to tackle a tough project in the deep woods. She donned her hardcore gardening clothes, long-sleeved shirt, her oldest gardening pants and steel-toed work boots, then took her tools from the shed, secateurs, loppers and two saws, and headed for the bamboo mini-jungle in the far corner of the yard. It was the neighbors' bamboo, but had spread onto their property. Bill worried about its invasive ways and would be delighted if she got rid of some of it.

As for the bamboo in her Asian-style garden, she'd assured her husband that the few graceful plants there couldn't spread because of the foot-deep plastic barrier with which each plant was surrounded. She didn't tell Bill that some roots had sneaked their way down beyond the plastic; she just saw to it that each tender new shoot popping up outside the barrier was lopped off.

Her arms weighed down with her tools, she marched through the woods to confront the bamboo. Within minutes, she was immersed in her work and had set aside all thoughts of the body in the garden.

Two hours later, she returned to the patio. Her next project would be to repot her cape primroses. These houseplants spent the summer on the patio, growing by leaps and bounds in the muggy summer air. Once she'd shaken the old dirt off the roots and supplied them with new dirt, she carried them into the kitchen and carefully watered them in the sink. She took out a big cookie sheet and set it on the corner of the counter, then put the plants on it so that they could drain properly.

With care, Louise cleaned the kitchen counters and sink with a soapy sponge and straightened her Grand Hotel dish towel behind the faucet. Only then did she realize it was two o'clock and she hadn't eaten lunch. She opened the refrigerator and got out the makings of a big sandwich. She thought she deserved one.

Bill sat in the green glow of his Art Deco desk lamp in his office in downtown Washington and tried to pull his thoughts together. Events were churning in the Middle

East, and he knew he had to leave the country soon. But his wife was sitting at home at this very moment, a police suspect in a murder. He had to do something to influence those overeager Fairfax County police and get Louise off the hook. Searching a phone number out of his wallet, he dialed Dan Trace.

"Glad you called," the lieutenant said, in his baritone voice. "Of course I can give you an update, provided you're circumspect about whom you share this with. It's okay to relieve your wife's tensions by telling her."

"You mean you've found the murderer?"

"No, but we have uncovered a lot of detail about Mr. Hoffman's business affairs."

"So have I. Louise heard something that could be important. Peter Hoffman was the informer who alerted the SEC ethics hotline to Downing's business tricks. Also, he was intending to flee the country."

"Uh-huh," said Lieutenant Trace. "We've heard that, too, probably from the same source, Mrs. Hoffman. We've finally been able to interview Lee Downing, and he's shed a lot of light on the purchase of Hoffman Arms. You probably know the broad parameters of the sale: The buyer and seller must agree on a value, which in fact is established by the IRS. It considers equipment, the goodwill or 'name' value of the company and its viability. In other words, is it up and running and healthy."

"So what happened here?" said Bill. "Rumor has it that Downing was unhappy with the deal after it was consummated. Did someone in fact falsify the books?"

Trace laughed. "They sure did, according to Downing. He charges that Hoffman, with Cunningham of course very much a part of the deal, inflated the business by almost one hundred percent. Hoffman probably wanted to get out of the country before Downing could unravel the details of the crooked deal."

Bill whistled. "How'd Hoffman manage all this?"

"Since a lot of his business was with the Defense Department, Hoffman saw that the books looked good. Orders were placed a year or more before the product was due, for weapons to be provided for, say, three years, with options to supply them for maybe ten more years. These factors were all woven into the value. But some orders were cancelled, it turns out, and others were only preliminary and had never been finalized. The irony is that this detail was all off-limits to Downing until after the fact, just because they were government contracts. Do you get the picture?"

"Yes," said Bill. "But it matters when Downing heard about this."

"Uh-huh," said Lieutenant Trace. "You put your finger on it. He says he didn't find out until after Hoffman was killed. This has to be established because it could be a motive."

"And the reason Downing couldn't just declare that the deal was invalid? The SEC investigation must enter in."

"It probably does," said the lieutenant. "I think Hoffman took a big roll of the dice. Decided Downing wouldn't risk a public flap over the sale of Hoffman Arms when he could face serious charges of industrial spying. It explains Downing's big profits of late. He's been the low bidder in at least two competitive bidding situations, because he's had a spy in his competitors' plants. 'First to market' is the name of the game in the competitive arms business, and Downing apparently made sure he was first to market."

"So what's your conclusion?" asked Bill. "Does this information help my wife?"

"Not totally. But it opens this mare's nest of possibilities. I can't talk about suspects with you, Mr. Eldridge, but you can figure out just as well as I can who the obvious ones would be with this set of circumstances in play." Then the lieutenant came forth with another bit of good news. "You might like to know that we've concluded further tests on Hoffman's body, and there's no evidence on the corpse itself to tie the crime to your wife. Of course, there's still the tarp with her fingerprints on it, the hat, and especially Hoffman's blood on Mrs. Eldridge's sweatshirt and on her gardening tool. I agree with Mike Geraghty that some of that could have been there just because Mrs. Eldridge uses that stuff when she gardens. But for the last two items, there's no explanation at all."

Bill tried to control his desperation. "There's a simple explanation, Lieutenant. The killer planted that evidence. Listen, I want you to understand in human terms what this is doing to my wife. Needless to say, it's depressing as hell. Fortunately, she has a good book and her gardening to occupy her time, because she's practically been ordered by your man Morton to refrain from talking to anyone. Her employers have benched her for a few programs just because she's been innocently caught in a terrible scandal. Not to mention the pickax, which scared the hell out of her. You still haven't got back to us on that."

"The technician who handled your toolshed is off on vacation. We haven't been able to get hold of him, I'm sorry to say."

"It seems too dumb a thing for a technician to do," said Bill. "Which leads to the possibility of criminal mischief on the part of someone else. Now let me continue. Our daughters are trying to plan an October wedding for Martha, and they're very upset about this. I, on my part, have to leave soon for Vienna. But I surely don't intend to go until I know Louise is freed from suspicion. We have lots of reasons for wanting you to find the real killer. Today is Wednesday. I think this Friday deadline of Morton's for arresting my wife is just plain nonsense."

"Mr. Eldridge," said Lieutenant Trace, "consider the

deadline shoved forward a bit. And lest I forgot to tell you, we're also looking into the consequences of Hoffman's will."

"I'd hoped you would."

"The will's interesting. I can't share the details with you, but it might bear on the case."

Bill said, "That's what they always say, don't they, when there's a murder—find out who profits."

"Who profits, and who loses out," amended Trace.

"Thanks, Lieutenant."

"One further thing, and I hope this doesn't upset your wife unduly. Apparently Mike Cunningham has filed a complaint because she entered his yard and did some damage. A statue was broken, I believe. He's very upset and is charging malicious destruction of property. Umm, I hesitate to mention this last item."

"What's that, Lieutenant?"

"He's also brought up some new details surrounding Mr. Hoffman's murder that involve your wife. I'd rather sit down and discuss this with you after I hear from Cunningham."

"Just what does that mean?" said Bill.

"Mr. Cunningham is implying he knows of some other connection between your wife and Hoffman."

Bill's voice was shaking. "Lieutenant Trace, my wife had no connections with Hoffman."

He could hear the lieutenant expel a breath on the other end of the phone line. "I know this is well after the fact and that right now Mr. Cunningham is very angry at your wife. That's why we have to go after this carefully. I'm to have a face-to-face with Mr. Cunningham tomorrow. As soon as I do, I'll get back to you and Mrs. Eldridge."

After Bill hung up, he tapped his pen on the desk. He'd hoped to make a cash settlement with Cunningham over the Aphrodite matter. If not, it was better being in court for malicious destruction of property than for murder. But what the hell kind of "connection" between Louise and Hoffman was Mike Cunningham trying to feed to the police? He sat back in his chair, trying to calm down and think. One thing he knew for sure: he was through cooperating with the police, for it hadn't gotten them anywhere. He wasn't about to tell his already troubled wife about this latest insinuation that she had something to do with Hoffman before his death.

Bill arrived home by eight o'clock, and he and Louise hurried off to Old Town Alexandria for a late dinner. Afterward, they bought ice cream cones on King Street and wandered down the brick sidewalks, window shopping as they ate. Home by ten, they found that the house seemed empty with the girls gone. On the plus side, it was more privacy than they'd had for some time.

Louise was going straight to bed, for she'd had a long day of gardening. But she decided her stomach would appreciate a small glass of milk and a few soda crackers before she took two aspirin to help her sleep.

She went to the kitchen, flipped on the overhead light and went to the refrigerator for the milk. She paused in thought, then turned around again. Even a quick glance told her something was wrong. Her gaze moved over the counters, the stove and, finally, to the sink. A rush of cold coursed through her body. "Bill," she called, "come here quickly."

By the time her husband arrived in the kitchen, she was standing and staring at the rough-hewn squares of tumbled marble behind the stainless steel sink. The protective Grand Hotel towel was nowhere in sight.

Her pristine marble tiles were splattered with a brown substance.

"My God," cried Bill, "what is it?"

She reached out and touched some of the discoloration. "It's garden soil. Someone threw a handful of it at the tiles."

"Who the hell was in here?" he demanded.

She stood very still. "I don't know. But this isn't a joke."

"And where'd they get the dirt?" Even as Bill said this, he walked over to the counter where the repotted house-plants stood, draining in the tray. "Huh," he said, pointing to the cape primrose, which was sagging sideways. "They scooped it out of here."

"Where's the Grand Hotel dish towel?" she asked in a hollow voice.

Bill searched around and pulled it out of a corner. "It was neatly folded and tucked in back of the toaster."

"It's as if someone's out to get me. It's all con-nected—innocent things at first, the re-arranged curio cabinet—"

"—the pickax, which could have killed you. And now this. Someone's been breaking into our house!" Bill pounded on the counter, and she jumped at the noise. "That does it, Louise. Somebody wants to harm you. Tomorrow, we get all the locks changed. Right now, we call Geraghty."

Louise slumped against the granite counter and stared across at her grimy tiles. "Please, not tonight, Bill."

"You're not safe in this house anymore."

"You're here tonight, so I'm safe. Let's have a good night's sleep. Then we'll call the police first thing in the morning." She gave him a pleading look. "I suppose I can't—"

"No, you can't clean up your tiles. Leave the dirt there so Geraghty and the skeptical Mr. Morton can see just what the hell some pervert is up to."

She said softly, "What else do you think this person has done in our house?"

He came over and put his arm around her, switched off the kitchen light and guided her down the hall to their bedroom. "There'll be plenty of time tomorrow to find out."

Lee Downing pulled his Lincoln town car into the curve of Dogwood Court directly in front of Mike Cunningham's house. He parked the Lincoln with the exaggerated care of one who had recently been drinking a lot of booze. Despite his best efforts, and for the umpteenth time, he scraped the tires against the goddamned curb. After emitting a few choice swear words, he grabbed a suitcase he had packed with papers, slid out of the car, locked it and strode toward the house.

He could see through the garage windows the bulk of Cunningham's car. That was a signal to all that he was home. Downing glanced at his Rolex watch. It was almost one o'clock. It had been a long day, including the shuttle flight home, three hours with the Fairfax sheriff's office, a good long session with his attorney regarding the SEC investigation, followed by a dinner paid for by the attorney—who would still net plenty off him—and a few hours of unaccounted-for time at the conclusion of which he'd had a few belts of scotch.

It was supposed to be the moment for a showdown with Cunningham, a man whom he'd started out liking almost as a friend, but whom he now despised. They were to sit in Cunningham's glitzy living room and get down to brass tacks, instead of playing the old game of accuse and deny. He intended to give the lawyer an ultimatum, an offer he couldn't refuse, because there was no way in hell that he was going to be screwed the way Peter Hoffman and Mike Cunningham had planned for him to be screwed, even if it meant airing his dirty linen in public. Especially when Downing had an inkling that Mike Cunningham had a secret. He was fairly sure that Cunningham was the one who'd conveniently removed Hoffman from the planet.

He tried the front door and found it open. Entering, he called, "Mike, I'm home. Late, I know, but better late than never."

Silence. Mike could be was asleep, though the man normally stayed up late. Downing did what seemed normal under the circumstances, went to the master bedroom door, which was ajar, and noted the bed was empty and neatly made. He called in a loud voice. There weren't many rooms in this house where he wouldn't have been heard, except downstairs in Mike's exercise room. He went to the stairs, opened the door and called again. Again he was greeted with silence. He went down the stairs and walked through the luxurious little panoply of exercise equipment. That would be a logical thing to do, just to be sure that Mike hadn't keeled over in some freak accident.

Mike wasn't here. He might be nearby, messing around with that young Swiss woman, Hilde, although Mike would have more logically brought the girl to his house, because Hilde, to his knowledge, didn't have a car. And it would be a little obvious for an attorney of his stature to trundle through the neighborhood to that studio apartment of hers to get laid. Or maybe not. Sex drove even important people to do very dumb things.

Even if he was down the street doing Hilde, would a paranoid guy like Mike Cunningham leave the front door open? A normal person wouldn't.

Downing went into the front hall, picked up the stack of mail that lay near the front door and tried to determine how many days it represented. One, maybe two days, maybe three. Downing had been in New York since Sunday night, arriving back in Washington early this morning. It would be hard to know when the man went missing, unless the neighbors noticed something.

Would he be thought foolish calling the police? He tried to put it in perspective. This was a neighborhood where one man already had been found dead in the past seven days. What the hell was he waiting for?

He started to call information, then cancelled that call and dialed 9-1-1.

28

Louise was still in bed, and Bill was in the bathroom, shaving, when there was a simultaneous ringing of the front doorbell and a loud knocking on the door itself.

With shaving cream on the side of his face, Bill peered around the bathroom door and said, "Who the devil is that?"

Louise slid out of bed and into her robe lying on the apricot bedside chair. "I'll see."

Bill raised a finger and warned her, "Look first, honey. Don't open the door if you see someone suspicious out there."

Without pausing to find her slippers, she hurried to the front door. Peeking through the vertical side window, her heart gave a thump. Looking in at her with wide, intent eyes were Dan Trace, George Morton and Mike Geraghty. She opened the door, though she didn't want to. The presence of these three men could mean nothing but trouble.

She set aside formalities such as "hello." "What on earth are you doing here?" she asked. "My husband and I were just about to phone you people."

Lieutenant Trace said, "Ma'am, we're pursuing a tip we

received a short while ago. Uh, what was the nature of your call? Is it an emergency?"

Yes, Lieutenant, it is: dirt splashed on my kitchen tiles, indicating an intruder has been in our home. She could tell by Trace's expression that her intruder problem would pale in comparison to whatever matter it was that had brought three officers to their house at seven-thirty.

"Why don't you tell me first, Lieutenant Trace, just why you're here."

"Is your husband at home, Mrs. Eldridge? I'd hoped we could talk to both of you at the same time."

Bill, who was still tying his robe, came up behind her. He said, "Hello, Lieutenant. Good morning, detectives. What can we do for you?"

"We have a serious situation, I'm afraid, Mr. Eldridge," said the lieutenant. "I don't know if you noticed police activity in the neighborhood late last evening."

"Nope," said Bill. "We were both too tired. What happened?"

"Mr. Mike Cunningham, your neighbor, is missing."

"He is?" said Bill. "What does that have to do with us?"

"Just a few minutes ago, the sheriff's office got a tip as to where he was located."

"And where was that?"

Louise gave a gasp, then prayed that what she feared wasn't true.

Lieutenant Trace looked calmly down at her from his great height. "We were told by this anonymous tipster that a person was digging in your vegetable garden late last night."

"No, no," Louise said, and took a step backward until she felt Bill's strong presence right behind her. She felt as if her body were melting. Bill kept her upright by putting his arms around her waist.

"This is ridiculous," snapped Bill.

The lieutenant shrugged. "Well, let's just see, shall we? It could be a prankster. But in view of the fact that Mr. Cunningham's missing, we have to follow this up." He gave Louise a smile. "Now, do you want us to get a court order or could we just, uh, go ahead?"

"What do you think, Louise?" asked Bill. "I say just let them dig up the vegetable garden. They'll get permission anyway, if they go to a judge."

Louise felt numb and cold. "Go ahead. How could we stop you?"

"But first," said Bill, "did this person say anything else?"

The lieutenant bowed his head. Louise could see George Morton itching to interrupt, but he didn't dare. Trace said, "Our tipster said the person was wearing a gardening-type hat, so we'll want to investigate that shed of yours again. And the person was using your garden cart."

"Oh, my God," she said, trembling, "the same tip you received before I dug up Peter Hoffman. Greg Archer, I bet that's who called you."

Bill's arms tightened around her.

The lieutenant shook his head. "I have no idea, Mrs. Eldridge. We couldn't determine who it was, man or woman. Let's just put first things first, okay, and see what we find in that garden. Now we'll give you and Mr. Eldridge time to get dressed and maybe have some coffee."

Louise and Bill dressed hurriedly and went first to the kitchen, where like an automaton Louise went through the machinations necessary to make Chemex coffee. Putting on the kettle, grinding the Kona beans, setting the coffee filter in the beaker-shaped pot, letting the water cool to just a few degrees below boiling, wetting the grounds first, then continuing to pour the water through the grounds until the glorious brown liquid rested in the pot. While she did this, Bill made toast.

When they'd settled at the table, he said, "Let's try to

relax and enjoy a bite. Let them dig up your garden and not worry about it. *I* know you didn't bury a body in with the onion sets. I was with you all evening."

"I might have tucked in a murder and a body burying after you fell asleep at eleven." They clung together and laughed. But her body was still trembling.

The next person at the front door knocked first and then opened the door. "Louise, Bill, it's Sam Rosen. Can I come in?"

Louise and Bill were still at the dining room table, drinking a second cup of coffee.

Their neighbor's eyes were wide with concern. "The cul-de-sac is filled with TV trucks again. Meantime, the cops out back are ruining our onions!"

"Sit down," she said. "I'll get you coffee. Black, right?"

"Right. They told me they got the tip early this morning. Just like the last one about Peter Hoffman."

Bill said, "You mean the press people are here already?" His eyes narrowed. "That's interesting—they must have been tipped, too."

Sam accepted his cup of coffee from Louise with a smile and a nod. "Look, we can fix the garden, maybe even get some fresh onion sets. But what bothers me is that someone's out to get you, Louise. It's damned puzzling."

She sighed. "I tell you, Sam, I don't know what to think. I'm at the end of my rope. I'm just going to hole up in my house and hope that the police can solve this thing. And before I forget, have you seen any strangers around our house? We've had a few funny incidents, as if someone may have broken in."

Sam laughed. "You mean strangers other than the constant stream of cops and press that hang around? Seriously, though, you know I'd tell you if I saw anything suspicious."

They heard a knock, and Lieutenant Trace came in. "Folks, I think you'd better come out and have a look."

Louise felt like a sleepwalker. She walked slowly out the front door with Bill and Sam trailing behind her. She turned around and exchanged a despairing glance at her husband when she saw the press people milling in Dogwood Court. They followed Lieutenant Trace the thirty feet to the yard's boundary. Even now, at eight-thirty, the sun shone down on half a dozen police technicians and a deep excavation that once was a growing onion patch. The carefully stacked timbers that supported both ends of the little garden had been dismantled and set in a neat pile. Black dirt was scattered in a wide circle. Because the soil was tilled for planting, it had been a quick job to dig it out. No one had bothered to save the onion sets as they dug, and they were strewn aimlessly about, like bent green pencils. "Oh," she moaned, an involuntary sound that came out when she saw all her and Sam's gardening work destroyed.

"Steady, honey," said Bill.

"Step closer so you can see," said Lieutenant Trace. Visible at the bottom of what once was their garden was a long, plastic-wrapped package. She could see clearly that there was a body inside.

"Oh, my God, no," she cried as she saw the face far down at the end of the hole, a big, handsome face. The body was garbed in white shirt and tan slacks, the feet much closer to the surface, in stylish sneakers. Cunningham. Faintness overcame her, and she would have fallen had Bill not stood in back of her and supported her weight.

"Easy does it," said her husband. Then she realized this was as hard on him as it was on her, and she willed her feet to hold her own weight.

"Is it Mike Cunningham?" Bill asked.

"We don't know for sure," said the lieutenant.

She stood teetering, looking steadfastly away from the body. "It's him, you know it is."

Trace's voice was stern. "You're really convinced of that, are you?"

Bill snapped at the policeman. "Of course, and so am I."

Trace raised both hands, as if quieting a crowd. "Okay, okay, don't get upset. We just wanted you to see the . . . situation as it now exists. Uh, Mrs. Eldridge, can you pull yourself together long enough to tell us if you see anything strange, anything foreign-looking, in the hole?"

Louise looked back down and tried not to shudder. Dully, she said, "The body's wrapped just like Hoffman's body was wrapped. This one is inclined, with the head lower than the feet. Now can I go somewhere and sit down?"

But Sam caught her arm and said in an excited voice, "Just so, Louise, just so! The head is down, and the feet are up. '*Zolstu voksn vi a di tsibele, mitn kap in elrerd un di fis aroyf*!' "

Lieutenant Trace gave him a polite look, the kind one gave to a person who was acting crazy. Perhaps he feared that their wide-eyed neighbor was having a breakdown. Louise knew he was wrong about that, for Sam was as well-adjusted a person as she'd ever met, composed and logical. He'd just come across something of extraordinary interest.

"Are you all right, Mr. Rosen?" said the lieutenant. "What is it you're trying to tell us?"

Sam said, "The person who did this was fulfilling an ancient Yiddish curse. '*Zolstu voksn vi a di tsibele, mitn kap in elrerd un di fis aroyf.*' "

"Which means?" asked Trace.

" 'May you grow like an onion, with your head in the ground and your feet in the air!' Actually, that's the mild translation. Literally, it's 'May you grow like an onion, with your head in *hell* and your feet in the air.' "

"Holy shit!" muttered Morton.

Mike Geraghty asked Sam, "So we think that's why this guy ended up in your onion patch, to fulfill a curse? You wouldn't know anyone who's familiar with that curse, would you?"

"Besides me, you mean?" Sam grinned widely. "Maybe you ought to add me to your list of suspects."

Still staring down at this extraordinary scene, Sam turned his attention to Louise. "Do you realize this is the literal carrying out of a curse that is centuries old? Now why the devil would someone do that?"

Morton's remark was barely audible, for he'd directed it at his colleague, Mike Geraghty. Unfortunately, the rest of them heard it too. "Maybe it's to throw us off the scent. Maybe it was someone who didn't like a guy who sued them for minor neighborhood offenses."

Lieutenant Trace came over to Morton and quietly said, "George, that remark wasn't called for." He turned back to Louise and Bill and Sam. "We want to search your house and also question your family, Mr. Eldridge. You, too, Mr. Rosen. Is it convenient for you all to come to the station?"

Bill retorted, "Not convenient at all, Lieutenant. I'm needed downtown. I'll have to make it fast if at all."

The lieutenant blinked his eyes, as if Bill had slapped him. Louise supposed he was rethinking the kind and compassionate manner he'd taken so much trouble to exhibit since he'd arrived at their house at the crack of dawn. The officer cleared his throat, then said, "I know your work is important, Mr. Eldridge. But so is mine. A murder has been committed here and, whether you like it or not, there's lots of *in situ* evidence tying your wife, or maybe even you, to the crime. Now we aren't going to be able to come up with better solutions if we don't have co-operation with people such as yourself. Get me?"

Bill looked over at him. Louise could tell her husband was completely frustrated, wanting to cooperate, on the one hand, because he wanted her off the suspect list, but being torn by the unusual demands from the State Department on the other. His response was silence. He didn't use words to answer the lieutenant, just curtly nodded his head in agreement.

29

In view of another body turning up, Dan Trace looked forward to a long afternoon and evening sitting in this small conference room and reinterviewing the principals related to the Peter Hoffman murder. What he had he wasn't sure of, but undoubtedly a murder related to the Peter Hoffman killing. A curl of pain went through his gut.

Was a serial killer of some kind at work in the Sylvan Valley neighborhood?

He hadn't liked Bill Eldridge's attitude at the house this morning. Mrs. Eldridge appeared stunned and out of it. According to the husband, there was no way his wife could have killed Mike Cunningham and buried him unless she did it after he fell asleep. It probably took more than an hour, maybe two, for one person to kill a man, wrap him in plastic and bury him in a garden filled with soft, deep soil. It took three men only fifteen minutes to unearth him.

Trace knew the murder had likely occurred somewhere after eleven. From nine to eleven, it wouldn't have been safe to commit the crime, for kids sometimes tramped through the woods near the Eldridge house. Bill Eldridge was asleep by then, and so were the rest of the neighbors. Everyone except the tipster.

He looked over the table at Mike Geraghty. Now there was a man who thought it incredible that the Eldridge woman could kill. Yet Mike, unfortunately, was blinded by his friendship with the Eldridges. Trace, too, thought Louise Eldridge was an unlikely candidate, but it was amazing how people could fool one.

Now that the Eldridge interviews were concluded, he was meeting with Mike and George Morton, comparing notes. "Let's talk about this Yiddish curse. Anybody believe that's what the murderer had in mind?"

Geraghty shrugged his big shoulders. "It could be significant, or it could be a fluke. The soil was real soft. Maybe the head got lower than the feet by accident, or because of the killer's general sloppiness."

"First of all, lots of people might know that curse,"said Trace. "There's Phyllis Hoffman, for instance. A small woman, but a small woman with a motive. It looks as if she's been left with only a small portion of her husband's wealth. And the person who engineered that unfortunate dispersal of Hoffman's wealth is now dead."

"She's also buff," said Geraghty. "We've found she spends a lot of time in a health club. She's stronger than we think." He leaned back heavily in his chair, forgetting it was stationary, and it groaned in protest. "On the other hand, Mrs. Hoffman is Jewish, and it's a pretty stupid murderer who broadcasts his or her ethnic background by fulfilling an ethnic curse. It's too darned obvious. Another one of our outlying targets of interest, Mort Swanson, is also Jewish. But I sure don't think a man that smart would do something that implicated himself."

Morton pulled himself up closer to the table, and Geraghty could see he was about to make a pronouncement. "Why go through all this mickey mouse when we have the murderess tagged already?"

"We do?" replied the lieutenant in a flat voice.

"Darn right, Lieutenant. Did you look at Louise Eldridge

this morning? She's a mess. She's lost weight, and she's
got the shakes. The woman looks guilty as hell. And she
doesn't go to work anymore, I've heard. They may even
have fired her. So how did all this develop? First, it's Peter
Hoffman bugging her, so she kills him. We have firsthand
testimony from at least four people that she set the guy up
by inviting him to her home."

Trace nodded. "That's right, we have to take that into
account. You mean she was going to kill him that night,
August fourth, I believe, but it didn't come off, so she
lured him back a week later to finish the deed?"

"Exactly," said Morton, his face happy and flushed as his
superior helped him make his case. "There's evidence ga-
lore—we all know that. Now we find Cunningham buried
in her yard. Here's a man she obviously hated."

Trace said, "How do you know she hated him?"

"Well, she deliberately smashed his garden statue,
didn't she? And she went to all the trouble to go to
downtown Washington to his office to rant and rave at
him."

Geraghty sliced his hand across the air. "Cut it for a
minute, George. That was Cunningham's take on those
events. He could have had it in for Mrs. Eldridge. Let's not
ignore another good candidate, Lee Downing. He was
swindled by Hoffman and Cunningham when he bought
Hoffman's arms business. We need to trace the movements
of both Mrs. Hoffman and Mr. Downing. And maybe Mort
Swanson as well."

Lieutenant Trace nodded agreement. "Especially since
I've just learned something that bolsters the theory that
Downing could be our man. Peter Hoffman was the one
who phoned the ethics hotline and dished the dirt on
Downing's industrial spying."

Geraghty said, spreading his hands wide. "There you
are, George. Just more reason to pin both murders on

him. A helluva lot more reason than to pin them on Mrs. Eldridge."

Dan Trace raised an admonishing finger. "Hold on, Mike. That's motive. But we have physical evidence pointing another way."

"And when we test the plastic on Cunningham's body, we'll have even more," said Morton. "We'll find Mrs. Eldridge's fingerprints again." He smiled triumphantly at Geraghty. "Evidence is evidence, Mike. She's the only one caught in the evidence net."

Trace stretched back in his chair. "Now why in the hell would someone like Louise Eldridge, who seems like a smart lady, kill two men and bury their bodies in her own yard? Doesn't make sense."

Geraghty said, "I agree. Especially after she's told us about those strange happenings at her house, the misplaced items in a cabinet, the pickax that nearly fell on her and the muddied tiles in the kitchen."

"Huh," scoffed Morton, "you gonna believe that? Those kinds of incidents are so easy to fake that it isn't worth talking about. She is a smart lady, I'll give you that. She figured no one would believe she'd do it again. I tell you, folks, she's our killer. She murdered Hoffman because he threatened her. She hated him. She polished off Cunningham because she thought he was on to her. He as much as told us that he had information that tied her to Hoffman's death. The guy got killed before he had a chance to tell us about it."

Geraghty shook his head. "Come on, George, the guy could just be blowin' smoke. He probably would have told any lie to get Louise Eldridge in trouble."

Morton scowled at his partner. "How do you know that? We ought to bring her in."

Dan Trace gave Morton a thoughtful look. "What you say makes some sense, George, but I still have to get over my disbelief."

At the phone's insistent ring, he said, "Excuse me. That will be the evidence technicians at the Eldridge house." Trace talked for a minute, then hung up. He looked at George Morton, then slowly turned his gaze to Mike Geraghty. "Speaking of evidence, they've found more."

After the police interrogations at the station, Bill and Louise arrived home to find the TV trucks and reporters circling Dogwood Court again. They reminded Louise of foraging jackals coming in after a kill, scrounging for the leavings from a crime scene now encircled with yellow tape. Ignoring reporter's shouted questions, she and her husband walked up the flagstone path. Louise carefully avoided looking at her onion patch, where police technicians still poked about. More technicians were in the house.

Bill hurried off to his office in the State Department, urging her to call the locksmith and also to contact Martha and Janie in Chicago, plus both sets of parents. He didn't want them to hear about a second body in the Eldridge garden through a news program.

Louise was sitting at the dining table and had just dialed up her mother. Elizabeth Payne said supportive things. "I feel positive, darling, that they'll soon find who did this. Your father and I believe you must just go about your business on the theory that this will all soon go away."

The remark made Louise's stomach pitch. Easy for her mother to say "go about your business." *People don't get it,* thought Louise. *I have only days, perhaps hours, before they come and throw me in jail!*

In the background, she could hear the sounds of the two police technicians searching the house. They were almost finished and had opened the door to the back bedroom that Martha used when she was home. After the girls left Wednesday morning, Louise had vacuumed and cleaned it to make way for the next guest, neatly closing the door behind her.

While she'd been able to hear the men's constant talking back and forth, now there was only silence. Had they left by the recreation room door?

Suddenly, one policeman appeared in the dining room, and she could see the man's eyes were bright with excitement. He said, "Ma'am, could you please come with us?"

She told her mother, "Mom, I'd better phone you back. I'm needed here right now." She followed the technician into the bedroom and immediately noticed the dirt on the carpeting at the base of an étagère, a three-shelved unit that held her most prized houseplants. He pointed to the hoya plant on the middle shelf, with its handsome fronds of shiny dark green leaves. It was filled with waxy pink blossoms, which occurred only seldom and were a cause of great pleasure. Any police technician looking for clues would have been led right to the plant, not because of those dramatic flowers, but because the plant's soil surface had been roughed up and the dirt spilled.

"Look what we've found in this plant," said the technician. Not far below the surface, she saw a small gleaming object. The technician took his pen and prodded the object until it was loosened further from the soil. It was a gold ring set with a big diamond.

Louise took in a deep breath and realized she'd been shafted again. She looked straight into the eyes of the policeman and said, "I've no doubt that this ring belonged to Mike Cunningham. Why else would someone have put it here?"

30

Louise's body felt heavy, too heavy for her bones to support in an upright position. For the moment, she had no further strength to know or care about what would happen to her next. She took the phone and went to the bedroom, collapsed on the bed and promptly fell asleep.

She didn't wake up until someone insistently rang the front doorbell. When she went to the door, she found only the locksmith. Why weren't the police here to lead her off in shackles? Surely the gold ring belonged to Mike Cunningham. With the help of a bloody sweatshirt and a "stolen" ring, Louise was neatly tied to the two murders. Why didn't they just come and get her?

She yawned heavily and decided to resume her normal activities until her time was up. First, she put a spare set of new keys the locksmith had given her into her favorite outside hiding place in case the family was stuck outside without them. Then there were Bill's parents to be concerned about. She went into the kitchen and made herself a cup of tea before she rang up Jean Eldridge. Her mother-in-law would need some warning that Louise might be headed for jail. While her father-in-law, Dick Eldridge, was solidly in Louise's corner, Jean had not always felt the same way. When she told Jean of the second body, it appeared to renew her old doubts about Louise. Louise parroted her own mother's optimistic sentiments that the cops eventually would quit buzzing around the Eldridge house and the press would quit talking about it on the evening news.

"Oh dear," said Jean in a condescending tone, "I can just imagine the headlines that are coming!" Louise could imagine them, too, something such as ANOTHER LETHAL "PLANT" IN TV TALK SHOW HOST'S GARDEN. Things would get even worse if the press learned about the way the body was buried and the possibility that it fulfilled a Yiddish curse.

"Oh, well," said Jean, "I've unfortunately come to expect things like this from you. Dick says it won't hurt Bill's career, but you know how I worry about that."

"Jean, you know I didn't murder anyone."

"I expect you didn't, dear. But you're involved somehow."

Changing the subject, Louise said, "I'm sure Martha's phoned you about the date for her and Jim's wedding."

"Yes," said Jean, "and we're looking forward to it." Louise waited for the "however" to follow. "However, it's too bad she didn't plan it further ahead. It took us by surprise. As it is, we're racking our brains trying to decide on a gift."

"They're registered, you know," said Louise.

"I know. Martha told me. However, they're not registered in the traditional places. I've never heard of 'REI.'"

A new wave of fatigue engulfed Louise. She was in no condition to talk to Jean. "I'll phone you later when I know more. Martha will give me some ideas of what they'd like best."

Next, she rang Martha's Chicago apartment, first getting her daughter's bubbly, optimistic message in the voice of a bride-to-be who was supremely happy. Just as Louise was about to pour out her story into the answering machine, Martha picked up.

"Swell," she said sarcastically, when she was told of the corpse in the vegetable patch and the discovery of Cunningham's pinkie ring. "Now someone's hiding things in houseplants. Ma, I think we'd better return home. You don't sound good. I can tell by the tone of your voice you're bummed out."

"I admit I'm bummed out, Martha," she said, "but there's nothing you or Janie could do if you rushed back here."

Even over the long-distance line, Louise could hear her older daughter's impatient sigh. "How are you spending your time? Staying home, I hope, with your doors locked with those new locks. Did it ever occur to you or Dad that you're in grave danger? Someone's been in your house, doing mischief and planting evidence."

"He hasn't heard about the ring yet. Hearing about it will just make it worse. He doesn't want me to be alone, but what am I supposed to do, hire a companion?"

"No," said Martha, "just call in some favors from your friends Nora and Mary. Maybe Sarah Swanson, too. They could take turns coming over and keeping you company while Dad labors late at the State Department. Well, maybe not Sarah, on account of her hubby."

"I think it's silly to suspect Mort Swanson."

"Ma, don't rule anyone out. Gee, I wish I were there." Her voice held a wondrous quality.

"I know what you're thinking, Martha. You're just curious, especially since Sam brought up the Yiddish curse hypothesis. Do you really think the killer was playing that out when he buried Cunningham? I wonder if it wasn't just chance."

"Depends," said Martha. "How low was the head in comparison to the feet?"

Louise flinched. The image was fresh in her mind: the

stiff body, its human features barely disguised by the see-through plastic tarpaulin. She'd recognized her neighbor's face jammed against the smooth material and could even see that his mouth and eyes were open as if in shock. She took in some quick breaths as a new thought came to her. "I just realized, Martha, the murderer's used up two of my three large tarps. Do you suppose his work is at an end or will he try to come back and use the third on another body?"

"Ma, that's crazy talk. Please don't lose it. I'm counting on you to be the serene mother of the bride in just six weeks. Calm down and stop letting your mind wander like that. Answer my question seriously. How low was the head? How high were the feet?"

"The, uh, plastic package was arranged so that the head was down a couple of feet, and located at the base of the trench that Sam and I dug. The feet, on the other hand, were just barely covered. The feet were definitely what you would call 'up.' "

"Cool," said Martha. "Well, I don't mean to say I enjoy it, but someone did that on purpose. The person didn't have to be Jewish, though. Lots of people know about those curses. I always liked the one, 'May you catch cholera.' But why would a Jewish killer plant Jewish clues?"

"That's the question," said Louise.

"I want you to promise you'll phone us every day. Or would you rather that Janie or I phone you?"

"One way or the other, Martha, we'll stay in touch. Where did you say Janie's gone off to?"

"She's out shopping for wedding clothes. We still haven't found anything. She says she's better off shopping without me. I'm helping Jim with the campaign, and I'm due at a rally in just a few minutes. You take care. I'm really sorry you have to go through all this. And especially sorry, of course, that you lost your onion crop."

"Don't be smart, Martha."

"Just trying to get a laugh out of you."

Louise stared at the beige walls of the Mount Vernon police station and tried to put her mind somewhere else. Outside on Route One, she could hear a constant surge of traffic moving in and out of the capital and wondered what normal people were doing tonight. Eating out? Shopping for mattresses? Going to the theater? Visiting relatives? Bill was busy at work at the State Department, laboring hard under his green-shaded lamp or, more likely, sitting in last-minute meetings to plan the Vienna trip. She didn't want to summon him here for the second police interrogation of the day and had arranged that he come in Saturday morning for questioning. He probably was still enraged over the one that occurred this morning.

No, she'd only call Bill if they arrested her for murder.

"So, Mrs. Eldridge," said George Morton, "how do you think that gold ring got inside your house?"

"I'm sure someone planted it there, Detective Morton, the same person who rearranged my antique collection, relocated my pickax and messed up my kitchen tiles." There was little emotion in her voice, for she had little emotion left inside her.

"Have you ever seen that gold ring before?" asked Lieutenant Trace. "I hear you immediately identified it."

"Mike Cunningham wore it every time I saw him. Which, I should add, wasn't that many times. You have to understand that I barely knew the man."

George Morton sat forward in his chair. "Just enough to dislike him a lot, right?"

She looked at the eager detective and pondered whether to tell him the absolute truth. She decided she would. After all, this was the age of opinionated women speaking their mind. "Right, I disliked him intensely. He wasn't my idea of a great human being."

Morton nodded, as if he'd extracted the information through torture. "And are we to believe all that stuff about a house intruder without any corroboration?"

Louise shrugged. "Believe it or not, Detective Morton, but it's true. But they'll never intrude again, because we've changed the locks." She turned to Lieutenant Trace. "Are you going to arrest me? If so, I hope you do it quickly, because I'm exhausted and I know the county jail is in Fairfax City. That's a trip of a dozen miles or so. I'll have to warn Bill. Then there will be the fingerprinting, of course, and the paperwork. With all the red tape, I won't get to sleep in a cell until probably midnight."

Trace looked at her oddly. "Yes, ma'am. But I don't think we'll arrest you tonight. In fact, you're free to go home. The usual caveats apply, Mrs. Eldridge. Don't leave the area, and please don't try to intervene in any way in our investigation."

She exhaled a deep breath. "Lieutenant Trace, I wouldn't think of doing those things."

Mike Geraghty and the other policemen stood up. "Come on, Louise," said Geraghty, " I'm givin' you a ride home."

As she went by George Morton, he stared at her, his mouth in a tight line. She felt like giving him a smile, but there was no sense tempting fate. Instead, she nodded formally as she passed.

The Coffee Pub wasn't Charlie Hurd's idea, but Hilde told him that she had to be up early, and nine o'clock was too late to start out for dinner in a restaurant in Washington.

He looked over the wooden table at her, trying to be more objective than in the past with this girl. It wasn't easy, since she looked so damned good to him. "Admit it, Hilde," he grumped at her, "you had the hots for this guy Cunningham."

The accusation didn't appear to bother her. Her gaze didn't flinch, and she had a quick answer. "You think because I had a tennis game with Mike Cunningham, a foursome, and that I went over to his house to see his photography, that I was in love with him? Charlie, you're being—what is the best word?—naive."

He blew out a breath. "All right, damnit, maybe you can say I'm jealous and for no good reason. You sure don't look bent out of shape by Cunningham's death."

Quietly, she said, "All deaths are sad. But Mike was no more than an older friend. A sort of counselor. Charlie, he was giving me advice on what to do next with my career—whether to stay in America or go back home and try to obtain a teaching position."

"What would you teach?"

"Germanic studies. Or perhaps European cultural history."

Charlie scratched his head. "Okay, I'll accept that. He was a hotshot lawyer. He had a very heavy rep in the District. But what's so interesting about what happened to him is the curse. Have you heard about the curse?"

"I heard about it this afternoon when I walked over to Dogwood Court. Everyone was talking about it. I have heard that curse, or perhaps I read it. There's a book—"

Charlie leaned forward. "The book of Yiddish curses. Of course you'd know about that. Do you think that makes our suspect a Jew? That means we'd have Phyllis Hoffman, Sam Rosen and Mort Swanson, of course." He looked for a reaction from Hilde, but again she was totally cool.

"Mr. Swanson? I couldn't believe that, Charlie. He is so kind, so good." Her gaze moved to somewhere in the middle distance. "And yet I know he's somewhat . . . suspicious. He does spend time with the widow."

"You mean Phyllis?"

She nodded her head. "But I could hardly think of him and Phyllis doing this terrible thing."

"Hell, I could." He mentally filed the fact that Hilde had seen Mort and Phyllis Hoffman together. And yet he was having feelings of remorse throwing Swanson's name into the suspect pile. "I know you're beginning to think of him as a father figure, but we can't totally ignore him. We need to be objective and consider motive. As yet, neither Sam Rosen or Mort Swanson appears to have one, so that leaves old Phyllis. But she doesn't look like the type of woman who cares a rat's ass about Yiddish curses. On the other hand, if this were a team effort between Phyllis Hoffman and the more erudite Mort Swanson, then you could understand . . ." His mind wandered for a minute. "I mustn't forget Downing," he muttered, almost to himself. "Downing makes sense."

"Downing?" repeated Hilde.

"Yes, he had a perfect motive for both murders."

Their meals had arrived. Charlie picked up his fork, but before he started eating, he looked over at Hilde and said, "It's all about motive. Without motive, there's no crime." He reached over and took her hand. "Now, I'd consider Sam Rosen on account of he's savvy and the kind of guy who'd catch the irony of burying someone in an onion patch. But he has no more motive than you do. But people like Lee Downing, Phyllis Hoffman and, forgive me, Mort Swanson, are the ones that I have to look into more thoroughly. Use all my resources, the Internet, local contacts, court and police buddies. In all cases, the question is, 'Where is this person coming from, and where has he been?' " He laughed. "It has sort of the same cadence, doesn't it, of that famous question about Richard Nixon from the Watergate hearings, which I doubt you know much about: 'What did he know, and when did he know it?' "

She pulled her hand away and narrowed her eyes as if she were analyzing his words. "Charlie, you are a very smart man, smarter than I am." She stopped, and her face colored.

"Huh," he said, "what were you going to say? I'm smarter than you thought at first?"

"Charlie, let me finish—"

"Naw, that's what you meant, and it's not very flattering. What did you think at first, that I was a dunce?" Then he caught himself. What was he doing getting angry at a gorgeous woman like this, a woman a guy didn't meet but once in a lifetime? Hurriedly, he said, "But since you no longer have Mike Cunningham to admire, hell, I'll be happy to take his place."

She gave him one of those devastating smiles. "I do admire you, Charlie, more and more each day. You are an excellent reporter and investigator and a fine human being. Promise me you'll tell me everything that you find out. In fact"—she looked at the slim gold watch on her wrist—"Sarah wants me to finish hundreds of those cat figures by a deadline, and that is why I was going to work tonight. But if you want me to do research with you tonight, I could postpone my work and come."

"Hilde," he said, reaching over and taking her hand, "it's like asking me, 'Am I human?' Of course I'd like you to come with me."

After an hour or so of sitting side by side in his apartment and poring over computer searches with this girl, who knew what might happen?

31

It wasn't until they'd had their second cup of morning coffee that Louise told Bill about the gold ring and her second police interrogation of the day.

"Goddammit," he said, "no wonder you look shot." He went to the kitchen and grabbed for the phone to call Lieutenant Dan Trace. Leaning against the kitchen counter as the call was put through, he impatiently tapped on the granite surface, trying to frame words that would adequately express his outrage.

Though it was only eight, the man in charge of the double murder investigation was in his office. When Bill made his case, Trace sounded abashed. "I know how you must feel, Mr. Eldridge."

"I don't think you do," replied Bill. "If you'd followed up on information we gave you about an intruder in our house, you'd know that the ring was just more fun and games on the part of that trespasser. And those include a life-threatening trick of setting a twenty-pound tool over the toolshed entrance so that it was bound to fall on the person who opened the toolshed door. It was only luck that it missed hitting Louise in the head. There's no doubt in my mind, and there should be none in yours, Lieutenant Trace, that our trespasser is your killer." He found himself breathing fast and tried to quiet his voice, even though he felt like yelling at the bastard on the other end of the phone line.

Trace hurriedly added, "We told you that we were hindered in tracking down the technician who handled the toolshed. He'd already worked an overtime weekend on the case, and then he took off for a canoeing vacation with some buddies at the Boundary Waters. Even his wife doesn't have a cell phone number for him. The guy claimed he needed to get 'all the way away.' "

Bill groaned with disgust. "Isn't that nice for him. Meanwhile, the one who's suffered for this is my wife. She's mistrusted and disbelieved by your local detective, George Morton, who acts at every moment as if she's going to be summarily arrested for murder."

Lieutenant Trace cleared his throat in the background. "In view of all this, Mr. Eldridge, there's no deadline hanging over Mrs. Eldridge's head. But don't forget, there's still a lot of evidence against her."

"Find the answer to the trespasser in our house and you'll find your murderer," snapped Bill. "Quit misdirecting your efforts, Lieutenant. I'm about ready to file charges against the Sheriff's Department."

"Uh, I wouldn't do that, Mr. Eldridge," said the lieutenant. "Not until we get this sorted out."

"As far as I'm concerned, you don't have much time left," warned Bill, and hung up. It was an empty kind of threat. What could he do to get the police off his wife's back? But it made him feel a little better.

After his angry conversation with Lieutenant Trace, Bill had a hard time leaving for work. But the pressures there were enormous.

Normally when he left for the office, Louise was ready

and eager to get into her own world and her own work. Today, she shuffled about the house in her gown and robe, her hair messy, her face unwashed. And why not? She had nowhere to go and nothing to look forward to except to peek at evidence technicians who might come around and look at the area where the second body had been buried or perhaps plead with her for a second search of the house.

"Bill, take care." Her voice sounded hollow.

He turned, his brow knit with worry lines. "You're the one who has to be careful, Louise. Remember what you promised. You won't put yourself in danger, and you'll try to stay in the company of friends. Invite Nora over. Or Mary."

"I will." When he left, the absolute quiet of the house pressed on her. Looking out the tall windows into the woods, she could see only gray. A storm was on the way. She went to the living room couch and picked up the morning paper, experiencing the final straw—the tremble had returned to her hands.

She plopped unceremoniously onto the couch and threw the paper aside. No matter what she'd told Bill, she had to get out of this house. She would go back to the yoga studio and sign up for more classes. Then she'd drive to WTBA-TV and barge her way into the studio if necessary. There, surely, she would be among friends. Her producer just couldn't kiss her off this way, not without Louise putting up a fight. At the very least, even if her co-host John Bachelder was there busily usurping her job, she could provide, as Marty so tactfully put it, "input" on those upcoming garden shows.

It took a half hour to dress up and put enough makeup on her gaunt face for someone to guess she was a syndicated TV host. She grabbed the numerous gardening notes that she'd been collecting for weeks and hurried off to the studio.

Marty Corbin tolerated her for an hour. Then her buff, dark-haired producer, the picture of good health himself, told her, "Go home, Lou. You've come back too soon. I told you that John would handle the next two programs. And when you do come back, I hope to see that you've gained a few pounds." A big, friendly, indicting smile. "You look scrawny. We know the camera adds pounds, but not that many."

She'd driven home and climbed into bed for a long nap.

The phone awoke her at four. "Honey," said Bill, "I don't know how I can get out of this late meeting. Damn but I'm frustrated!"

"Bill, take it easy. What's so new about your working late?"

"I feel as if I'm letting you down."

"It's all right, I know how busy you are. They want you to go overseas right away, don't they?"

"Yes, but I'm resisting. It's bad enough that I can't be with you after what's happened. I'd like to be there with you."

"Don't worry. I'll phone Nora, and she'll either come over here, or else I'll go to her place."

"That makes me feel better. And just so you won't feel so hopeless about all this, I have a little project for you. . . ."

Ron Radebaugh strolled along the edge of the patio, inspecting Louise's plants, as she walked by his side to answer questions. "Now why is this yellow peony in bloom in late August instead of May?" he asked her. At the patio table, Mary Mougey was setting out five place settings, while her husband, Richard, poured wine. In Louise's kitchen, Nora was making a salad. From a far distance they could hear thunder roll.

"It's a tree peony," she told Ron. "It's the kind that re-blooms in late summer."

He nodded his approval and moved on to the next group of plants, then turned to her again. "And what's this?"

"*Cimicifuga purpurea.* Nicknamed 'snakeroot.' Do you like it? I just divided it and will happily give you a clump."

"Nora and I would love a clump." He stole a look at her. "Are you also dividing those dynamite daylilies?" he asked, pointing to an array of rose-colored flowers with deep maroon throats.

"Ron, I'll happily give you some of those, too."

He grinned down at her. "I don't come to visit your garden often enough." Looking into this gray-haired man's rugged face and gentle brown eyes, Louise wondered why Nora had ever been tempted to stray from their happy home.

Just then Nora came out on the patio with a big black bowl. "Here's the salad. Time to eat!"

Her neighbors, laden with carryout, had made their friendly invasion of Louise's place as soon as they discovered that Bill was delayed at the office and she was alone. She was hardly dressed for company. Because she'd needed solace after her mortifying visit to the TV station, she had changed into her oldest gardening clothes. In these clothes, she could be her real self, just a woman who loved family and gardening.

Richard took a ceremonial taste of the white wine in his glass, closed his eyes and smiled. "Friends, I think you'll like this one from our cellar. A nice little 2002 Greco di Tufo, from the Campagna region." Cellar was a bit of a stretch, thought Louise, since like many Sylvan Valley residents, Richard and Mary's house was on a concrete slab. The modest wine cellar was part of a kitchen addition on the first floor.

"Pretty high-class wine to accompany Chinese carry-out," said Ron, serving himself some moo shu pork from among the white cartons on the table.

Another thunder roll sounded, this one closer. "Are you sure we don't want to move inside?" Louise asked the others, looking up at the roiling clouds forming above the tall trees. "The storm's coming."

"We always prefer sitting amidst your flowers," said Mary. "Let's not move in until we have to."

As they ate dinner, they talked about other things, about the Radebaugh's planned vacation and Richard's second thoughts about quitting his job. It was not until they were finished that Ron asked, "Anything new, Louise, from the police? I hear they were poring over your property again today."

Nora tossed her head in what seemed like a futile gesture. "Let's not talk about murders this evening. I find it very debilitating."

Mary Mougey laughed. "My dear, what else is there?"

"Yes," said Richard, nodding his long face. "It's all the neighborhood will be able to think about until they take that yellow police tape down. Later, maybe we can have a party to celebrate the fact that a killer is no longer loose in the neighborhood." He slyly added, "Though our numbers will be a bit down, now that Cunningham's among the deceased—"

His wife put a small rebuking hand on his arm. "Richard."

Nora said, "Murder and mayhem isn't 'all there is.' " She held up a small volume she'd brought with her. Her gray eyes widened hopefully. "I could read you a poem. This is Billy Collins's latest." The others looked at her without responding, and their poet friend's shoulders slumped in discouragement. "He once was poet laureate."

"Sure, darling, do read us one," said Ron, reaching over and caressing his wife's arm.

Nora shook her head. "No, though the poems are charming and thought-provoking." She laid the book on the table. "I'll leave it here for Louise to enjoy later. I think maybe it's better for us to talk about what's happened."

Louise looked gratefully at her friend. "I could use your help. You've heard about how the police found Mike Cunningham's ring in our house. I could be arrested any time now."

Ron quietly asked, "Since the ring was in your house, why wouldn't they suspect Bill just as well as you?"

"Because I'm already a suspect in Peter's murder, since they found my bloody sweatshirt in his grave. Because I am supposed to have a motive. And because I allegedly had the opportunity to kill both of these men."

"Ridiculous!" cried Mary.

"Bill knows I'm feeling desperate," continued Louise, "so he suggested that I write down everything I can remember about that party on August fourth, and anything that happened afterward. He thinks I might recall something important."

"For one thing, Peter dreamed up a phony conversation with you that night," said Mary, recounting it almost sentence by sentence. "And finally he said, 'Of course, Louise, I'd love to talk to you . . .' He was just acting."

"What amazed me," said Ron, "was that the police didn't slap the guy in jail for going over to your house and practically assaulting you."

Louise said, "That's because George Morton believed his story. And he had corroborating witnesses: Sam Rosen, Greg Archer and even Mort Swanson. Hoffman was expert at twisting reality."

"It kept him from landing in jail for assault," said Ron.

"He said something extraordinary to Hilde Brunner that night, too," said Mary. "I remember it. He said"—

Mary's voice now became low and intimate.—" 'My dear girl, you are like a dream.' "

The others laughed at her imitation of a lothario. Louise recalled that remark, too, for though she was ashamed of it now, she'd wished her husband said things like that to her.

Nora said, "It was rather banal, don't you think?"

Richard laughed. "Men dream up those remarks and then practice them in front of the mirror before they deliver them."

"I also recall he likened her to a Botticelli," said Nora. "Or was it Titian?"

Mary, who was fanning herself now, said, "It's because Hilde is a dream with that rosy hair and coloring and lovely figure. Peter was always bowled over by every pretty woman who crossed his path."

Louise said, "The way he said it sounded odd."

"I agree, Louise," said Mary, "but I'm really impatient with our police. Why should we have to sit here and deconstruct everything said at a neighborhood party to try to save the reputation and future of an honest woman like you? Surely with all their manpower, they can find the person who did these ghastly things. There must have been a dozen police milling around your yard yesterday and today."

Nora added, "And especially with all the information that Bill has dug up for them." Nora had always admired Bill, sometimes to the point where it was uncomfortable for Louise, back before she knew Nora's loyalty as a friend superseded any predatory thoughts she might have about her husband. "He's so smart," she told the others. "Louise tells me it's he who led the police to uncover the murky business deals of Lee Downing."

Louise filled them in on the details, after which Richard said, "Everything points to Downing. No question."

"Martha played tennis with him," recalled Louise. "She

thought he was awfully tough. Do you remember him saying anything that might be useful?"

Her friends shook their heads. Ron leaned back in his
chair. "I read him as a fairly ruthless entrepreneur, not
much into talk, just into making those quarterly results
meet market expectations." He cocked an eyebrow. "I con-
clude from what you said that he has plenty of trouble
now with the SEC."

"How about Mike Cunningham?" persisted Louise.
"Did he leave us with any hints? Personally, I can't remember one meaningful thing he ever said to me, though he
did divulge a few details about the Hoffman Arms sale."

Nora sniffed and said, "I remember nothing but sexual
innuendos."

Mary lowered her eyes. "I don't like to speak ill of the
dead, but the man was horrible."

The silence that followed her statement indicated the
others' agreement.

A few raindrops fell on them. Louise saw her guests wor-
riedly looking at the lowering sky. "You need to go home
before the storm breaks," she told them.

Ron frowned and looked at her. "But Louise, have we
helped you at all?"

"I honestly don't know," she replied.

By the time they'd cleared the table and cleaned up the
few dishes, the winds had risen and the tall windows of the
house hummed with the vibration. "Let me help you close
the drapes," said Nora, stepping over and pulling one of
the cords. "This is the kind of storm that breaks double-
paned windows."

Louise bade her friends good-bye and said she might
come over later. "I have new locks, though, and they
make me feel quite safe. Maybe I'll stay home and read
Billy Collins." They hurried away, and Louise threw the
bolt on the front door and went to the family room and

closed the drapes. She told herself that now she should settle down with the poetry book. But she was too unsettled. She wondered if she would ever relax again.

Realizing she'd forgotten to lock the outside garden toolshed, she opened the curtains and the door and hastened across the patio to do so, then hurried back into the house.

Again her thoughts went back to the murders. She and her friends had gone over that infamous August fourth party. What had they forgotten?

One thing was obvious: almost everything Peter Hoffman did and said while he was at the party was calculated ahead of time. It was theater. The only unprogrammed moment now stood out clearly in Louise's mind. He'd expressed amazement at the sight of Hilde Brunner, almost as if he recognized her.

Why would he recognize Hilde?

She wished Martha and Janie were still here so that they could talk this over. Taking a glance at her watch, she decided to phone her daughters. She was doubtful she'd catch them, since it was eight o'clock in the Windy City, and Louise couldn't picture the young people staying home in Martha's apartment at eight o'clock on a nice summer night.

32

L ouise felt as if she'd caught a lifeline when her call was answered.

"We're eating a pizza from Old Chicago and watching a reality show," said Janie. "Last night, Ma, we went to Andy's Lounge. I loved it. A jazz place, you know—really old Chicago at its best with Billy Goat Lounge just down the street. I tripped over a rip in the carpeting at the club, so my ankle's in an Ace bandage. But the music was worth it."

"You sound wonderful, Janie. Um, have you found Martha a wedding dress?"

"I think so, Ma," said Janie. "I've certainly tried. I've been out shopping by myself every day since we got here. Today, I limped out and shopped and put another dress on hold. I think it's the one. The busy bride-to-be has to get herself over to the store and try it on. But you're the person we're worrying about. How are you? Have the cops found the killer?"

Should she tell her daughter the truth, that her hands were shaking again, that she was losing weight and being criticized for it by her producer, that she was essentially falling apart? "They haven't found the killer. But I'm doing pretty well in spite of that. So you're having fun."

"Actually, Ma, it's the first time I've been treated like a grown-up by Martha in my whole life. She's always been a grown-up, while I have always been the kid. And Jim Daley, why, you'd think I was just a friend instead of Martha's little sister."

"That's wonderful. Janie, I need to talk to your sister for a minute to get some information about . . . well, about Elsebeth."

"Elsebeth?" said Janie in surprise. "Sure. I'll put her on in a minute, but first, I can only warn you—take a gun."

"What are you talking about?"

"I know you, Ma. I can tell by your tone of voice that you'll be out in the neighborhood poking around again. And we're not there to stop you. Just take a weapon if you go somewhere, because I have a feeling in my gut that the murderer lives in the neighborhood. Do you promise?"

"I promise."

"Now I'll put Martha on."

"Ma, how's it going?" asked Martha.

"At your father's suggestion, I've been doing a lot of thinking. God knows I don't dare do anything else or the police will descend on me. But I recalled some odd remarks made by Peter Hoffman the night of that party. There was one in particular. It was about Hilde."

"About Hilde? I thought Hoffman didn't know her."

"He didn't."

"What did he say to her?"

"It wasn't what he said so much as the fact that he seemed to recognize her. And then I remember another incident about Hilde. She and Elsebeth argued over language."

"Ma, it didn't amount to anything."

"Elsebeth is the most amiable woman in the world. If she was annoyed, there must have been a reason."

"Believe me," said Martha, "it was trivial. The Swiss and

the Germans and the Austrians all have their own way of
using the Germanic language. This was just a little argument, not even an argument, about the word for 'salad
greens.' I didn't think it was important."

"You didn't?"

"Not then. But why don't you call Elsebeth? We never
had a chance to talk about Hilde. She probably could tell
you more about why she disapproved of her. You're not
thinking—"

"I'm not thinking anything yet, Martha. As a matter of
fact, I'm just sitting here alone as a storm breaks overhead, grasping at straws."

"Elsebeth, it's Louise Eldridge."

"Oh, Louise. I'm sorry to hear about this latest horrible
discovery in your yard. It was all over the news. Are you all
right? Do you need my help there?"

"Not right now, but thanks for the offer. I've called
about a small thing that's bothering me. I just talked with
Martha, and she suggested I phone you and see if you
could straighten it out. It's about that young woman you
met last Monday when she came over for lunch."

"Yes. Hilde. The Swiss girl who's Martha's friend."

"Hilde's not really her friend," said Louise. "She'd just
barely met her. She's here for the summer and lives in the
neighborhood."

"Oh. If I'd known they weren't close, I might have said
something to your daughter that day."

"Did you think there was anything strange about Hilde?
Martha told me you didn't seem to like her."

"Oh, I didn't dislike her, but I certainly disapproved of
her. She isn't who she says she is."

"She's not?"

"She's certainly not Swiss."

"Are you sure?"

Elsebeth made some chuckling noises. "I could tell at once. She doesn't have that singsongy way of talking that the Swiss have. And the salad. She insisted on using the German word '*Vogerlsalat*,' when any Swiss would have called it '*Nüsslisalat*.' But I didn't quarrel with that. It was when I said '*Servus*.' That's a German greeting for both 'hello' and 'good-bye.' A Swiss would have answered me with '*Ciao*.' Most people know that as an Italian greeting, but the Swiss use it too. Sometimes they spell it the German way—T, s, c, h, a, u—'*Tschau*.' "

"So she's German."

"Well, no. I would say with her accent that she's Austrian."

Louise felt as if someone had hit her in the solar plexus. Kristina Weeren was also Austrian.

Now she knew why Peter Hoffman had thought Hilde was "like a dream."

Hilde was not like a dream but more like a nightmare.

"Elsebeth, thank you."

"*Tschau*, Louise."

"*Tschau*."

It was impossible to wait, impossible to stay home when she thought she now knew the truth. If only she had someone to go with her she would feel much better. Where was Charlie Hurd, for instance, when she could use him? She looked at the reporter's number posted on the refrigerator. His phone rang, but Charlie didn't answer. It was useless to leave a message.

She thought about her husband's warnings and Janie's. She knew that if she were to go out, she needed a weapon in case the strange scenario she suspected turned out to be true. Standing arms akimbo in the living room, she considered getting Bill's Beretta out of its locked box in the bedroom closet. But guns had always repelled her, and she doubted she'd shoot very straight. She had other perfectly good modes of defense.

Unlocking the series of locked doors as she went, she retrieved her secateurs from the toolshed, noting that the rain was now beginning to fall in large sheets. Ducking back into the house, she thrust the sharp tool and her telephone into the pocket of her Japanese gardening pants. She was now ready for anything.

33

Louise got out of her car just as a huge lightning bolt tore the sky, followed by a thunderclap that made her step back in fright. Only a fool, she thought, would go out in a storm like this one unless she had a mission. And she did. She pulled the hood of her rain poncho closer around her face and tied the string fastening under her chin. The top half of her was dry, though the bottoms of her old gardening pants were soaked the minute she left the car. She ran up the driveway.

Then she saw the fire. She'd heard of it, but had never seen it before. Saint Elmo's fire was so spectacular that she had to stop and watch, even though rain streamed down her face and lightning threatened to bolt her to the ground. Like a light show, flame-like pulses of static electricity danced back and forth along the wide roof of the Swanson house.

The thunder and rain masked the sound of the door opening, but suddenly she saw Hilde standing in the studio entrance. She glanced quickly at Louise and then at the atmospheric marvel occurring above them on the rim of the roof.

"Hurry! Come in!" Hilde cried.

Louise was happy to get away from this alarming display of nature. She hurried into the studio, but immediately was on guard, knowing that it could be as perilous inside as it was outside in the storm. Suddenly, her protective rain poncho became like a prison, and she felt the sweat forming in her armpits.

Looking over at Hilde, she saw that the young woman appeared off-balance, and Louise knew why. The time was right to knock her further off her composed center.

"*Servus*, Hilde."

"*Servus*," repeated the young woman reflexively. She gave Louise a startled look. "What are you doing, practicing your German?"

"No, my Swiss-German. Except you don't necessarily know the difference, do you, not being Swiss, or you would have been more apt to respond with '*Tschau*.'"

Hilde stood near to her, looking strong and unyielding. Only her eyes betrayed her nerves. "How clever you must think you are."

"Elsebeth assured me you were definitely not Swiss," said Louise. "Your accent and your usage indicate you're Austrian."

Hilde sighed in aggravation. "It's what I would expect of a woman like that."

"How did you manage this change in identification?" asked Louise, meanwhile looking furtively about for avenues of escape.

"It was so easy," exclaimed Hilde. "A kind friend who asked few questions lent me her passport and identification. That is why only the annoying Charlie Hurd found out. He searched through all the records of the trial and didn't find anything. But when he talked to a court employee, he discovered that Margit *Hilde* Weeren represented Kristina Weeren's family at Hoffman's trial. To make sure, he ransacked my purse and saw the passport photo. He realized it wasn't me. And then you—you and your trifling concerns about how I was using the language."

"You're Kristina's sister. That's what I finally guessed. I didn't know Charlie suspected you, too." Louise wished Charlie was with her right now. As she spoke, she continued to measure her situation. She wanted to put some distance between herself and Hilde, but she didn't want to be trapped in this big room. Hilde blocked the nearby exit door. Louise sauntered a few steps down the studio aisle, noting tables full of eight-inch-high clay cat figures. She tried to remember how many exits there were in this workshop. She could see only two—the one she'd entered through, and a connecting door to the main house thirty feet from where she stood.

But she was safe, wasn't she, with her cell phone and her secateurs in her pocket?

Louise turned back and confronted the young woman. "So what's to be done now, Hilde? Did you suspect I was coming over here tonight?"

Hilde smiled and looked down at something in the aisle behind her. Louise's breath caught in her throat when she heard a long moan of pain. "Charlie came before you," she said.

The reporter sounded awful, as if he were dying. Louise said to Hilde, "It would be best for you if we could help Charlie. I've told people I was coming here, and they'll be looking for me." She could have kicked herself for not doing exactly that.

"Why would I help Charlie?" said the Austrian woman, her voice calm and cold. "As you said, I'm out for vengeance. Peter Hoffman killed and dismembered my sister. Since then, both of my parents have died, my father by his own hand, my mother from grief and depression. And nothing much was done to that *Ungeheuer*, Hoffman. So I came to the States to set things right. Once I was here, it was easy to arrange a job and to meet him, almost the minute he was freed from the mental hospital."

"Why did you bury him in my garden?"

"I wanted to get revenge on everyone who caused or benefited from my sister's suffering." Tears flowed down the young woman's cheeks. Louise now knew Kristina's pain was as fresh to Hilde as when she'd first heard of it. "I was outraged at the way you testified at Peter's trial. Everything you said helped the lawyers justify that he was crazy."

"No," cried Louise, "you couldn't think that."

Hilde's face reddened with anger. "But I do think that. I remember your words. You told how he broke into your writing place and attacked you: 'He was wearing a white parka. He was totally out of control, and looked like a huge enraged animal as he came after me.' What did you think the jury would do once you'd said that?"

"But Peter Hoffman was acting quite mad when he attacked me in my own house. Oh, God, Hilde, I only tried to tell the truth."

"You told it too well," said Hilde. "And you profited from Kristina's death. You wouldn't be a TV personality today if you hadn't been involved with Peter Hoffman."

Louise realized that Hilde was right. She'd endured her share of guilt feelings over that matter in the past. The brief celebrity she'd experienced at the time of Kristina's murder was the primary reason a TV producer had plucked her out of her housewifely anonymity and made her into a garden show host. "But you should also remember that I'm the one who identified Peter Hoffman as the killer."

"But you profited. I was going to get you one way or another, with the pickax"—she smiled coldly—"or the planted clues. If I didn't succeed in getting you arrested as the killer, I was going to make you my next victim."

"Kill me, too?" This bald admission somehow made Louise feel calmer. Now she knew just how cold-blooded this young woman was.

"Yes. It was annoying when the police didn't charge you. I smeared Peter's blood on that sweatshirt and that garden tool for nothing. Then I was sure they would act once they found Mike's gold ring in your house. But they didn't even do it then. What is the matter with those police?"

Louise fleetingly pictured Mike Geraghty. Had he pleaded with Dan Trace to delay action on Louise? "If they'd jailed me, you'd have been home free. How did you get in the house?"

"So easy," mocked Hilde. "A woman who is so childish that she keeps her spare door keys in an artificial rock shouldn't feel secure from burglars. It was so enjoyable to see the effect my little tricks had on you."

"The sympathetic, helpful young neighbor."

"Indeed. The observant young neighbor. I knew your family's every move."

"But there's no way you could have gotten away with a third killing." Hilde tossed her head in an arrogant gesture. Louise realized the young woman still felt she had control over the situation and wondered how she could use this overconfidence to her own advantage.

"Don't be so sure. I'd planned for you to commit suicide." She gave Louise a malicious smile. "Everybody agrees you're a 'wreck,' so why wouldn't they believe you'd take your own life? I even have the pills for it. It's an assortment of codeine products that you left in your medicine cabinet. I would have combined them with others I had on hand, and that would have been the perfect ending. But your unexpected arrival has ruined that

plan. Now I will have to leave both you and Charlie behind."

Louise looked around in desperation, knowing this
woman meant what she said. Without batting an eye, she
would kill them both. Louise needed to buy time. Maybe
the Swansons would arrive back home and interrupt this
grim standoff, though she hated the thought of drawing
friends into the web of this killer.

A little flattery was in order. "You're very clever, Hilde.
Tell me more about how you did all this."

"When I was told by authorities that Peter Hoffman had
concluded his hospital stay after four short years, I applied
through the Foreign Artists' Association for an internship
as Sarah's apprentice. I spent my leisure time learning
about the neighborhood and watching your frenzied gardening habits. Finding out from Sam about your electric
'cartita' to carry plants around. Discovering from him that
you never locked your toolshed. While the Eldridge family
was away, I had no trouble tempting Peter into the com-
mon woods in back of your house. I placed your edging
tool conveniently near where I wanted to attack him.
When I'd hit him once, he fell down but was not uncon-
scious, and I told him how good it felt to attack him the
way he'd attacked my sister. Then I beat his head until he
died."

"You found the cart at Sam's house."

"I knew it was there. Nothing was by chance. I brought
his body onto your property and buried it. The first body
required a great deal of digging."

Louise heard another moan. Poor Charlie. He could be
dying there on the concrete floor while Hilde went through
this recital of her crimes. The young woman turned to the
noise, but didn't move. "I'll take care of him soon enough."

"Why did you kill Mike Cunningham?"

"Hah! Another *Ungeheuer*, or what you call 'monster.'

That creature also was profiting from my dear sister's death by millions. Do you realize he bargained with that pig Hoffman for a large part of his fortune?"

"Was that provided he succeeded in getting Peter into a hospital and not a prison?"

"And also because he brokered the sale of Hoffman Arms. That was a crooked deal, you know. He told me a little about it, not everything, but enough for me to understand what an advantage it was to him, like an Enron deal. And then of course he wanted to sleep with me." Her eyes glistened with the excitement of telling the tale. "Most men want to sleep with me as soon as they meet me."

"Like Charlie."

"Yes, Charlie, too, though Charlie was nicer than Mike. I had great satisfaction burying that crooked lawyer in your vegetable garden. The digging was so much easier there." She smiled again. "You and Sam did such a good job there."

"Thanks," replied Louise in a sarcastic tone. She was dripping with perspiration under her plastic poncho, and any moment now she looked for the heart palpitations to start. It was something that happened to her in desperate situations, but something she could ill afford right now, with both Charlie's and her life at stake.

The fact was that Louise was cornered, and the woman's story nearly told. But she had her cell phone just inches away, so she should be safe. She didn't want to take out the phone until she'd heard one last detail of Hilde's murderous ventures.

"Tell me about the Yiddish curse."

"Oh, that. Mike Cunningham was *verflucht*—cursed, that is—from the moment I met him. The charming vegetable garden was not done, of course, when I struck down Peter Hoffman. I had to find him another grave. Then I saw you and Sam planting onions. I immediately

thought of the beauty of humiliating my enemy by burying him with his 'head in hell and his feet in the air.' "

"The literal translation. You're a real student of history,
Margit Hilde Weeren, a believer in Old Testament justice.
But now you'll have to come to terms with what you've
done, because the Fairfax County sheriff's department
doesn't operate on Old Testament justice." The time had
come to alert the authorities. But when Louise plunged
her hand in her pocket for her phone, she heard the hor-
rifying sound of her pants pocket ripping apart.

34

Her pants pocket tore asunder and the little phone slid down her leg through the hole and clattered across the floor, halting under a table. She just barely caught the secateurs, which were caught in the pocket's torn fabric before they, too, slid beyond her reach.

Hilde rushed toward her, a long metal tool in her hand, something with which to smooth clay. Louise had no time to retrieve the phone from under the drying table. Instead, she clutched her snubby secateurs as if they were a sword and prepared to confront Hilde. As she saw the young woman flying at her, she realized that it was an uneven fight, for her weapon was a fraction of the size of Hilde's.

She knew the only answer was flight. Forgetting what she should have known, she rushed down the outside aisle and nearly fell after she tripped over a prone body. She kept herself upright by grabbing onto the drying table, sending cat reproductions flying through the air and crashing onto the floor. Several landed on the body, which reacted with a reassuring groan.

"Ow!" It was Charlie, and now she was certain he would live, provided she could lure this murderous woman out of the studio.

"Charlie, hold on!" she cried, and raced onward to the exit door, reaching it only a few feet before Hilde did. She wrenched it open and dashed into the pelting rain. She didn't have to turn around to know that her young assailant was directly behind her.

Only one solution came to mind, and it wasn't a very good one. She must get to the street before Hilde did and hope that someone in this monsoon was willing to stop and help her. She dodged into the front yard and, like a skier doing the slalom, skidded back and forth down the hill through Sarah Swanson's native plants and shrubs, panting noisily as she went down the steep hillside, stumbling sometimes over the river rocks used to mulch the plants. Hilde followed, making straining sounds like a feral animal. *And she is an animal,* thought Louise. *She's killed twice and has no reason not to kill again.*

She grazed the big clump of oakleaf hydrangeas, batted down several of the smaller, less tough native grasses and a kerria shrub, and nearly entangled herself in a Sir Harry Lauder's Walking Stick. She evaded the low pines, for they were dark patches that were easier to see in the rain. She was nearly to the bottom of the hill.

Ahead of her was the *Crataegus crusgalli,* a tree that she knew. Hope swelled in Louise's heart, for this tree could save her. Behind her ran Hilde Brunner, still groaning intermittently from the strain of pursuing an enemy who could destroy her. Between groans, her breathing was noisy and raspy like Louise's. Louise increased her speed and headed for a collision with the innocent-looking tree. Just as she was going to crash into it she swerved to the left, so hard that she tripped and fell and rolled down onto the sidewalk.

"Oww!" she cried, as she skidded onto the concrete sidewalk. The entire right side of her body throbbed with pain, and her right leg felt as if it were broken.

Then she heard Hilde's scream. With her vision blocked by Louise, Hilde must have continued straight ahead when Louise swerved. She had done what Louise had planned, crashed into the hawthorn, whose inch-long thorns must have pierced her skin. Louise struggled to her knees, then gradually to her feet. After a moment, she found she could stand up. Hilde was writhing on the ground underneath the tree and howling like a resentful baby, yellling out, "*Scheise, Scheise, Scheise!*"

She didn't know what to do. She could try to find a stray tree branch and brain her, or stab her with the secateurs that she still clutched in her hand, but that would be like killing a baby seal. Yet she knew that if this young woman had another chance, she would kill Louise in an instant. Hilde had to be taken out of action.

Headlights of a car turning the corner off Rebecca Road onto Larch Road penetrated the rain. They were like beacons of hope to Louise, the equivalent of a light-house light to a foundering ship in the ocean. She said, "Thank God." If she'd ever needed help, it was now.

The big dark Swanson car slowed in the street near her. Sarah Swanson rolled down the passenger side window. "Louise! What on earth are you doing out in this—" She spotted the figure on the ground. "Who is that . . . is that Hilde? Is she hurt?"

"Yes, it's Hilde, and I must tell you—"

Mort had now lurched the car into park and swung out of the driver's seat. He hurried over to Hilde, whose angry cries had turned into pathetic-sounding moans. "Hilde, my little one!" he called. "What has happened to you? You are all bloody!"

"Ooh, Uncle Mort, help me!"

With each step a small agony, Louise struggled after him, as he arrived at the prone girl's side. "No, no, Mort, leave her there! She'll hurt you!"

"Nonsense," he rebuked her and crouched down and took Hilde in his arms and held her like a child. Without warning, the young woman sat up straight and reared back with one arm. Emitting a loud bellow, she thrust the arm forward and struck Mort Swanson in the head. He slumped over, and Hilde discarded her weapon, a large river rock, onto the ground. She stumbled to her feet and stood there shaking her head, trying to focus on Louise, who was only a dozen feet away. Deep scratches marred her bloody face and rain streamed through her tangled hair. Within seconds, she seemed to collect herself and placed her feet wide apart in the stance of a young warrior ready to strike. Louise knew that it was to be a contest between the two of them.

"Hilde," she warned, "you've done enough harm."

Her young adversary laughed out loud, a harsh, irreverent laugh. "You think you can stop me?" sneered Hilde. "You're old enough to be my mother!"

Louise measured the situation. It was hard to tell who was injured more seriously in the race down the hill. It must mean something that Hilde didn't immediately dash forward to attack and instead stood with her legs unnaturally wide apart. Despite her gimpy leg, Louise felt invincible. Adrenaline was running through her body like a river. Once her opponent came to her, she was ready for hand-to-hand combat. She gripped the secateurs more firmly in her hand. This wretched person had framed her for two murders and had beaten two of her friends, Charlie and Mort, to the ground. Now she thought that she could run over Louise as easily as running over a helpless old lady.

Louise forgot her gimpy leg and rushed toward Hilde, bringing her down to the ground and landing on top of her, with the secateurs flying out of her grasp. Now it was a tussle, and Louise could barely keep the younger woman from throwing her off.

"I can help stop her, Louise," said a strong voice in back of her. It was Sarah Swanson. She was standing over the two of them.

"Sarah, don't get into this," Louise pleaded. All her attention was on keeping the young woman pinned to the ground, knowing it was worth her life. "Hilde is a murderer."

"I gathered that," said Sarah, bitterness in her voice. "Who else would strike out at a man, a sick man at that, who'd treated her like his own daughter?"

"I'll take care of her." Louise glanced up quickly at her friend and gasped. Sarah was holding a foot-long gun and had it pointed straight at Hilde's heart. Hilde had seen the weapon, too. The fight suddenly went out of her. She wilted back on the ground like a spent flower. Louise loosened her hold, sat back and tried to catch her breath.

"Good!" Sarah cried. "And don't move again. My husband had better not be hurt, Hilde, or I'll kill you with no hesitation at all."

Louise had to do something quickly. She got to her feet. In the calmest voice she could muster, she said, "Let me hold that gun. Then you can go to Mort."

Sarah's voice was dangerously harsh. "You're hurt, Louise. You can hardly walk. Get out of the way now. I'll handle Hilde." As she tried to shoulder her aside, Louise decided she'd have to use force to take the weapon from her friend. At that instant, a car careened around the corner. She saw the headlights of Bill's Camry, turned on bright in his attempt to see through the rainstorm. He parked at an angle so that the lights lit up their little tableau. Sarah stopped in her tracks and shielded her eyes with one hand. Bill leaped out, stuffing his phone in his pocket as he ran toward them. "Hey, what's going on?" he cried.

"Bill, hurry!"

He touched her shoulder and said, "Thank God you're safe, Louise," then quickly moved to Sarah's side. "Sarah," he said quietly, "let me take that gun while you tend to Mort."

Sarah looked up at him with a mixture of tears and rain on her face. She handed over the weapon, then ran to her husband.

Bill shook his head. "I can only guess what's happened here."

"Keep that gun aimed at Hilde. She's Kristina Weeren's sister and has been out for vengeance. Not only did she kill two people, but she's injured both Charlie Hurd and Mort, I don't know how badly—"

"Charlie's hurt, too?"

"He's in Sarah's studio. I think he's pretty bad off. If you hand me your phone, I'll call the police."

"I've already called them. But Hilde—I can hardly believe it."

"Yes—Hilde. And Bill, never tell me again that your timing's off. Your timing's perfect."

As her husband focused his attention on the beautiful, bloody-faced villain in their midst, Louise could hear police sirens in the distance. Finally she felt safe. She gave way to the pain in her injured leg and slid down onto the puddly sidewalk. Unlike some Sylvan Valley sidewalks, it mercifully had no jagged edges sticking up.

35

Bill took a final look out the front door and then joined Louise in the living room, where she lay on the couch, wearing her reading glasses. In between phone calls and visits from neighbors, she was reading her book.

"I see a U-Haul and some wooden crates being stacked at Sam's front door," said Bill. "Sam and Greg are standing out front, talking."

"Arguing, or just talking?"

"Talking, but they both look kind of unhappy. Did Sam and Greg break up?"

Louise, her injured leg stretched out on the living room sofa, sighed. "I hope that I didn't have anything to do with it, but I'm afraid I did. I can see why Greg might think I monopolize Sam on Saturdays."

Bill grinned. "That's because you do. I just accept that you both are compulsive gardeners."

"Maybe Sam didn't like the fact that Greg was so anxious to point the finger at me in those murders."

"Greg did see a person in sweatshirt and hat riding that cart at the time Peter Hoffman was killed. Dan Trace told me that, amidst his effusive apologies last night. But he doesn't think Greg was the one who phoned in on Mike

Cunningham. He believes that person was Hilde herself, or rather Margit Hilde Weeren."

"Greg suspected me of murder, Bill. And he may have embellished his story to make it worse."

"You don't know that for sure, do you?"

She looked over at her husband. "No, I don't." Why did he always have to put his finger on the truth? She was having guilt feelings enough about possibly ruining her friend Sam's life. Talk about the need to apologize. Even with her gimpy leg, she needed to get over to her neighbors before it was too late.

She sat forward. "Uh, Bill, why don't you hurry out and peek at them again."

He did as instructed and came back. "Well, now they're going back in the house. They're bringing the crates back in."

Relief flooded over her, and she sat back and sighed. "Maybe they're giving it another try."

"Louise, you didn't do anything on purpose."

"The trouble with me is that I've never gotten to know Greg. Actually, I know Hilde better than him. I even have a certain empathy for her."

"Are you serious?"

"I'm just saying that after I heard her story, I could see how she did these terrible things. Peter Hoffman was wealthy and hired the best lawyers. He spent only a brief time in a comfortable mental hospital as his punishment for killing and dismembering her sister. It ruined her parents' lives as well as hers, and now she's totally alone in this world. If that had happened to you or me, what would we have done?"

Bill shook his head. "We wouldn't have gone after the perpetrator like she did, and the auxiliary players as well. She thought you'd also profited from her sister's death. You might have been the next person on her list."

She gave her husband a sober look. "I didn't want to tell you, but her idea was to kill me and make it look like suicide. Then she could have calmly finished her summer internship and returned to Europe."

He whistled between his teeth. "I knew you were in danger. But I didn't know what direction the danger came from. Why did you begin to suspect her?"

"Only when you asked me to write down that journal. When they came over last night, Nora and Ron and Mary and Richard and I talked about the weird things Peter said at the party. That included the big fuss he made over Hilde. When I remembered how he looked at Hilde as if he knew her, I began to concentrate on her instead of the usual suspects. I recalled she'd had a disagreement with Elsebeth Baumgartner. So I called Elsebeth and learned the truth. We would have known much sooner that Hilde was Kristina's sister if either Martha or I had talked to Elsebeth after she met the girl, for she knew right away that Hilde was flying under false colors."

Bill chuckled. "The Swiss flag was not her flag."

"You can honestly say this was a volunteer effort, Bill, with family and friends helping. Without Martha getting out and getting acquainted with people, we'd never have come to know about Hilde, nor would we have been able to tell the police about Downing's antagonistic relationship with Mike Cunningham. Mary was the one who learned that Peter tattled on Lee Downing—"

"Not that business corruption had a thing to do with this," said Bill.

"How does all this leave Phyllis Hoffman, I wonder?"

"Better off than when Cunningham was claiming the major part of Hoffman's assets. On the other hand, she'll have Lee Downing trying to cut into them. In spite of whatever the SEC charges him with, he was swindled by Peter Hoffman in that sales deal."

Louise winced as she moved her sore leg. "At least I know our injured friends are improving. Charlie Hurd's still in the hospital, but he's improving. He wants to write what he calls a 'groundbreaking' first-person story about his encounter with a killer."

"We could expect no less of Charlie," said Bill, smiling.

"And then Mort. He's out of the hospital and at home with Sarah. He told Sarah why he's been so troubled."

"And why was that?"

"He knew more than he told police. He knew the bare outlines of Mike's and Peter's deal with Lee Downing. Though he tried to stay out of it, he suspected the worst kind of deception on their part. And he knew more about Phyllis Hoffman than he wanted to, even suspected these might be contract killings that she'd arranged."

"They certainly did benefit her."

"But she was his client, so he was reluctant to tell police his suspicions. It turned out they were groundless."

"That sounds like Mort," said Bill, shaking his head.

"Last night, when they brought over dinner, I heard news from Nora and Ron and Mary and Richard."

"Oh, what of our troubled friends?"

"Not so troubled as they were. Nora and Ron are taking a quiet vacation on an island south of Cancun, to celebrate her fiftieth birthday."

Bill smiled. "Maybe turning fifty will do it for her."

"And Richard's going back to work three days a week. He's very happy."

"He's one of those men incapable of being retired, or anyway, not at fifty-five." He moved closer to her on the couch, as close as her leg would permit. "Now let's talk about us, Louise. It's going to take me a while before I regain that sense of safety that I usually feel. I think I let you down, deserted you—"

"No, you didn't, Bill."

"The only answer is for you to come with me to Europe."

She laughed in delight. "What a hardship. I'd love to."

"We'll leave early next week. You can wander the streets of Vienna while I'm in meetings, or else sit around and get your leg stronger. Then we can spend a week in Tuscany. You might even gain a few pounds eating good pasta."

"Not a bad thing," she said, drily, thinking of Marty Corbin's criticism of her scrawny frame. She was happy to leave her job for a while. "Before we leave, though, we're going to have a little supper for our friends, just like I promised."

"Isn't that taking on too much? How can you whip up a fancy dinner in two days?"

She tossed her hand in a careless gesture. "Martha's given me lots of tips. I'll chop some truffles into scrambled eggs for course number one. It's supposed to be very gourmet. Then we'll have roasted guinea hen for the main dish. Martha says it's easy. She'll stay in phone contact while I'm cooking in case I have a problem."

Her husband looked down at her with furrowed brow. "If you say so, Louise. And of course we're due home the first week in October, because of the wedding. By the way, how are the wedding plans? The girls must have it all together by now."

The smile vanished from Louise's face. "Not completely."

"What's wrong?"

"I know it will work out in the end. Janie's been shopping on a daily basis. But she can't find a wedding dress that Martha will sit still for."

"What's the problem?"

"They cost too much."

Bill smiled broadly. "Too much materialism for our nonmaterial girl. Why don't they try a secondhand clothes shop?"

Louise peered at him over her reading glasses. "Why didn't I think of that?"

36

L ee Downing tapped his forehead, trying to remember who that general was in the Vietnam War known for proclaiming that he was beginning to "see the light at the end of the tunnel." Ah, yes, his excellent memory prevailed. It was Westmoreland. However, the general had been wrong about that war, because America didn't win it. But Lee was going to win his little war. Indeed, he could see light at the end of the tunnel, a flood of light.

Granted, he'd been through a bad patch recently. Outside of a little fun he'd had with Mike Cunningham and those party girls, the month he'd spent in Washington, D.C., had been a nightmare. To be cheated so royally by two other businessmen had made him lose some of the faith he had in himself; it had shaken him to his roots.

But things were looking up. His two adversaries were dead. Now it seemed as though he'd get out of this SEC mess with a fine—a huge fine, but a fine was better than going to court any day.

Getting the SEC off his back left him free to deal with Peter Hoffman's widow. The woman was sitting on millions, but several of those millions were his. If she had a reasonable attorney, they ought to be able to settle, especially if a mediator was brought in. The outcome of this messy Hoffman Arms deal was extraordinary. To think that both Hoffman and Cunningham were removed from the scene by a mere girl! So much better than if he'd been stuck with getting rid of the two. Of course, he would have had no hesitation in doing so. Peter Hoffman was already dead by the time he'd figured out the extent of the scam. Lee was about a day away from calling in his muscle men to get rid of the other cheating bastard, Cunningham. But Hilde Brunner—or whatever her real name was—did it for him.

Hoffman's little blond wife shouldn't be that much trouble. After all, she was only a woman. Then, with a twinge in his chest, he remembered Hilde, who was also only a woman.

How had she fooled them all? She'd murdered swiftly and smoothly, and almost gotten away with it. Had it not been for Louise Eldridge's constant little pickings at the scab, no one would have known who'd killed the two men, and Lee would have remained under suspicion. So he could thank the Eldridge woman for that much.

The twinge faded, and he began to feel more confident. He had nothing to fear from Phyllis Hoffman except a prolonged lawsuit.

Phyllis Hoffman sat straight-backed on the living room couch, a couch that would soon be given to the Goodwill. A pad and pen were on her lap, for when one moved one's household, one needed a list. She wrote down "Buy new house," "Set date for moving," "Get movers," "Buy new furniture." Fortunately for her, after Mike Cunningham's demise, Peter's and her mansion was available again. The realtor was holding it for her.

But first things first. She'd close on the house soon, but she didn't intend to get into the mundane job of sorting and moving her household effects until she found out what Lee Downing was up to. Mort Swanson had warned her that Downing might act fairly quickly, suing Peter's estate to get compensated for overpaying for Hoffman Arms.

Phyllis stared out into the street and thought about the possibilities. She could settle with Downing. That might be the best way, since it seemed Peter had generous offshore accounts to be dipped into. Mort would prefer this, of course, instead of having to fight it out in court.

If the man became a major pest and wanted too much, Phyllis had another recourse. She could call up her Russian friend Sophie. Seeming to know that Phyllis had lots of challenges since Peter's death, Sophie had approached her again with some enticing details. She'd said that her brother was a sophisticated man. He didn't only work on the East Coast. He traveled in his job and was perfectly willing to follow someone home to West Texas to get the task done.

WILLING VOLUNTEERS IN THE GARDEN

Volunteers among the human population are special people who step up and help others who need them, easing their suffering and making their lives more enjoyable. Volunteers among the plant population are much the same. They spread themselves around our gardens and yards, making our labor less arduous and at the same time brightening our lives. They are particularly helpful to the busy gardener, the lazy gardener and the gardener with emerging back problems. They're less suited to the neatnik gardener, for a garden where volunteers have their way can get out of hand unless carefully controlled.

We're talking here not only about plants that seed themselves or otherwise manage to move themselves to other places in the garden, but also those that enlarge themselves through root, tuber or bulb development, multiplying themselves from one plant into a drift of plants.

Some varieties need little encouragement in these natural processes of nature, but the best environment in which to generate volunteer plants is a soil with good tilth that has been nurtured with compost and fertilizer.

Plants that seed themselves can provide constant surprises. Imagine how you might feel to see your garden turn scarlet in the spring. This can happen if you allow the beautiful deep red seedlings of the herb red orach to spring up unchecked. It is just one of scores of self-seeding plants that will make your garden a constantly changing delight. Scores of colorful volunteers will emerge if you allow even one plant go to seed in the fall. Seedlings can be thinned, with extra plants going to friends and relatives. Or you could leave a patch of them to grow up through various dramatic stages into a five-foot-high red jungle!

Similarly, chartreuse will predominate should you let dill spread in your garden and artistically fill in the spaces between such perennials as lilies, clematis and roses. In maturity, they have a lacy splendor that can't be rivaled. Shake a packet of seeds onto a patch of garden, and you'll create enough potential dill plants to last for years. Plants will not only reseed, but spread far and wide.

Another willing garden volunteer is the beautiful bronze variety of the fennel plant. It will reappear vigorously from seed in your garden. With its fine filigree foliage, the plant grows five feet tall and, best of all, will attract the parsley worm. Gardeners in the know will plant both fennel and dill for the express purpose of attracting this creature. The parsley worm is fetching, with white, yellow and black stripes. When disturbed, it has a cunning defense weapon. It pulls up a Y-shaped horn from behind its head that emanates a rancid-butter smell and discourages its enemies' approach. But the magical thing about it is that it turns into the swallowtail butterfly. And there is nothing like having beauteous butterflies fluttering through the garden in late summer.

The beauty of letting herbs such as dill and fennel prosper in the garden is that they're handy to be harvested for culinary purposes. There's nothing nicer than going out to snip off plant tops to put in a green sauce or a salad.

Those who wish to be spared the job of thinning seedlings

should remember this simple rule: deadhead the seedpods that form on your plants, and you'll have few seedlings. The prudent gardener allows a few seedpods to mature and disperse, removing the rest.

To control those plants that spread by root growth, use the murderous overhead ax method. This easy way of dividing plants works especially well with tough clumps of iris, aster or polygonum.

Few plants exceed the snapdragon in range of color. It willingly reseeds itself, sometimes cross-pollinating and creating new color tones of surprising subtlety. After a couple of years, plants in these special hues may disappear, never to be seen in that exact shade again. Another good thing about snaps is that deer don't seem to like them as part of their diet.

For vigor, nothing exceeds the cosmos. One packet of seeds is all you need to have a lifetime of cosmos plants. This annual is not fussy about soil, and it comes in a variety of colors—the familiar white, pink and rose, as well as vibrant orange shades and the new chocolate-hued plant. The same is true of sunflowers, which, with their bold blossoms, make colorful punctuation marks in the perennial border.

Some wildflowers will positively wallow in good garden soil. One example is the native white yarrow, with its filigree foliage and rather insignificant flowers. A few clumps of it add special grace to a garden's texture. Garden experts might sniff to hear that volunteers such as native yarrow are allowed in one's garden, for they deplore this lack of discipline and even term some of these plants weeds. Yet, one gardener's weed is another gardener's treasure. Grasses such as miscanthus will also spread, given the right environment. This is another case where control is needed.

It is always good to have a groundcover willing to spread

and proliferate. Among the willing are wooly thyme, snow-in-summer, creeping phlox and basket-of-gold. They like to go places and clamber over rocks, and in so doing make a wonderful show. Think twice, however, about letting English ivy loose, remembering that it has roots as tough as steel. In contrast, other plants with shallower roots can be removed with a quick swipe of the gardener's gloved hand.

Volunteer plants work their wonders in shade gardens, too. A patch of *Anemone sylvestris*, with its twelve-inch-high white nodding flowers, will grow bigger and more handsome year after year, as will plants such as May apples. So will prominent-leaved hosta plants and little beauties like grape hyacinths. The columbine is another reliable self-seeder.

Oriental poppies proliferate over time, until eventually from just one poppy you will have a field of poppies. Of course, we all know about iris and how they reproduce, sometimes so rapidly that they overwhelm us with their needs. These plants need division about every three years and should be reset with space between them on rich little mounds of soil.

Another robust grower that spreads both through roots and seed is lamb's ears or *Stachys byzantina*. Its gray, fuzzy leaves make a nice contrast to green-leaved plants and look splendid when teamed with pink roses. When it volunteers in some offbeat place, you can just let it grow unless it threatens to smother another nearby valuable specimen.

The tall, well-structured plume poppy (*Macleaya microcarpa*), which does well in many parts of the country, is as architecturally pleasing as a plant can be. It has large, handsome, lobed leaves, grows about five feet tall and produces pale peach flowers in late summer. As an additional bonus, it volunteers readily, popping up here and there by virtue of its long, horizontal roots. But still it does not overwhelm the place.

The plume poppy's leaves are classier, but similar in contour to the hollyhock's. Unlike the hollyhock, they are not prone to rust and bug injury. Yet hollyhocks have their place in the volunteer-oriented garden bed, too. They are among the most dependable volunteers, springing up in odd and delightful situations—and sometimes exactly where you don't want them. They deserve to live until and unless their leaves begin to deteriorate. Then, you can just chop them down. Newer hollyhock strains, incidentally, do not seem as sensitive to insect damage.

If volunteer plants appear in places where they are not needed or welcome, don't forget your fellow gardeners. While some variety may be proliferating in your garden bed, a friend or neighbor might be longing for some of these plants. Extra volunteers can be moved, given away or thrown into the compost pile.

And you can purchase plants with the express purpose of having them spread and take over a portion of your landscape. It's always a challenging experiment. And a gardener who doesn't mind being surprised in the spring will love being part of it.